SAVAGE VOW

IVANOV CRIME FAMILY, BOOK ONE

ZOE BLAKE

Poison Ink Publications

Copyright © 2020 by Zoe Blake & Poison Ink Publications

All rights reserved.

No part of this book may be reproduced in any form or by any electronic or mechanical means, including information storage and retrieval systems, without written permission from the author, except for the use of brief quotations in a book review.

Cover Design by Dark City Designs
Photographer: Wander Aguiar
Model: Jonny James

CONTENTS

Note from Zoe Blake	v
Chapter 1	1
Chapter 2	9
Chapter 3	17
Chapter 4	25
Chapter 5	38
Chapter 6	48
Chapter 7	55
Chapter 8	59
Chapter 9	68
Chapter 10	76
Chapter 11	84
Chapter 12	96
Chapter 13	108
Chapter 14	114
Chapter 15	121
Chapter 16	126
Chapter 17	135
Chapter 18	142
Chapter 19	149
Chapter 20	152
Chapter 21	161
Chapter 22	170
Chapter 23	177
Chapter 24	181
Chapter 25	193
Chapter 26	204
Chapter 27	215
Chapter 28	218
Chapter 29	225
Chapter 30	234
Chapter 31	245

Chapter 32	253
Chapter 33	263
Chapter 34	267
Chapter 35	275
Chapter 36	278
Chapter 37	283
Chapter 38	290
Epilogue	293
Traditional Russian Recipes	297
About Zoe Blake	299
Also by Zoe Blake	301

NOTE FROM ZOE BLAKE

Here is the beautiful romantic Russian poem which helped inspire this book.

Among Worlds
Amid the worlds, 'mid luminaries' gleam,
One Star I know whose name I keep repeating.
It's not that of my love for Her I dream:
It's that with others all is mirthless cheating.

And when oppressive doubt I have to fight,
Her answer only have I sought and heeded.
It's not that She is emanating light:
It's that with Her around no light is needed.

- Innokenty Annensky

Среди миров
Среди миров, в мерцании светил
Одной Звезды я повторяю имя…
Не потому, чтоб я Её любил,

NOTE FROM ZOE BLAKE

А потому, что я томлюсь с другими.

И если мне сомненье тяжело,
Я у Неё одной ищу ответа,
Не потому, что от Неё светло,
А потому, что с Ней не надо света.
- Innokenty Annensky

CHAPTER 1

*S*amara

Washington, D.C.

"We're going to get caught!"

Ignoring the warning, my boyfriend tugged harder on my arm.

The clatter of music and laughter from the party faded the farther Peter pulled me down the dark corridor. When I glanced back, I could just make out a shaft of light as it stretched across the marble-tiled entrance to the great hall. The servants had moved the ancient furnishings out and rolled the Persian carpets up to make room for the celebration. Hired catering staff dressed in ill-fitting tuxedo jackets passed around silver trays with either caviar canapés or glasses of Veuve Clicquot while everyone smiled and pretended to like one another.

From where it was tucked away on a thickly wooded lot along the Rock Creek Parkway, visitors could be forgiven if they thought they'd arrived at a creepy gothic manor. My friend Nadia's massive granite house was probably over a hundred years old.

The estate screamed old money and tradition, even though it was far from the truth.

It was only what they wanted people to think.

Instead, it was all just smoke and mirrors.

But I wasn't allowed to talk about such things.

Peter's warm hand was sweaty as it clung roughly to mine. As he dragged me down the shadowed labyrinth of hallways, he stopped before each threshold, twisting one doorknob after another to see if they were locked. Soon, the muted rattle of metal against wood and Peter's soft curses replaced the music. He finally found a door the servants had neglected to secure. We slipped inside, and Peter softly clicked the door shut.

The room was mostly dark, only hints of moonlight filtering through the gauzy silver curtains covering the floor-to-ceiling windows.

We didn't dare turn on a light.

I took a few careful steps inside, not wanting to bump into any furniture. Although I'd played in my best friend Nadia's house since I was a child, I hadn't been paying attention, so I wasn't sure which room Peter had pulled us into. I knew the first floor on this side of the house mostly contained a mixture of bedrooms, gaming areas, and offices.

A distinct scent clung to the air, the unmistakable mark of the room's occupant.

Closing my eyes, I inhaled.

It was a warm woodsy scent with a hint of ginger and spice.

My eyes snapped open.

I knew that scent.

"We have to leave."

"What?"

Clasping Peter's forearm in a tight grip, I bent my knees and tugged, throwing my weight backward. "Please, Peter. We can't stay in this room!"

My slight frame was not enough to budge him.

"No. All the other rooms are locked. Besides..." He snatched me around the waist, then yanked me against his chest. "This one has a bed."

Peering over Peter's shoulder, I widened my eyes as I could just make out the ominous outline of the four-poster bed.

That was *his* bed.

Clawing at Peter's fingers, I freed myself from his hold.

I had to get out of here.

"No, Peter. You don't understand!"

I couldn't be caught in this bedroom.

In *his* bedroom.

Of course, I should have known *he* would be here tonight.

It was Nadia's eighteenth birthday, after all.

It had been five years since I last saw him, but it didn't matter.

Ten years, hell, twenty years could pass, and it still wouldn't matter.

I would still be terrified of him.

I wasn't sure why I was nervous.

It wasn't like he cared—*if* he even knew who I was.

I stopped myself from asking Nadia if he would be attending her birthday party at least a million times.

Because it didn't matter.

If I kept telling myself that, it might actually be true. It *had* to be true. Besides, I had my own life now. I even had a boyfriend. I wasn't that foolish little girl with a crush. Not anymore.

But that scent.

His cologne.

Bleu de Chanel.

The unmistakable scent of *him*.

Goose bumps rose on my arms.

He was here.

Pivoting on my heel, I clamored in the darkness for the doorknob, desperate to return to the party. Back to the music and light and dancing, to people and laughter... and safety.

As soon as I managed to open the door a sliver, it was wrenched from my hands and slammed shut.

Peter took hold of my shoulders, spun me around, and pushed me against the door. "You're such a fucking cock tease."

The dim lighting threw his face into shadows, contorting his features into harsh lines. His breath had the fetid yeast smell of stale beer from the drink he'd stolen from the bar before the party began.

"What? Why would you—" Confusion scrambled my thoughts.

He clawed at the neckline of my dress, tearing it.

"Peter, stop!"

His palmed my breast, ruthlessly squeezing it. My eyes teared at the searing jolt of pain.

"The saintly Federovs and their virginal daughter. Your family thinks they are so much better than everyone else," he jeered as he forced his knee between my thighs.

Digging my nails into his wrist, I struggled to break free. "Let me go!"

"I'm tired of hand jobs and dry humps. Come on, Samara," he whined as he crowded closer and tried to kiss me.

I stretched my head to the side, avoiding his lips. My mind could not keep up with Peter's crazy display of emotions. Angry one second but pleading the next. I knew he wasn't happy with my decision not to go all the way, but he was insane if he thought I was going to have sex with him at my friend's birthday party with my mother and father just down the hall.

Craning my neck, I kept pulling on his arm, trying to dislodge his painful grip on my breast. "Peter, get off me!"

His free hand went for the zipper of his jeans. "I'll be quick. I'll even pull out, so you won't get pregnant."

This isn't happening.

Although we could never talk about Nadia's family business, I knew security guards always patrolled the grounds. Maybe if I cried out, I'd get lucky and one would be in earshot and come help me. With the loud music, there was no chance of anyone from the party hearing me. As I opened my mouth to scream, there was the soft *shush* of a sliding door opening. The cool rush of midnight air brought with it the acrid scent of cigar smoke.

Peter released his grasp, whirling around.

We both stared as the immense, dark figure of a man walked in from the stone patio that ran along the north side of the bedroom. He appeared as if out of a dark mist, a malevolent figure, like in *Dracula*, the book I was enthralled with.

It was *him*.

Gregor Ivanov.

Nadia's older brother.

In the barely lit room, he was still deep in shadows, but I knew it was him.

My gaze followed the glowing end of the cigar he must have been smoking outside.

Without saying a word, he stepped inside and leaned

against the front of the desk. He took another slow drag from his cigar; the end glowed brightly like an evil, all-seeing eye. When he exhaled, a halo of sweet tobacco smoke encircled him. With slow deliberation, Gregor set the cigar aside, slid open a side drawer… and withdrew a revolver.

My hand flew up to cover my mouth.

Peter ducked behind me.

When Gregor's chilly voice finally broke the tense silence, my body started at the sound.

"Were you aware that Russians did not invent Russian roulette?"

Flicking the chamber open, he reached into the drawer a second time, then raised his arm. The bright casing of a single bullet caught the moonlight.

"An American author made it up for a short story," Gregor continued as he slid the bullet into the revolver chamber with a click.

"Who is this guy?" Peter whispered over my shoulder.

"Shut up," I hissed through clenched teeth, afraid to even move my lips. My body tensed so tightly it felt like brittle glass. I was sure the slightest loud sound or sudden movement would make me shatter.

Gregor straightened to his full height.

Peter and I both gasped.

"Still, everyone believes it must be true. Probably because we Russians are so crazy, no?" Gregor said as he took several steps toward us.

Peter's fingers dug into my shoulders as he pushed me forward.

My fingertips turned to ice, and all the feeling left my body. My tongue felt heavy when I tried to form my next words. "Gregor, it's… Samara, I'm Nadia's—"

"I know who you are, Samara."

My heart lurched at the sound of my name on his lips—at the seductive way he softly rounded the *R*.

Despite both of our families living in America now, Gregor had been sent back to Russia just over five years ago because of some hastily covered up scandal at his college. So his accent was thicker, giving his voice a decadent darkness that was almost mesmerizing.

My brow furrowed. How could he know who I was? The last time I'd been around him, I was nothing more than his little sister's awkward friend, barely thirteen years old. He hadn't known I was alive.

Without warning, Gregor reached out and snatched Peter by the collar, dragging him out from behind me. Peter's gangly limbs flailed as Gregor manhandled him across the room. He tossed the man into a chair in front of the cold fireplace. Instinctively, I surged forward a few steps with my arm outstretched but caught myself.

Placing his hands on the armrests, Peter immediately tried to get up. When Gregor raised the gun, Peter fell back onto the seat. His high-pitched voice broke as he stuttered, "We didn't mean to come into your room."

Gregor cut his grey gaze toward me.

I hugged myself around the waist, trying to stop my body from trembling. His steely eyes surveyed me from head to toe.

He took a step forward.

With a gasp, I stumbled backward. I couldn't help it.

As much as the man enthralled me.

He terrified me more.

Always had.

Except now, he was even bigger and scarier with *way* more tattoos. Even in the darkened bedroom, I could make out the outline of an image on his neck and several more on his hands, making the tailored suit he wore a mockery of civility. The man radiated dark energy and barely leashed anger.

His eyes narrowed. I could tell my reaction displeased him.

Switching the gun to his left hand, he kept it trained on Peter. After giving him a warning look, Gregor returned his attention to me. He raised his right arm.

Instinctively, I moved back again. The hard look on his face stilled me. After holding my gaze long enough to freeze the blood in my veins, his eyes lowered to the torn neckline of my dress.

Glancing down, it mortified me to see the top of my pink lace bra exposed. Despite the low lighting, I could already see the beginning of a bruise on my soft flesh from Peter's rough handling.

Using two fingers, Gregor pulled aside the fabric, exposing more of my skin to his gaze. Using just the tip of his middle finger, he caressed the outline of the bruise. I hissed in air through my teeth when he touched a particularly sensitive spot.

His jaw tightened. The steel of his eyes turned to molten fire.

Turning his head, he looked at Peter as he cocked back the hammer.

Peter's eyes widened as he threw up his hands in pitiful defense. "No!"

His plea fell on deaf ears.

Without saying a word, Gregor pulled the trigger.

CHAPTER 2

*S*amara

My scream drowned out the hollow metallic click.

It took a full moment for me to realize something wasn't right.

Gregor had pulled the trigger, but the gun hadn't gone off.

Peter was running his hands over his chest as if he, too, couldn't believe he wasn't dead.

"Are you familiar with the laws of probability theory?" asked Gregor in a casual tone as he spun the revolver chamber.

Peter looked past him to me before answering. "What the fuck is this?" he sputtered.

Gregor raised the gun again, pointing it directly at Peter's face. His voice was deceptively calm and even. "In Russian roulette, the probability you will die on the first shot is sixteen point six percent. The probability you will die on the second shot goes up… to twenty percent."

Gregor pulled back the hammer.

Peter shook as streams of sweat stained the armpits of his shirt. "We didn't touch or take anything of yours. I swear!"

Gregor turned and pierced me with a glare. Without looking at Peter, he growled, "Now that is where you're wrong. You touched something of mine."

My stomach flipped.

His meaning seemed clear, and yet it was impossible.

He couldn't mean *me*?

The idea was ludicrous.

Still keeping his gaze trained on me, Gregor pulled the trigger a second time.

The hammer slammed down, but again the gun didn't fire.

My knees buckled, and I collapsed to the floor.

"Please, please stop!" I begged.

A dark stain spread over Peter's crotch. He had pissed himself.

Gregor spun the chamber.

"What is your name, boy?"

Boy.

Peter *was* a boy compared to Gregor.

He was my age, eighteen, and was all limbs and skin and bones like a typical teenager.

Gregor was twenty-six but looked older in that scary he's-seen-and-done-some-serious-shit kind of way.

Where Peter was awkward-looking and gangly, Gregor was handsome as hell and powerfully built. The type of man where even an expensive suit always fit a little snugly over his heavily sinewed arms and chest. He still wore his jet-black hair long so it curled a bit at the ends. Even so, it was his eyes which ensnared me. They were the most startling grey. Bright silver one moment. Smoky steel the next.

"P... P... Peter."

"Peter what?"

Peter inhaled a shaky breath. "Peter Fischer."

Gregor threw a hard glance over his shoulder at my kneeling form. I knew that look well. I had already gotten it a thousand times from my father for dating a non-Russian boy.

Gregor cocked his head to the side as he stroked the barrel of the gun. "So, Peter Fischer, you come into my family's home and trespass on our hospitality by taking advantage of one of our guests?"

"Look, me and my girlfriend were just—"

"Don't say that," interrupted Gregor.

"What?"

"She's not your girlfriend. She's not your anything. Not anymore."

My cheeks burned. The possessive undertone of Gregor's words was unmistakable, yet still made little sense. Maybe he was angry because I was his sister's friend and Peter had hurt me? Or, like he said, because I was a guest in his family's home?

"Is that what this is about? Dude, you can have her! Good luck!" Peter nodded in my direction. "The bitch's legs are locked at the knees."

My mouth fell open as my cheeks burned.

Gregor walked over to Peter, placed the gun at his temple and without preamble pulled the trigger a third time.

The gun made a hollow click.

"Stop doing that!" Peter screamed as his face and neck became a mottled hue of red and purple.

Gregor sneered. "What? Does the little American boy not have the stones for a silly Russian game?"

He spun the gun chamber and raised the revolver to his own temple as he pulled back the hammer.

Horrified, I stretched out my arm. "No!"

Gregor pulled the trigger.

It clicked but did not fire.

All the air left my body.

Gregor spun the chamber again and raised his arm a second time.

I didn't know what was happening, but I knew it was all fucking madness.

Crawling on my knees, I lunged for Gregor's legs. "Stop! What are you doing? Don't!"

I knew the laws of probability theory. You didn't grow up in a Russian family and not learn the odds of Russian roulette. That was the fourth shot. This would be the fifth, which meant there was a fifty percent chance the gun would fire. Gregor knew that as well as I did.

I clawed at his suit pants. "Please, Gregor. Please, stop."

He reached down and brushed my cheek with the back of his knuckles. I snatched at his hand and opened it, pressing my cheek against his palm. "Please," I whispered against his warm skin.

"Would those pretty green eyes fill with tears for me if I died, malyshka?"

Malyshka.

Gregor Ivanov had just called me *malyshka*. Baby girl.

"Yes! Please, Gregor. Please, stop!" I begged, pressing my lips against his palm. I could smell the hint of tobacco and gun oil on his hand and felt the slightly calloused touch of his fingertips along my jaw.

"Why don't I leave you two alone?" Peter snarled.

"Shut the fuck up," Gregor snapped as he pointed the gun at Peter's crotch and pulled the trigger.

The hammer clicked down. The gun didn't fire.

Peter flew out of his seat. "You're fucking insane! You know that?"

Afraid of getting trampled by the two angry men, I scrambled out of the way and back onto my feet.

Gregor grabbed Peter by the front of the shirt and swung him wide, slamming him against the wall before placing the gun under his chin. "Five empty shots in a six-cylinder gun. Do the math, boy."

Peter's toes barely touched the ground as his hands scraped for purchase along the wall. "I don't know what you're saying!"

Gregor cocked his head in my direction. "Samara?"

I licked my dry lips before responding. Nervously clutching the neckline of my torn dress together at the base of my throat, I croaked, "A hundred percent. There's a hundred percent chance the gun will fire this time."

Peter's eyes widened in horror as he whimpered.

Gregor's voice lowered to a dark rumble in his chest. "If you so much as look in Samara's direction ever again, I will hunt you down and kill you like a rabid dog in the street. Do you understand me?"

Peter tried to nod his head, but the gun pressed under his jaw prevented him.

"If there is so much as a whisper about what happened here tonight at her school, I will rip away all that you hold dear. Have I made myself crystal clear... Peter Fischer?"

"Yes, sir! I promise!"

Gregor released him.

Peter crumbled to the floor as his knees gave out. He slithered a few feet back on his ass before scrambling to his feet and scurrying through the door without even giving me so much as a backward glance.

The room fell silent again.

My heart was beating so fast I was lightheaded and sick to

my stomach. It was going to take me a week to process everything that had just happened.

Portland Cool Grey. The color of his eyes.

Indanthrene Blue. The color of his tie.

Transparent Earth Red. The color of blood.

Picturing the aluminum paint tubes and their tiny white labels inside my artist oil paint kit, I recited the colors in my head to calm myself, a strange coping mechanism I'd had since I was a little girl.

Twisting my fist into the collar of my dress, my curiosity overrode my fear of being alone with him. I had to know. "Would you have pulled the trigger?"

Gregor turned those inscrutable eyes on me.

For half a second, he didn't move or respond.

I was about to turn and leave, assuming I, too, had worn out my welcome, when he moved so quickly the breath was knocked out of my body.

One moment I was standing in the middle of the room, the next, he pressed me against the wall, towering over me. His hips leaned into mine as his right arm rested high over my head, caging me in. His warm spicy scent enveloped me. The sensation was overwhelming… and terrifying.

Still, he didn't speak.

I licked my lips and watched as his gaze zeroed in on my mouth.

"Answer me," I demanded with more boldness than I felt.

"Would I have pulled the trigger?" he repeated.

I nodded.

He lowered his right arm. The cold barrel of the gun grazed my cheek. I sucked in a breath. He pointed the gun off to the side and cocked the hammer. I squeezed my eyes shut and braced for the gunshot, but only heard the same hollow metallic click. Opening my eyes, I watched as Gregor tossed the gun onto the bed.

"But… I don't…."

Lifting his left arm, he held up a bullet between his thumb and forefinger. He had never truly loaded the gun. It had all been a twisted game from the start.

My brow furrowed. "Why would you do something like that? You scared him to death!"

"He deserved to be punished for touching you."

He said it so matter of factly. As if we weren't discussing terrorizing my now ex-boyfriend with a fucking gun!

I shoved at his chest. It was solid muscle, so of course he didn't budge. I hated that I had to crane my head back to meet his gaze. It made me feel small and vulnerable. "No one asked you! I can take care of myself!"

"Malyshka, you can't honestly think I was going to let him assault you like that and just walk away unscathed? He's lucky it's my little sister's birthday, and the house is filled with witnesses, otherwise I would have beaten him within an inch of his worthless life."

"I don't understand. Why do you care?"

I hadn't laid eyes on this man in over five years. I was just his little sister's friend. I was nothing to him.

He reached down to pull back the fabric of my dress, exposing the top of my breast and shoulder. His fingertip traced my collarbone before slowly moving down to caress near the bruise marks. His brow creased, and a small tick appeared high on his cheekbone just below his eye. He breathed heavily through his nose as if he were trying to calm himself down. His anger was palatable.

"He hurt you," he said matter-of-factly, his voice gruff and low. "When I entered from the patio, even before I saw your face, I could *feel* your fear. If I hadn't come in when I did? That little bastard would have…."

It hadn't occurred to me he might actually be shaken and

upset at Peter's treatment of me. Gregor almost appeared human in this moment. Vulnerable.

"Yeah, but he didn't."

He cupped my jaw and gazed down at me, his eyes as hard as flint. Gone was my brief glimpse of his unfamiliar human side. He was back to being the scary, inscrutable man I knew him to be. "It will never happen again. Do you understand me? I'm here now to make sure of it."

What was that supposed to mean?

Alarm bells raged inside my head.

He ran his thumb over my bottom lip before continuing. "From this point forward, you are under my protection. I will expect you to behave accordingly and not put yourself in these types of dangerous positions again. I *will* be obeyed in this, malyshka."

Under *his* protection?

Obey him?

Malyshka?

No.

Something was wrong here.

I couldn't think straight. Too much had happened in the last hour.

My head was spinning.

Nothing he said or did was making any sense to me.

My eyes welled up as the trauma set in.

Frustrated, I swiped at a tear that fell down my cheek. "Stop calling me that!"

"What?"

"You know what."

"Malyshka?"

"Yes, malyshka! I'm not you're malyshka. I'm not your anything! You can't just come in here and start dictating rules to me!"

"That's where you're wrong. You're mine now."

CHAPTER 3

*G*regor

She looked beautiful when she cried.

The tears brought out the gold in her deep emerald eyes and made them sparkle.

Beauty was not the problem where Samara was concerned.

I had been summoned back from Russia because our families decided we would wed as soon as she graduated, which was in only two weeks.

It was the same old story.

It all came down to money.

The Federovs were a venerable old-world family with ties back to the Czars. They had significant political and business connections both here in the States and in mother Russia. Their name carried a great deal of weight in the drawing rooms of Europe and in embassies around the world. Unfortunately, Samara's father was an imbecile who pissed away most of the family fortune. He then panicked and got into bed with some dangerous people. So being the caring patriarch that he was, he'd put the only thing of value he had left on the auction block... his precious daughter.

He was willing to sell off her hand in marriage—and all the benefits of the family name that went with it—to the highest bidder, in exchange for a hefty dowry and protection from the rather nasty Nigerian criminals who'd ensnared him.

It was all very medieval.

Naturally, since our families had been linked both socially and through some minor side business dealings for generations, they decided we could not allow another family to outbid us for Samara's hand. Plus, this connection would give our more, shall we say, *shadowed* business ventures the veneer of respectability, once our name was formally attached with the Federov one.

Parading her around at all the various society dinners and charity events would open new diplomatic doors, which was a polite way of saying backdoor entrances to corrupt leaders, military officials and politicians who controlled massive spending contracts.

Yes, it would be a lucrative deal for both families. In fact, since her father was in such dire straits, we had already transferred a considerable amount into his offshore accounts to ensure everyone's complicity.

Of course, none of this had been told to Samara yet.

Until all matters had been decided, it was none of her concern. She would do as she was told.

As the eldest, the duty of marrying her ultimately fell on my shoulders... whether or not I liked it.

It didn't help that my first glimpse of her in five years, I find her alone with some boy, pressed against the wall with her legs spread like some whore.

Her father had assured us that Samara was a good, obedient girl who had had a sheltered upbringing and was still a virgin. I assumed with her being a close friend of my little sister that it must be true.

Now, I was not so sure.

Her body trembled within my embrace. She was so small and delicate. As I trapped her against the wall with just the threat of my height alone, it was like cupping a baby bird in my palm. Watching the tiny bundle of feathers and thin bones twitch and shake with fear.

"What are you talking about?" she asked. Her eyes stared at the knot of my tie.

I placed a finger under her chin and forced her gaze up.

"You were a very bad girl to let that boy drag you into a room alone."

She opened her mouth to speak.

I shifted my hand and placed a finger over her lips.

"Don't. I'm already angry, and you've already earned yourself a severe punishment. Don't make it worse."

"Punishment?" Her green eyes widened at the word.

Running the back of my knuckles down her cheek in more of a threat than a caress, I said, "Yes, malyshka, punishment for being so foolish and reckless."

The pulse at her throat jumped. "You're crazy if you think I'm going to let you punish me, Gregor."

I pulled on one of her long dark curls. "It's adorable that you think you have a choice in the matter."

That was when my little bird started to fight.

Samara kicked and thrashed within my embrace, struggling to get to the door.

Grabbing her around the waist, I roared, "Enough!"

She instantly stilled.

Good girl.

Lifting her high, I crossed the room to the upholstered chairs in front of the unlit fireplace. I sat down in one and placed her on my lap. Compared to my considerable size, she really was a little thing. The thought of getting my thick cock inside what was sure to be her tight pussy had me reaching between us to adjust myself as my shaft thickened and lengthened.

Samara squirmed.

I groaned and grit out between clenched teeth, "Be still."

For emphasis, I raised my hips up slightly so she could feel the hard ridge of my cock press against her bottom. Her eyes widened.

"Exactly," I quipped.

I took a deep breath and reminded myself it was my little sister's birthday party. If we weren't missed already, we would be soon. They were probably getting ready to cut the cake. Now was not the time to sink my cock deep inside my soon-to-be wife. There would be plenty of time for that later.

I positioned the chair closer to the windows so I could see more of her in the moonlight. Her ivory skin seemed almost to glow. In the soft light, I couldn't quite make out the pink shade of her lips, but the bottom one was slightly fuller than the top, which formed a cute little cupid's bow. Like when she was young, she still wore her dark hair long and in curls down her back.

Looking down her slender neck, I observed the bruises on the top of her breast. I pulled the fabric of her neckline aside. Samara objected, grabbing my hand to stop me. One hard look and she relented.

Seeing the dark smudges on her perfect skin, I uttered a curse under my breath. "I'll kill him for hurting you like this."

"He… he didn't mean it."

"You're defending him?"

"No. It's just… it's fine."

I pulled the fabric down a little further and exposed the pink lace of her bra. Her breasts weren't large, just enough to fill a man's hands. Perfect.

With a single fingertip, I traced the scalloped lace edge. "Samara, it's not fine. He touched what's mine. I can't let him get away with that."

Samara played with a button on her dress, avoiding making eye contact. "Why do you keep saying that?"

"Saying what?"

I knew what she was asking. I just wanted to hear the words on her lips.

"Why do you keep saying that… that I'm yours?" she whispered.

There it was. I was a little surprised how much I enjoyed hearing the words *I'm yours* coming from her. For me, this really was supposed to be just a business transaction with some fringe benefits. My plan had been to wed and bed her and then return to Russia and my life and other women there. Perhaps I would stay in the states a little longer after all.

For a slip of a girl there was something about her that intrigued me.

A spirit that sparked behind her eyes.

For whatever reason, I was definitely feeling possessive of her.

When I saw her in the arms of that fucking boy, I wanted to tear his throat out, especially after I saw the fear in her eyes.

She was mine and mine alone, bought and paid for, and no one but me had the right to touch her.

It was a heady emotion to realize I was going to be the only man in this special creature's life.

Or at least I was *supposed* to be the only man, assuming she was untouched as her father claimed.

"Because you are, malyshka."

I knew she didn't understand. How could she? And I was a bastard because I had no intention of explaining it to her... not yet.

I cupped her jaw and pulled her head down. Using the tip of my tongue, I teased her bottom lip, then the top. I traced the seam. Her mouth opened just slightly with a gasp. Still using only the tip, I flicked along the edge of her teeth and coaxed her own tongue to spar with mine. Her mouth opened a little more.

I groaned against her lips. "That's it, baby, open for me."

My tongue swept in. She tasted of peppermint candy and champagne and innocence.

Shifting in the seat, I pressed my cock against her hip as I forced my tongue deeper into her mouth. She whimpered, and her small hands grasped at my chest. She was such an ingenue, so untried.

Her mouth broke free. She tilted her head back and away, trying to catch her breath. "Please, Gregor. Wait! I need to—"

But I didn't stop... I couldn't.

I dragged my teeth along her jaw; I swept my tongue down her throat, tasting her pulse. My hand skimmed her waist to cup her breast, my fingers seeking and finding the small pebble of her nipple. Rolling it between my finger and thumb, I pinched it hard.

Samara's hips rose up as she cried out. She pushed against my chest, once more straining to break free. I knew I was overwhelming her, probably scaring her more than that boy did an hour ago, but I was too far gone to care. Her innocence was like a drug.

Moving my mouth across her cheek, I captured her delicate earlobe between my teeth and bit down as my hand moved from her breast over her belly to between her thighs. As my tongue traced the shell of her ear, I lifted the hem of her dress.

Her small hands grasped my wrists. "Wait, Gregor. We can't."

Her skin was a creamy ivory, pure and unblemished. Her hands looked like the tip of an angel's wing resting against the savage darkness of my tattoos, which displayed countless symbols of violence and power. A stark allegory of the corrupting influence I was about to have on her perfect little suburban life.

I shook her off and raised the hem. Pushed my fingers into the waistband of her panties.

I could feel the soft down of her pussy against the back of my hand as I pushed her panties lower on her thighs.

"Gregor! Stop!" Samara begged as she squirmed on my lap, which only inflamed me more.

"Are you a virgin?" I asked against her neck.

"What?" she gasped.

"You heard me, Samara."

"You have no right to ask me that!"

"I have the right of a husb— Just answer me," I ground out.

"No."

"No, you aren't a virgin or no you won't answer?"

Her cheeks flamed as she averted her face. "You're a bully and a brute and I hate you! Let me go!"

She struggled in earnest as she tried to get off my lap. That would not happen, not before I had my answer.

Grasping her by the hair, I wrenched her head back and took possession of her mouth, swallowing her screams. Ignoring her legs as they kicked, I pushed my hand between her legs. I ran two fingers along the seam of her pussy, pleased to feel the evidence of her arousal. With my middle finger, I teased her tight entrance, slipping in to the first knuckle. Her body clasped tightly around me. I groaned as I imagined the same sensation around my shaft.

Freeing her lips, I growled against her mouth. "This may hurt, malyshka."

With no warning, I thrust my finger in deep, pushing hard till I felt the thin delicate membrane of her maidenhead. She was still intact.

Fuck, she was tight.

It was going to be a struggle to get my thick cock inside her.

"You are lucky you are still innocent or I would have had to kill the man who had robbed me of what was rightfully mine."

I pulled my finger free and slipped it inside my mouth, tasting her.

Her pretty lips opened on a shocked gasp, but she didn't respond.

Knowing I'd been rough with her, I pulled her panties up and her dress hem down as gently as I could.

She lowered her head. I brushed her soft curls away from her face and forced her to meet my gaze.

Her emerald eyes sparkled with gold flecks as tears streamed down her flushed cheeks. She hopped off my lap and took several steps away from me. Swiping at her tears, she swore, "I hate you Gregor Ivanov, and I never want to see you ever again."

Rising, I adjusted my still painfully hard cock in my pants before closing my suit jacket. "Well, malyshka, that's going to be difficult, seeing as how I'll be your husband two weeks from now."

CHAPTER 4

Samara

"I won't marry him! I won't!"

It was excruciating having to go through the rest of Nadia's party as if my entire world hadn't just been turned upside down. After my humiliating encounter with Gregor, I snuck into Nadia's bedroom and borrowed a sweater to cover my torn dress. After brushing my hair and fixing my makeup, I returned to the party right as the accordion player started to play and everyone sang the song from the Cheburashka cartoon.

As everyone was singing the chorus, *it's so sad that a birthday can only happen once a year*, I caught Nadia's eye. Surprisingly, she looked as miserable as I felt.

The lights dimmed, and everyone turned to watch as her mother walked through the doorway holding a big cake decorated with eighteen candles.

Nadia and I seized the moment.

She clasped my hand. "I have to talk to you!"

"Me too!"

"Usual place?"

As Russians it was in our blood not to trust electronics, so they had taught us even from an early age not to have important conversations on cell phones. Our houses were less than a block apart so since we were little girls, I used to sneak out of mine and meet her inside her playhouse, which was tucked away inside some trees in the back of her yard. The security guards always knew we were there, so we were never in any real danger.

I nodded. "Two am?"

She nodded.

"I'll tell Yelena." My other best friend.

I moved away from Nadia just as her parents reached her with the cake and made my way across the room to Yelena. I bumped her with my shoulder and mouthed *two am*. She nodded.

We both watched as Nadia pasted on a fake smile and dutifully blew out her candles. Everyone cheered and surrounded her. They all started pulling on her ears and shouting out each year till they got to eighteen. A silly Russian custom no one really knew the origin of.

As I watched over the tops of their heads, there was no mistaking when Gregor joined the party. I shivered despite the warmth in the room.

He was leaning against the doorway, looking like the devil himself.

Keeping his dark gaze trained on me, he slowly raised a glass to his lips. I watched as he pulled an ice cube into his mouth and then crushed it between his sharp teeth.

I swallowed.

Pivoting away, my cheeks burned as I heard his laughter over the chatter of the crowd.

* * *

"You can't make me marry him!"

We were back at my home, and I'd finally confronted my father about what Gregor had said. Part of me felt silly for even bringing it up. I mean, the idea was ludicrous. I was technically still in high school! Besides, this was the twenty-first century and America; they didn't do arranged marriages anymore. The whole idea was archaic.

My stomach twisted into a sick knot when my father told me it was true.

"I won't do it and that's final," I said.

I stood in front of my father, hands curled into fists. The man had never made it a secret that I disappointed him. I was a girl, not the boy he desperately wanted. I knew I was guilty of ruining my parents' marriage. After me, my mother wasn't able to have any more children. I destroyed his chance at a legacy, and he never missed an opportunity to remind me of it. But even so, I thought the man at least cared a little for me. To give me away in marriage as if I were nothing more than a piece of property he was unloading was colder and more heartless than I ever gave him credit for. Apparently, he hated me far more than even I realized.

My father turned to face me. He struck out, the flat of his hand catching me on the cheek so hard I staggered back. His hand was icy and wet from the chilled vodka bottle he had been holding, but the slap felt like fire on my skin.

"You will do as you're told! You're finally going to be good for something."

My eyes swam with tears as I fell back onto the sofa, nursing my bruised cheek.

My mother raced into the study, her gaze shifting between the two of us as she exclaimed, "Boris, what have you done?"

With my arms wrapped around my stomach, I rocked back and forth, staring at the carpet beneath my feet.

Prussian Blue.

Chrome Yellow Deep.

Vandyke Brown.

Gold Ochre.

My mother sat next to me and awkwardly rubbed my back. It felt strange and unfamiliar, like she was going through the motions of being a caring mother, mimicking something she had seen in a Hallmark movie, probably.

My father paced in front of us. The vodka in his hand sloshed over the side of the glass as he gestured wildly with his hands. "Don't take that tone with me, Alena! You like this big house? A new car every other year? Your trips to Europe? Jewels? Well, those things cost money!"

My mother swiped the air with her arm. The heavy gold bangles around her wrists clanged and rattled. "So? We have plenty of money for those things."

"Had. We *had* plenty of money. It's all gone." My father turned his back and returned to the sidebar to pour himself more vodka.

"What do you mean, Boris? How could it be all gone?" my mother asked as she abandoned me and followed him across the room.

My father shrugged. "Poor investments. Business deals fell through. Nothing for you to worry about."

"Nothing for me to worry about? You say that we are broke now!" My mother snatched the bottle from his hand and poured herself a drink. Picking up the glass, she took a long swallow. She must have been upset. My mother rarely drank vodka. She preferred wine or champagne.

"We *were* broke. I have fixed it!"

She gestured in my direction, her gold bangles clanging. "What? By selling our only daughter?"

"You act like I have given her hand to some stranger in the street. Our family has known the Ivanovs for generations. She will be well provided for."

My mother frowned. "Yes, we have also known that the Ivanovs deal in—"

My father cut her off with a harsh curse.

They both looked at me.

I wasn't surprised. My entire life there was always some kind of secrecy around Nadia's family and how they earned their money. Not even Nadia knows.

I stood up. "Papa, this is wrong! You can't just give me away in marriage as if I'm your property."

My father raised his arm and pointed at me. "It's done, and you will obey me in this."

"I don't understand any of this. Why does he even want to marry me? He barely even knows me."

"He's marrying the Federov name, you stupid girl," he responded viciously. "It has nothing to do with you. He wants the connections and reputation my family name provides. You are nothing to him but a means to an end.".

I crossed my arms over my chest. His words stung, but I refused to be cowed. "Well, I won't marry him. And you can't make me."

My father sighed. "You have no choice. I've already taken the money."

"Well, give it back!"

My mother came to stand before me, wringing her hands. "What would be so bad about being Gregor Ivanov's wife? He is rich. Handsome. You will have a pleasant home and good powerful sons."

I knew the moment my father threatened her with poverty, my mother would shift her loyalty to his side. I wished I could have said it surprised me.

I was alone in this.

What was wrong with Gregor? I couldn't explain it.

When I was a little girl, I used to have the biggest crush on him. I mean, it was to be expected. He was my best friend's big and strong older brother, but even then there was something dark and scary about him. He terrified and intimidated me from the moment I met him.

He had this way of sucking all the energy out of a room when he entered it, like a vampire seducing his victims with a charm that belied his cold, dead stare. Everything revolved around him. Someone like me wouldn't stand a chance in his dark and twisted universe.

I would lose all sense of self, all identity.

Now that he was older and his own man, he was even more terrifying.

The thought of being his wife made me quake.

Sure, the man's kisses could melt my bones, but I wasn't delusional enough to think I would keep his interests for long. I was a teenager in his eyes. A little girl. His sister's friend. He was probably used to sophisticated women. Women who knew how to kiss a man. My cheeks burned at the recollection that he could tell I must be a virgin by how badly I kissed.

There was no way a man like Gregor would want to be saddled with a sheltered suburban girl like me. He would resent me for it from day one. We would have a miserable marriage and wind up hating one another.

"What about college? Art school?" I asked, grasping at straws as my pleading gaze looked from my mother to my father.

I loved to paint and had hoped to go to college to learn more about art technique and history. I knew I had talent. I just needed someone to believe in me. Someone who looked at my paintings and *understood* what I was trying to convey. I always hoped that perhaps if I became a celebrated artist, my parents would see that I had worth and a voice. Now I see what a stupid, immature fantasy it had been to think they would one day see *me* for who I was... and not their disappointment for who I wasn't.

My father shrugged and turned away, not wanting to meet my eye. "You could always do those hobbies later. If your husband permits it."

I was crestfallen. A hobby. That was how my father viewed my desire for a career in art. Nothing more than a distraction from my true purpose, which apparently was to marry and secure a dowry for him.

"Papa, please."

He cleared his throat. "My mind is made up. You will do as you are told. You have no choice. Now go to bed."

I cast a pleading glance at my mother. She lowered her head. She wouldn't go against her husband, not even for her own daughter, especially not if it meant losing her position in society or having to sacrifice her enormous home and jewels.

It was final. They were going to force me to marry Gregor Ivanov the day after I graduated.

* * *

"Nadia, are you up there?" I whispered.

"I'm here!" she whispered back.

Glancing around and seeing no one, although I knew we were probably under surveillance by the guards on her property, I grasped the first wooden slat nailed into the wide tree trunk and slowly climbed the makeshift ladder up to her treehouse. Then lowering my head, I stepped inside.

Unlike most treehouses, her father had this one professionally built, so it was rather beautiful inside. Kind of like a one-room cottage nestled in a tree. As we got older, we moved all the toys and tea sets out and replaced them with thick rugs and lots of large cushions and glass-enclosed candles. We had lined the walls with shelves for Nadia's favorite books, and there were cabinets for my painting supplies. The place now had an exotic yet cozy feel.

Like me, Nadia had changed into yoga pants and a hoodie. Nadia was the baby of the family. She had two older brothers, Gregor and Damien. She looked nothing like either of them. Where they were tall, she was petite. Where they had dark hair and eyes, she had strawberry blonde hair and light blue eyes. They often teased her about being adopted. Both of her brothers were a lot older than her by at least eight years. She was kind of an *oops* baby. So the poor thing always felt a bit awkward and out of place among her own family. They were all so sophisticated and social where she was shy and preferred books to people. It killed her mother that Nadia would rather wear Doc Martens and a baby doll dress than Chanel.

Nadia slumped back onto a pile of pillows. "This was the worst birthday ever!"

I bit my lip. There wasn't a doubt in my mind she had no idea about our families' plans for Gregor and me. They never told her anything. And I had absolutely no idea how I was going to tell her.

"I finally worked up the courage to talk to Mikhail," she said as she stared at the ceiling of the playhouse, which was still plastered with little plastic glow-in-the-dark stars from when we were younger.

"What did he say?"

Nadia shrugged. "He told me I was a silly little girl and that I should go back to my big party before I was missed."

"Oh, Nadia. I'm sorry, but you knew it was a long shot. He's your family's head of security. Your father and brothers would kill him if he was caught with you."

Before she could respond we heard rustling below us.

"Nadia? Samara?"

Crawling over to the open doorway, I poked my head out. Yelena was below. I waved her up.

Once inside, Yelena pushed her long blonde hair away from her face and settled down on one pillow. Of course, she was still in her cute party outfit. Leave it to Yelena to climb a tree in a dress. She was the true fashionista out of our little group.

"No offense, Nadia, but that party sucked," she huffed. Then turning to me, she raised a suggestive eyebrow and asked, "And what were you and Peter up to for so long?"

Peter was the least of my problems right now. "We broke up."

Nadia patted my shoulder as she made a sympathetic sound.

Yelena shrugged. "Never liked him. Never trust a Gemini."

To Yelena, the Zodiac could make all of life's decisions.

I played with the strings on my hoodie. "Listen, I don't even know how to say this, so I'm just going to blurt it out."

Both girls sat up, alerted by my tone that something was wrong.

My eyes filled with tears.

"Oh my God, Samara, what's wrong? Is it Peter?" Nadia asked.

I shook my head.

Yelena stroked my upper arm. "We've been besties since we could walk. You can tell us anything."

Picking at the pillow beneath me, I avoided their gazes. "Nadia, I don't want you to get mad at me."

Her brow furrowed. "Samara, I could never be mad at you. Tell me, what's wrong."

I took a deep breath and blurted it all out. How her

brother caught Peter and me. What Gregor said about us marrying and how my parents confirmed it. The only part I left out was Gregor checking to see if I was still a virgin.

That part was too humiliating to share, even with my closest friends.

Pulling my hoodie sleeve down over my hand, I wiped my cheeks. "I'm sorry, Nadia, but I don't want to marry your brother."

Nadia leaned over and gave me a hug. "I don't want you to marry my brother either!"

I pulled back. "What?"

She shrugged. "I know you had this big crush on him when we were younger, and I know girls think he's cute and stuff...."

Yelena interrupted. "Uh... Nadia. Your brothers aren't cute. They're hot as fuck. Even though they're both a pain in the ass, especially Damien."

She said Damien's name with such animosity that Nadia and I exchanged a look.

Yelena brushed us off. "We had words earlier. I... might be in a little trouble."

"Wait. What? Why?" I asked.

"It's nothing. We're talking about your problem right now."

"Yelena...."

"I'll tell you both later."

Nadia twisted the gold fringe of the pillow she was sitting on. "I love Gregor, but he can be really old-fashioned. I know what he wants in a wife, and Samara is not it. No offense!"

"None taken!" I quickly assured her.

"It's just. Look. It's not like I wouldn't love it if you were truly my sister and all that, but... you're not the only one he scares. He terrifies me sometimes too, and he's my brother! The guy's intense! I still don't know why they sent him back to Russia. It's a big family secret, but I know it was something bad... really bad." Nadia had twisted the fringe around her finger so tightly the tip was turning purple.

We all fell silent for a moment.

Finally, I slumped against the wall with a groan, then said, "I'm in real trouble, aren't I?"

The shock of the situation was wearing off, and the reality was setting in. If I didn't do something drastic, then I would find myself married... *married*... in less than a month. All my dreams would be over. Never mind the fact that my husband would be a man who both terrified and enthralled me. With every kiss, I would lose a piece of myself until there was nothing left.

Yelena pointed at me with a long red fingernail. "You have to run."

Nadia and I both looked at her.

"What?" I asked, not sure I heard her correctly.

"You have to leave. It's your only option. If you stay, your parents will force you to marry him."

"I don't know anyone. I don't have any money. Where would I go?" I argued, even as the idea took root. She was right. It was my only option.

Yelena sat up straighter, and her bright blue eyes lit with excitement. "I have money, and I'm coming with you."

We knew Yelena's home life was shit. Her mother was dead, and her father was a drunk who occasionally hit her. Even in the low light of our treehouse, I could see the shadow of a bruise on her cheek.

We never talked about it.

There were a lot of things we never talked about.

It was just how things were with our families.

Nadia and I always suspected it was one of the reasons Yelena claimed to love makeup and would never be seen without lipstick and foundation on. The real reason was she needed it to cover the bruises.

Nadia raised an eyebrow. "What do you mean you have money? How much money?"

The corner of Yelena's mouth quirked up. "Over a hundred grand."

My mouth fell open. "Yelena! How?"

"Seriously?" Nadia exclaimed.

"That racetrack scheme my piece of shit father was working on. I reworked the algorithm and hit big. Really big." She turned to Nadia. "By the way, it's why your brother Damien is *pissed* at me." She waved her hand in the air dismissively. "Something about bringing on the attention of the feds to some mob scheme."

I took a deep breath. "So we're really doing this? We're running?"

Yelena's smile vanished. "All kidding aside, if Damien is right, I could be in some real trouble with some pretty nasty people because of what I did. I need to get out of town. Now."

We both turned to Nadia.

Tears streamed down her cheeks. She shook her head and whispered, "I can't go."

We didn't bother arguing. She was right. Her brothers would never stop looking for her if she left with us.

We huddled together and hugged.

I whispered against Nadia's hair, wanting to believe what I said was true. "We won't be separated forever. All this will blow over. Gregor will marry someone else, and whatever Yelena did will be forgotten. And then we'll come back, okay, Nadia?"

We stayed in the treehouse planning our escape till the early morning hours.

As I crept across the damp lawn back to my house, I

looked up at the gloomy windows of Nadia's home. I could have sworn Gregor was watching me.

I shivered.

Everything would be fine.

He would be mad for a week or two and then forget all about me.

CHAPTER 5

Gregor

It really was a tragedy I couldn't shoot the man and be done with it.

I rubbed my temples and exhaled slowly, hating with every fiber of my being that I needed this piece of shit alive. The wooden spindle chair groaned and creaked as Boris Federov shifted his considerable bulk.

Boris wiped the sweat from his brow with the sleeve of his suit jacket, leaving a greasy stain on the grey flannel. "She'll be back. She's just having a tantrum. Typical teenager stuff."

Samara had been missing for over a week now. Although my little sister still refused to answer any questions, I learned that because of Yelena Nikitina, Samara's escape was well funded. This was problematic for me. Money bought a great many things.

For our two little runaways, it meant flights out of the country, discreet hotels, and access to fake IDs and paperwork.

For me, it was supposed to have meant an innocent, biddable wife from a well-connected family.

Marrying into the Federov family would have given the Ivanovs the prestige and status my father had craved his entire, bitter life right up until the end, allowing entry into the upper echelons of high society around the globe.

None of that really mattered to me. In my eyes, it was more about business.

Bribes. Blackmail. Power. Politics. Malice. Murder.

All just part of the job.

To the everyday person, I was Gregor Ivanov, CEO of Ivanov Imports. To those who knew better, I was Gregor Ivanov, head of a massive criminal enterprise. I'd taken the helm after my father's death four years ago and more than doubled our family wealth by securing countless, lucrative business relationships, both through fair means and foul.

You see, I never bothered with the petty drug and prostitution game.

Leave that to the gangs and the Italians.

My real trade was in weapons and information.

If you had it, I wanted it.

If you didn't want me to have it, all the better.

Weapons were lucrative but information was the true power.

I didn't just know where all the skeletons were buried... I was the one who buried them.

Because I was the man with all the information, the money... and the power.

Which was how I found out Boris Federov had crossed a line, borrowing against money he didn't have and gambling with his life and future by getting into bed with the Nigerians.

So being my father's son, I struck a deal.

I purchased Federov's daughter.

It was as simple as that... or at least, I told myself it was that simple.

It was just business, nothing personal.

Just cold-hearted business.

When I first learned she had fled, I assumed she'd be caught within a few days, figuring she was hiding at a friend's house. It was understandable. Learning your father had arranged your marriage to someone you barely knew—and in all honesty, probably feared, had to have rattled her.

I'm sure me chasing off that asshole she called a boyfriend didn't help matters in her mind.

The trouble was I didn't care. This wasn't about her.

This was about business, and right now, her little teenage tantrum was interfering with my plans. We already had to suffer the embarrassment of cancelling the wedding. I didn't give a shit about the pageantry of the affair; I cared about the seventy-five million-dollar weapons deal it scuttled. Weddings were an excellent cover for dark dealings. It was much easier bringing a general from the Russian 14th Army based in Transnistria and a third world dictator together under one roof when you could claim they were extended family here for a wedding.

I worked with Dimitri Kosgov and Vaska Rostov for months to smuggle a small arsenal of tanks and surface-to-air missiles out of Transnistria and into Morocco. Now they sat in a warehouse gathering dust waiting to be transported out. There had already been one attempt to seize the weapons, which fortunately my head of security, Mikhail Volkov, and Dimitri had taken care of, but there would be others.

Having the diplomatic ties of the Federov name as I traveled with my blushing new bride would have helped mediate the matter.

My little malyshka was definitely becoming more of a problem than I anticipated.

She certainly had shown more spirit than I was expecting.

When I made the deal with her father, she was nothing but a fragmented memory to me, a pretty girl in pigtails who played with my sister. I remembered her being a shy and squirrelly little thing who always seemed to hide whenever I entered a room but that was about it. I hadn't even asked to see a photo. At the time, the chit's appearance was of no importance.

To me, she was a means to an end. Nothing more.

I was after her family name and an heir. She didn't have to be pretty for me to fuck a baby into her belly. Especially since I had no intention of truly honoring our vows. I would return to Russia and my life and women there for the better part of each year while she kept my home and raised my children here.

Then I saw her.

Standing there in the moonlight.

I couldn't believe it when I heard that asshole utter her name.

Samara. *This* was Samara.

My Samara? My future bride.

In truth I had been expecting a skinny somewhat awkward girl so I wasn't prepared for those generous curves that made a man just want to grab her by the hips and thrust in deep. Her skin was so pale and flawless it looked luminous. In that instant, I wanted to drive my fingers into her thick hair, which fell in a riot of auburn waves over her shoulders, and twist till her head fell back so I could claim those gorgeous full lips for my own.

Those beautiful emerald eyes wide with fear.

That fuckwit boy is lucky I didn't snap his neck then and there.

Then later, I certainly wasn't prepared for the physical shock the moment I touched her.

Tasted those lips.

Felt her innocence pressed against the tip of my finger as her body writhed within my embrace.

In that moment, everything changed.

A primal need to seize and conquer rose within my blood.

In retrospect, I should have realized she was barely more than a child.

No wonder I had terrified and overwhelmed her.

No wonder she had fled.

I had been a monster.

In short, I had been my father's son.

The bastard was dead. I was king of the savage Ivanov criminal empire, and yet still his dark shadow stretched over my life.

My earliest memory as a child was my father beating a man to death with his bare hands.

I remembered every detail of that moment. The sick copper smell of fresh blood. My father's bruised knuckles. The splatters of crimson across the wall and floor, and most especially, the pitiful moans.

What made it worse was the man lying at my father's feet had been my beloved uncle.

My uncle had betrayed the family. That was the only explanation I received at the time and would ever receive, even decades later.

Still, the message was obvious.

Our loyalty to family came first, and we never betrayed family.

The Ivanov family had enough wealth to last for generations, but what we didn't have was prestige.

In my father's eyes, our family was still scrounging for scraps after losing it all in the Bolshevik revolution. He had been obsessed with reclaiming our status and honor, but unfortunately, you cannot buy back the past but you can buy the future.

Tilting my wrist, I wound the dial on my Maîtres du Temps platinum watch. "You've cost me not only a great deal of money but a great deal of embarrassment and inconvenience as well."

"Gregor, I promise you…."

"That's *Mr. Ivanov* to you."

The older man bristled but swallowed his pride. Pride had no place when you were a useless beggar dependent on others for your survival. Boris Federov would have nothing if I hadn't stepped in and replenished his fortune… for the bargain price of his virgin daughter.

Clearing his throat, he continued, "Mr. Ivanov, I promise you. Samara is a good girl. She'll return soon."

Rising to my full height from my position leaning against his desk, I crossed the room and circled around his chair. "You assured me your daughter was obedient and would fall in line with our plans."

Boris sputtered and coughed. "And… and… she will! This isn't her fault. It's those slut friends of hers. They're a bad influence."

I rubbed my jaw with the back of my hand before reaching into the inner pocket of my suit jacket and pulling out my brass knuckles. Slipping them onto my right hand, I positioned myself in front of Boris. I waited as his beady eyes shifted from my metal-encased knuckles, to my face, the men who were guarding the two entrances to his home study.

The man's body jerked with fear as I reached over and

picked a small piece of lint off his shoulder. My voice was deceptively low and calm. "My little sister happens to be one of your daughter's closest friends. Are you calling her a slut?"

Before he could respond, I bent my arm back and threw a hard punch straight into his jaw.

The chair tipped backwards and crashed to the floor as Boris howled in pain. Climbing out of the chair, he fell to his knees and raised his arms in a placating gesture. "No! No! I wouldn't disrespect you or your departed father that way!"

Grabbing him by the collar, I wrenched him to his feet as I kicked the chair upright. Tossing him back into his seat, I rested my hands on the armrests. "It occurs to me that your daughter might not be lost after all."

Boris tilted his head to the side and spit out the blood which had pooled in his mouth. "What are you saying?"

"I'm saying you are a deceitful, disloyal bastard who may have gotten the extremely dangerous idea of double-crossing me by selling your daughter's virtue to a second bidder."

"How dare you call into question my honor!" he raged.

I punched him a second time.

Boris started to bellow as snot dripped from his nose and blood from his mouth.

Fuck, I really hated this part of my job. Not the violence, that was necessary. I hated the distasteful crying.

Turning away in disgust, I ran the tips of my fingers over the cool surface of a large Fabergé egg on his desk which was suspended on a gold pedestal. From its intricate emerald and gold design, it resembled the Empire Nephrite, one of the missing eggs which disappeared after the fall of the Romanovs. The beginning of the end for my family name. If it were in fact real, it would figure that a man like Federov would have one of the lost imperial treasures casually displayed on this desk. An obscene gesture of wealth and influence.

Turning back to the matter at hand, I said, "I'm afraid we have a problem then. I have paid you a great deal of money for a product you haven't delivered on."

"I... I... can't give you the money back. I've already spent most of it. I had creditors and obligations," he blubbered.

Fortunately, for him. I didn't give a damn about the money, not anymore. Fifteen million was nothing to a man of my fortune.

I didn't want my money back... I wanted her.

Now.

I wasn't a patient man, so being denied something I already considered mine did not rest easily with me.

Boris continued to spew venom. Nothing was this man's fault. Not his staggeringly poor financial management or judgement, not his daughter's disappearance, nothing. "This isn't on me. The bitch is your problem now. I can't be held responsible if you can't get her down the aisle. And I shouldn't be expected to give the money back!"

And now... he'd just crossed a line.

Storming back over to him, I snatched him up by the front of his shirt. "That's my future wife you just insulted," I growled. Raising my arm, I slammed my fist into his mouth over and over again. A final cut to the jaw rendered him unconscious. I tossed his heavy, dead weight to the floor.

"Take care of this," I said over my shoulder as I pulled off the bloody brass knuckles and threw it to one of my men.

Leaving the study, I headed to the front stairs and upper level. It took only a moment to find Samara's bedroom. Perhaps there was a clue to where she and Yelena were hiding. It was apparent her parents weren't going to search for her. If she was going to be found, it would be up to me.

The hunt was on but first I needed to learn more about my prey.

If I was expecting a foolish girl's room filled with pink

pillows and unicorns, I was disappointed. The walls were covered in posters of famous paintings, mostly the Impressionists, which happened to be one of my favorite art periods, as well.

The carpet was stained with small drops of paint and just about every surface was cluttered with brushes, paint tubes, and other paraphernalia.

She was an artist.

I didn't know that.

But where was her artwork?

Her parents' taste could best be described as garish. Their house was filled with gilt-framed, unremarkable works including a rather unfortunate portrait of a panther stretched out on a gold-limbed tree.

Crossing to a small door on the other side of the room, I threw it open and pulled on the small chain to turn on the light. The narrow walk-in closet was filled with canvases. Her clothes were crammed into the corner to make room for the haphazardly stacked paintings.

Selecting one from the top of the nearest pile, I carried the canvas back into her bedroom where the light was better. It was actually a student's study of *Christina's World* by Andrew Wyeth. The original painting was famous for its realism juxtaposed with its surrealist tones. Wyeth meticulously painted each blade of glass invoking a profound image of the American pastoral landscape.

Samara had made the subject her own, giving it a more Impressionist slant. Instead of a realistic portrait of a field of grass, it was more an expanse of tawny gold with flecks of captured light.

It was the subject which most grabbed my attention. In the original, the viewer focuses on the sense of longing and isolation of Christina as she pulls her broken body across the field toward her home.

In Samara's version, there was a haunting desperation to the figure. I couldn't help noticing the subject's dark brunette hair and slight body had been altered to more accurately reflect Samara's auburn locks and curvy figure. She had painted herself into the portrait.

The raw despair and anxiety on display unsettled me.

It made me want to pull her into my arms and promise to chase all her monsters away.

That was impossible of course... since I was the monster chasing her.

CHAPTER 6

Gregor

Chicago, Illinois - Three years later

"You're sure it's them this time?" asked Damien as he flipped the knife he usually kept in his boot between his fingers. He was as anxious as I was to see this chase finished. The stakes had risen over the last few months.

"I'm sure."

For the three years while I had been chasing my fugitive bride, Damien had been chasing her friend. Yelena Nikitina had gotten under my brother's skin. Unlike with Samara, we weren't the only ones looking for Yelena. The stupid girl had fucked up, badly. She had pissed off the wrong people, and if our source was correct, they were closing in. Since Yelena was on the run with Samara, that put my girl in the crosshairs, which made it my problem.

The good news was that same source gave up their location.

Chicago.

The moment we heard, Damien and I both dropped everything and ordered our private plane ready. We would not waste the best lead we had gotten in over a year.

We both had a mutual purpose, to find the girls and bring them back under our protection.

I cracked my knuckles and stared out the window of our private plane as they finally lowered the landing gear. Soon I would be in the same city as Samara. I still couldn't believe it had taken me three years to find her.

Three years of searching.

Three years of wondering if she was safe. If she was even alive.

Three years of imagining the worse.

And I had no one to blame but myself.

There was no point in denying it.

Three years of searching had allowed for quite a bit of self-reflection. I had barreled into Samara's life and ruthlessly laid claim to her. For all intents and purposes, I now owned her in my mind. She was mine to do with as I pleased. The wedding itself was a mere formality.

Besides, if I hadn't taken the girl, who knows what her father may have done.

Her father was desperate, and desperate men did dangerous things.

Boris Federov was still a liability and could not be trusted.

Just another reason I was desperate to find Samara and bring her back under my protection… where she belonged.

As far as I was concerned, she was mine.

Bought and paid for.

I owned her.

It was now my job to protect her. If necessary, from her own father... just not from me.

Recognizing my fault in how I handled letting my bride-to-be know about her upcoming nuptials didn't change anything between us. She would still need to be taught a lesson. She could make choices in life, but those choices had consequences.

Samara would have to face those consequences.

I was, after all, still my father's son... nothing had changed.

Not with my father's death, and not now.

She was still mine.

I had every intention of making sure she knew her place and that I would not tolerate any disobedience from this point forward.

I wasn't sure when a passing fascination became a full-blown obsession, but somewhere between tasting those sweet, innocent lips of hers and knowing she had run off, the single driving force of my life had become finding her and claiming her as my own.

It had robbed me of something precious and unique. She was there, in my arms one moment, and then gone the next. Even now, years later, a darkness rose inside my chest every time I thought about it. Any sympathy I may have had towards her hardened as the months went by. Months of having to rein in my anger and frustration over not knowing where she was... or who she may be with.

I was certain her father was hiding her from me, but as the weeks and months passed, it became obvious her parents were clueless.

Even putting my little sister under surveillance accomplished nothing except fracturing our already strained relationship. There was a good chance Nadia would never forgive me for chasing away her best friends.

Samara and her friend Yelena had vanished without a trace.

It helped they were bankrolled by some track winnings of Yelena's but still. They were two young women. I had a powerful network of politicians, policemen, businessmen, and thugs at my disposal, and yet nothing.

For three years.

Nothing but mistaken identity leads and cold trails.

I had come close once in Boston. Breaking through the door of the apartment they shared, I could still catch the scent of Samara's perfume, Coco Mademoiselle, in the air. Despite trying to catch them off guard in the middle of the night, they somehow knew we were coming and fled. I remember touching the pillow I knew to be Samara's and feeling the warmth still clinging to the soft fabric.

Everything I knew about Samara came only from glimpses of her life through the belongings she was forced to leave behind every time I got too close.

A perfume bottle and a few dresses in Mexico.

A battered wooden case filled with oil paints and brushes in Los Angeles.

Three thoroughly read copies of *Dracula* found in New Orleans, Houston, and Vancouver. Obviously, her favorite book, and now mine.

Always Chinese chopsticks in the utensil drawer nestled among countless packets of soy sauce, but never a fork or plate.

My mouth quirked up at the corner... and countless McDonalds' receipts for Cafe Mochas and Egg McMuffins.

All dead leads until now.

The girls had gotten complacent.

They must have assumed we had stopped looking for them and settled in Chicago.

And that's when I finally found her.

They should have known better than to try to settle down in a city I traveled to frequently and where I had extensive contacts.

I flipped opened the file on the table in front of me. There was a stack of black and white surveillance photos.

Samara's loft was barely more than an open space. The massive windows gave a perfect view even of the bedroom—which was little more than a mattress on the floor—and several metal racks for clothes. Most of the photos were of her painting. She typically wore dark jeans with wide cuffs, a paint smeared t-shirt, and her hair tied up in a messy bun with what looked like some kind of bandana wrapped around her head.

I continued to flip through the photos with interest.

One photo after another showed her eating Chinese food straight out of the container. Staying up late watching what looked like old black and white films. Living in an apartment with barely any furniture and generally taking lousy care of herself.

What this little girl needed was discipline, I thought as I paused on a photo of her laying on her stomach on the bed. She was surrounded by what looked like art books and yet another half empty Chinese food container.

In another photo, Samara was dressed in some kind of vintage-looking dress. Her head was tilted back as she held a bottle of perfume close to her throat, Coco Mademoiselle by Chanel. I imagined what it would be like to lick her neck and taste the bitter sting of the perfume on her skin.

"Rockabilly."

"What?"

I turned to Damien, trying to focus on what he just said as opposed to my rising cock.

"The dress. It's a rockabilly style. Trim waist. Nice flare. High collar."

I can't help but give him an incredulous stare. "What the hell?"

I'm trying to rectify the image of my six-foot-three brute of a brother chatting about dainty trim waists and dress styles.

"What? You fuck enough models you learn about fashion. It's obvious Samara is all about the vintage 50s look. Red lips, cuffed jeans, the whole nine."

"Worry about your own girl, Versace."

I returned my attention to the file in front of me. The final black-and-white photo was of Samara sleeping.

Only the window directly facing the mattress on the floor seemed to have a curtain, which on this particular night she had forgotten to close.

Despite the slightly grainy appearance, I could tell she had fallen asleep with her makeup on. The dark outline of her lips was unmistakable against her pale skin. No doubt it was a deep, crimson red. She slept on her back with one arm resting above her head. It was easy to imagine that delicate wrist wrapped with a leather restraint and secured to the end of the bed.

There was at once a surge of anger and possession.

Anger that she was so foolish and careless enough not to realize there was a camera recording her every intimate moment while she lived in this fishbowl she called an apartment. I would put a stop to that immediately.

And possession knowing that soon this wild little creature would be under my complete control.

Soon, I would once again feel her warm, soft skin under

my hand and taste those sweet cherry lips as I swallowed her cries. My cock hardened at the thought.

Soon.

I checked my watch. We had just enough time to make it to the art gallery where Samara now worked under the assumed name of Gwen Stevens. I had made an appointment with her there today under the false name of Davidson.

After three years… the hunt was almost over.

CHAPTER 7

*S*amara

Balancing the phone against my shoulder, I pinned the wig cap into place.

"I'm running a little late, but I'll be there before Mr. Davidson arrives, I promise!"

I still refused to be seen in public without some kind of disguise, just in case. Yelena had stopped wearing one over a year ago. She was braver than I was.

Juggling the phone to my other shoulder, I pushed a bobby pin into place behind my ear.

"Yes. I had the boys pull the paintings I think he'll like out of storage. I'm getting ready now. I'll be there in twenty. I promise!"

Hanging up the phone, I ran over to the bed and dumped out my purse. Rifling through the contents, I grabbed my makeup bag, unzipped it, and dumped that out, too. Shifting through the various tubes of lipstick, eyeliners, and compacts scattered around my rumpled sheets, I searched for my favorite red lipstick. It was a classic red matte straight out of the old femme fatale noir films I love. Call me superstitious, but it was my good luck charm.

Taking off the lipstick top, I swung back to the mirror and smeared on a perfect cupid's bow. With my long auburn hair and bangs tucked up into the wig cap, I selected a neat blonde bob wig. It was a blunt cut just below my ears. I gave my head a shake to make sure it was secure.

Stepping back a few feet, I stared at my reflection. "Hello, Mr. Davidson. I'm Gwen Stevens. I'm Gwen Stevens. I'm Miss Stevens. I'm Gwen."

I repeated the name a few times till I felt more in character. The key was to believe in the lie. I needed to become Gwen Stevens, Art Consultant.

Over my shoulder in the mirror's reflection, I could see who I truly was—Samara Federova, a failed artist and for all intents and purposes a fugitive bride.

My apartment wasn't so much an apartment as a massive open-air loft. It used to be an old pencil factory. I chose it for its high ceilings and massive windows. Great for natural light. I dedicated most of the space to my painting studio. I filled the place with stacked canvases, easels with half-finished paintings, several workbenches filled with brushes, paints, and rags. I didn't even have a sofa, and the bed was just a mattress on the floor.

It wasn't for a lack of money; I had plenty of that in an offshore account thanks to Yelena and her racetrack betting schemes.

It was just I'd rather spend it on clothes and paints than something stupid like furniture, especially since we moved around so much.

Although after three years, we were finally putting down some roots.

It had been ages since we had a close call. The rumors of Gregor and Damien looking for us had all died down. It was time to build some kind of life. Which was why I got this job at an art gallery and my first apartment on my own.

My eye caught on the tarp-covered canvas in the center of the room. Underneath it was my latest painting in a series I was calling *Little Girl Lost*. This one had a girl dressed in a magenta dress tumbling down a hill into a black void as she reached out in vain for help. I thought the series was some of my best work. Unfortunately, I had only sold one of my canvases so far—my favorite.

It was a girl dressed in an emerald green dress and, like the others, she was tumbling through a void, but unlike the rest, a firm masculine hand had latched onto her wrist… saving her. I had titled it *Little Girl Saved*.

We were hiding out in Boston at the time, and I was so thrilled when a small gallery agreed to showcase my work. I couldn't believe it when they contacted me and said they had a buyer for the painting, and they wanted to meet me. *They bought one of my paintings.*

Yelena was furious when she learned I had used my actual name. It was stupid and rash and I shouldn't have done it, but I selfishly wanted my actual name on my art. She made us leave town that night. She was right, of course. I had put us both in danger. Still, I couldn't help wondering what would have happened if we had stayed in town a little while longer. If we had risked it. Would I have sold more paintings? Would it have been the start of my career as an artist?

Shaking my head, I focused. It didn't serve any purpose to dwell on what wasn't.

If I couldn't sell my art, at least I could be around it and help other artists sell theirs.

I'm Gwen Stevens. Gwen Stevens. Art Consultant. Gwen.

Sweeping my arm over the bed, I shoved all the contents back into my purse and ran out the door.

Never noticing, in my haste, I had left behind the one thing Yelena warned me to never, ever be without—a small leather portfolio with my extra fake IDs, passports, and cash, in case we ever had to leave and weren't able to return to our apartments.

Little did I know just how much I would come to regret it.

CHAPTER 8

Samara

I TOOK the train to the Bridgeport neighborhood and made it to the gallery with only a few minutes to spare.

"Hello boys!" I greeted Sal and Jimmy as I walked through the door.

Sal gave my ass in my black dress pants a once-over, which made me uncomfortable. "Hey ya, Gwen."

"Let's get this art on the walls. The client will be here soon," I said pointedly, avoiding his blatant stare.

I directed where I wanted each of the paintings to go, then hustled over to my desk to check emails before Mr. Davidson arrived.

Most of these executives were posers. They didn't understand what good art was any more than they knew about fine wine. It was all just a shell game. They thought art made them look big and important to their clients and associates, so they were buying culture and class. It was one big con. I was just being a little more honest about it.

That's why they hired someone like Gwen Stevens. She told them what to buy, and they acted like they knew what she was talking about and opened their wallets. They got to look good to their *Forbes* list cronies, an artist got a painting sold, and I walked away with a nice commission. Everyone was happy.

I got a nice one on the hook for today.

Julius Davidson. CEO of Brecht Industries. According to their website, they were looking to merge with some large Japanese company and soon, which was probably why he wanted to acquire some art for his building's lobby and his office. He needed to make the impression of wealth and sophistication.

Which was why he needed Gwen Stevens, Art Consultant.

After looking around the gallery to see that all the paintings were in place, I straightened my cardigan before smoothing the back of my wig down. Finally, I checked my lipstick in the reflection of the glass door.

I'm Gwen Stevens.

I was ready.

A black Escalade rolled up precisely on time.

"He's here," I throw out over my shoulder. I don't have to turn to know that Sal and Jimmy have made themselves scarce through the back door. They won't return till they get the all clear text from me.

Composed, I watched as the back door of the Escalade opened.

I couldn't see Mr. Davidson's face. He was turned away and talking to someone still inside the vehicle.

Then he turned to face the gallery entrance.

And my heart stopped.

It's him.
He found me.
Impossible.
No.

Maybe my eyes were playing tricks on me.

It wouldn't be the first time I had seen Gregor's face in a crowd. Every man over six feet tall with black hair in a suit gave my heart a lurch till I got a closer look.

This man's black hair was brushed casually back from his face, displaying painfully sharp cheekbones, but he was still mostly in shadow inside the car.

As he stepped from the vehicle, he smoothly buttoned his suit jacket over what was no doubt a muscular, flat abdomen. Being friends with someone like Yelena meant learning to recognize the tailored lines of a bespoke suit. The silver pinstripe suit fit him to perfection. As he adjusted his cuffs, I was certain I glimpsed cut black stone cufflinks. Black diamond? Perhaps black sapphire.

Everything about this man said money… and power.

Gregor.

A flutter of unease rippled through me.

It *was* him.

Gregor Ivanov.

I stood frozen to the spot. Unable to move.

His hand was already on the handle of the glass gallery door.

It was too late to run.

Would my wig and the passing years be enough of a disguise?

I no longer looked like the naïve teenager I once was.

Three years on the run will do that to you.

My face was more angular. My cheekbones higher and sharper. The slightly plump curves of a suburban teenager with no cares had been replaced by the lean muscle of a woman who constantly looked over her shoulder and saw monsters in every shadow.

The last time he had seen me was in a dark bedroom, and the time before that I had been little more than a girl. Besides, I was probably only one woman among thousands to a man like Gregor. He probably couldn't even remember my eye color.

I've got this.

I'm Gwen Stevens.

Taking a step back, I waited for him to open the door.

The moment he did, I knew I was fooling myself.

I don't have this.

It was Gregor.

He had found me… and I was fucked.

"Good afternoon, Miss Stevens, I assume? I'm Julius Davidson."

I was momentarily taken aback by his casual tone.

It took a second to register what he had just said. Julius. He had introduced himself as Julius.

So, we were both going to do this subterfuge?

That's right.

I forgot how much Gregor liked his twisted games.

This was just another version of Russian roulette.

His voice was low and dark, every word uttered with a precise clip on the end, as if he were using his sharp white teeth to bite off the edges.

Fine.

Let's play, Gregor.

"Good afternoon, *Mr. Davidson*. I've been expecting you," I said, perhaps a bit too breathlessly, as I extended my hand.

His own warm hand engulfed mine in a strong yet gentle grip. I remembered the feel of his hands. Large and slightly scarred. Callused, but not rough. Heavily tattooed. The most visible image was a swallow on the back of his right hand. I remembered googling it once. A swallow tattoo symbolized fidelity and loyalty. It fit. Gregor wasn't just the loyal leader of the Ivanov family; he *was* the family and embodied all the power and savagery that name symbolized.

"Julius," he corrected, piercing me with his platinum gray eyes.

Platinum Gray eyes.
Chromatic Black hair.
Butter Pecan lightly tanned skin.

"Julius," I whispered back as I lowered my eyes, slightly shaken from his gaze.

He slips the single bullet into the chamber and spins it.
Breathe.
You got this.

"I'm looking forward to seeing what you have arranged for me this afternoon... Gwen."

First pull of the trigger.
Misfire.
The chamber spins.

He knows, my mind screamed.

I wasn't fooling him for a second.

The way he said my name, with the subtle pause and emphasis.

My sense of self-preservation screamed at me to run, although I knew it was too late. I wouldn't get two steps across the gallery before he grabbed me.

I needed to play this charade out.

See what he had planned for me. For us.

Interlocking my fingers to hide my nervousness, I walked ahead of him, keeping my head low and cocked at an angle.

I'm being silly.
Everything is fine.
I'm Gwen Stevens.

"You mentioned this acquisition was for your corporate

headquarters. I thought something sleek yet engaging, forceful yet approachable would be best."

Stopping before the first painting, I refused to turn around, keeping my face averted and my focus on the wall ahead. Every nerve ending felt his presence behind me. He was so close; I could feel the brush of his warm breath on my exposed neck. Why did I have to choose the bob wig for today?

Dammit.

I inhaled a warm woodsy scent with a hint of spicy ginger.

Bleu de Chanel

His cologne.

Gesturing towards the painting, I continued. "This is a widely in demand artist among the exclusive circles. You could acquire his work for a fraction of what it will be worth after his show in New York next month."

"I see," Gregor murmured from his powerful stance behind me.

The hum from his words sent a shock to my system. I didn't just hear them; I could *feel* them.

"You'll notice the use of form and color, the unnatural brush strokes. Ingenious. As you can see, I have arranged to have several pieces of his here today as an exclusive showing."

"He appears to be a rare talent," Gregor said obligingly.

Why did it sound like he wasn't referring to the painting?

He cocks the hammer back.

I took a deliberate step to the side, then a few additional steps away from his unnerving presence.

He smoothly followed. The light scrape of his shoe on the hardwood floor was the only sound in the quiet gallery space.

This time, I stood perpendicular to the wall. I was now firmly on the defense.

"Here is another sample of his work. Notice the use of geometric shapes."

"A unique talent." Gregor stood before me, not looking at the painting.

There was the faint rustle of his suit as he lifted his arm. Before I could step back, one strong finger hooked under my chin and lifted my face.

Was now the moment?

Was he going to rip the wig off my head and drag me out of the gallery?

Taking a step closer, he stared at my red lips before asking, "Can I see the rest of the paintings?"

Pulls the trigger.

Another misfire.

My mouth dropped open in surprise.

That was not what I was expecting him to say.

I watched as what I thought was a spark of something intense flitted across his dark eyes before they were quickly shuttered.

He was playing with me.

He was enjoying this.

He spins the chamber again.

How many misfires had there been?

What was the law of probability that I would survive this little game of his?

"Yes... yes, of course," I stuttered as I lifted my jaw and turned my head away. "Here is another artist they will be showing in California next Summer. This is one of her early prints. Notice the use of a stark white background to enforce her message of spirituality through shape and form."

"What about that one?" he asked. Placing a hand at my

lower back, he guided me to the end of the gallery. As we stood before the painting, he did not remove his hand.

Shifting my foot, I meant to slide out of his grasp before responding.

The slightest, subtle press of his hand warned me not to move.

I obeyed.

"This is a Simes. A notoriously anti-social painter who only deals with a very select number of consultants and refuses to show his work in any public forum."

"Well, aren't you the lucky girl?"

"What?"

"You've been chosen."

He pulls back the hammer.

Chosen.

To marry him?

He pulls the trigger.

Heedless of the silent command of his hand on my back, I broke contact and stepped back.

He followed.

I took another step back, hitting the wall. My breath came in gasps.

"I don't know what you mean," I whisper, desperately trying to read his set features.

He leaned down, his lips so close I could smell the hint of mint on his breath. "Simes. You mentioned he is very selective in who he chooses to work with."

The gun goes off.

Misfire.

Another spin of the chamber.

"I think I see what I want… I'll be back later to claim it," he said, almost against my mouth.

He then straightened and turned on his heel. His confident stride took him back to the entrance to the gallery.

There was a slight rush of cool air from the open door. It brushed over my heated cheeks.

Without moving, I watched the pavement outside as his driver opened the door for him.

He entered, and within moments, the sleek Escalade pulled away.

Only then did I release the breath I was holding.

I had survived... but for how long?

And why?

The chamber spun again.

The hammer cocked back...

Bang.

CHAPTER 9

*S*amara

Tearing off my wig, I pushed my long, tangled hair out of my face and called Yelena again. "Yelena, call me back. Code Red! Code Red!"

I had already left her four voicemails.

Where the fuck was she?

We had to get out of town. Now.

Worst case scenario, if I couldn't get ahold of her, we had a Plan B in place, for just this scenario. We would meet up at a small house we bought in Montreal and decide where to go next.

Still, I would feel better knowing she was safe.

If Gregor was here then that meant that his brother Damien probably was as well. I know he and Yelena had sparred with one another in the past. Plus, he was probably really pissed that she continued to work that racetrack scam. If Gregor found me then there was an exceptional chance

Damien had found Yelena. *Fuck!*

Gregor's car had barely pulled away from the curb before I was grabbing my purse and sneaking out the back door. I had changed cabs four times on my way back home in case I was followed.

It was probably all for nothing.

If he knew where I worked then he knew where I lived, but I clung to a sliver of hope.

I had no choice.

Fuck.

I wish I hadn't been so stupid as to leave my fake passports and IDs at home. Yelena had taught me better. I should have had them with me at all times. I was in a hurry this morning and got sloppy. Now I had no choice but to risk going back because I obviously couldn't use the Gwen Stevens ID and credit cards anymore, and I definitely didn't have enough cash on me to flee to another country.

Maybe it'll be okay?
Maybe he hadn't recognized me after all?
He did leave.
Why did he do that?
Was it just to mess with me?
To get in my head?
Well, it's fucking working!

Finally, I was back at my loft. There was no sign of his Escalade on the street.

With shaking hands, I punched in the key code to enter the building

I paused in the hallway and placed my ear to my apartment door. Everything seemed quiet and still. Holding my breath, I carefully slipped the key in the lock and turned it, cringing when the lock gave with a loud metallic click. I paused. Nothing. I let out the breath I was holding. Pushing the door open slightly, I peeked inside. Nothing seemed amiss.

Shuffling inside, I pivoted to close the door quickly.

A man's arm reached over my head and stopped it from closing.

Letting out a shocked scream, I dropped my purse and keys on the floor, my gaze rose to face a pair of platinum gray eyes.

Gregor stood before me like a vengeful god.

"Welcome home, *Gwen*." His voice was dark and low… controlled.

I opened my mouth to scream.

His hand closed around my throat. "Tsk. Tsk. Tsk. I can't have you screaming like that, malyshka."

My fingers clawed at the back of his hands.

"You've been a very bad girl, Samara."

His grasp prevented me from speaking. After he could see I would no longer try to cry out, he lowered his arm. Straightening his suit cuffs, he ordered, "Now be a good girl and invite me in for a chat."

It was hard not to feel like Mina inviting the fiend Dracula in.

Like Dracula, Gregor seemed to exude a dark energy which fed on my own fears and desires.

Knowing I had no choice, I complied.

"Won't you come in?" I responded through clenched teeth as my hand grasped my throat.

Taking a step forward, I shook as he made his presence known directly behind me.

This was bad.

Very bad.

I quickly scanned the open area of the loft. There was no sign of his brother, Damien. We were alone. Was this why

Yelena wasn't answering her phone? Had Gregor's brother already captured her?

Fuck!

If I had any chance of getting out of this, I needed to reach my bed. Under the pillow was one of two .38 specials Yelena and I bought for protection when we were in Mexico the first few months we were in hiding. Taking a few more hesitant steps, I waited till I was close, then lunged for the mattress. Falling across it on my stomach, I slid my hand under the pillow.

There was nothing there.

Horrified, I turned on my back and looked up at Gregor. He was standing close to the bed, legs spread wide as he towered over my prone form. Reaching behind him, he pulled the revolver free from his waistband. "Looking for this?"

With a cry, I rolled onto my stomach and tried to scramble away across the rumpled bed sheets. He grabbed my ankle and pulled me toward him. Reaching down, he fisted my hair and lifted me up.

"Ow! Ow! Ow!" I cried out as I reached up to try to dislodge his grasp.

Gregor dragged me across the room and pushed me against one of the wide, timber support beams that dotted my loft space.

I watched as he inhaled deeply but said nothing.

As if he needed a moment to control his emotions.

This was not a man to piss off, I reminded myself.

As I waited for his next move, I looked him over. While still handsome as hell, his face now had an even harder edge to it. The sharp angles of his jawline and lowered brow heightened the sense of dangerous power he exuded.

I stayed silent. My fingers gripped the smooth wood of

the beam behind me in an effort to ground myself and my rioting emotions.

Gregor ran the back of his knuckles over my cheek. "You shouldn't have run, Samara. You've caused me a great deal of trouble."

"I'm sorry," I whimpered.

What else could I say?

"Are you?" he challenged.

His dark gaze lowered to my breasts as his fingers undid the first button of my cardigan.

Oh God.

"Please. Please don't hurt me."

Gregor looked into my eyes. I could feel his warm fingers brush my skin as he undid another button.

"If you don't want me to hurt you, then you need to be a very good girl and not anger me."

Grabbing my jaw with his full hand, he pushed my head back till it connected with the beam. I watched in captive silence as his gaze moved from my eyes to my open lips and back.

"Tell me why," he ground out.

He didn't honestly expect me to tell him why I didn't want to marry him?

To his face?

"I... I... please." I faltered.

He lowered his head. His mouth brushed mine. "That's not an answer, malyshka."

His other hand moved to span my belly. My entire body trembled. I could feel the scorching heat of him through my thin sweater. My traitorous body hummed as I waited to see if he would slide his hand higher or lower. How could a man who terrified me deep in my bones make my body quake like this? It was wrong. Sick. *Dangerous.*

My fingernails dug into the wood beam. "Please, Gregor. Just let me go. You could have anyone you wanted."

"I want you. I *own* you."

I watched as his eyes flashed with unmistakable need as the possessive power of his words rang in my head. I realized I would never be free of this man. No matter how long or how far I ran he would always give chase. I just couldn't understand why. This couldn't possibly be about the money he loaned my father? I hadn't spoken to my parents since the night I ran, but surely my father had paid him back by now. It had been three years.

My teeth chattered with fear. I had to clench my jaw to even speak. Taking a deep breath through my nose, I risked it all. "You don't own me. You'll never own me, because I'll never marry you."

Squeezing my eyes shut, I turned my head and braced for the violent blow I was certain was coming.

I didn't care.

I was tired.

Tired of running.

Tired of always looking over my shoulder.

Tired of watching the real me slowly disappear in the mirror.

I just wanted it to end.

My tiny bit of rebellion in speaking my mind had taken the last of my resolve.

If it hadn't been for his powerful presence pressing into my front, I would have collapsed to the floor as my knees buckled.

After an agonizing stretch of silence, nothing happened.

I hesitantly peeked at him through my lowered lashes.

His dark gaze studied my face as his jaw tightened. "You don't have a choice."

"Why would you want to marry someone who doesn't

want to marry you?" I cried, desperation making my voice high-pitched and thin.

He leaned down to whisper in my ear. "I have my reasons."

His lips skimmed my cheek before crashing down to claim my mouth. Balling my hands into fists, I beat on his shoulders and chest as I twisted my head away. With a growl, he clasped my jaw in his hand and pushed my head back.

"Open for me," he commanded.

This time when his head swooped down, I had no choice. The tips of his fingers pressed into the sides of my face, forcing my jaw open. His tongue swooped in to take possession.

This was the kiss that had haunted my dreams every night for the last three years.

He gave no quarter. His tongue dueled with mine as his free hand cupped my breast. He tasted of mint and tobacco and of bittersweet memories and longing. With a cry, I kissed him back, my fingers clawing at his lapel as I stretched up onto my toes. His hips ground against my own. The threatening press of his hard cock against my stomach both terrified and excited me.

This was precisely what I was worried about… this all-consuming feeling of being swallowed whole, body and soul, by him.

I pulled away, gasping for air. Clinging to him even as I yearned to be set free.

"Please," I begged, crushing the silk of his jacket in my fists. "I can't give you what you want. I can't be the girl you want."

Three years of independence had strengthened my sense of self and showed me what I did and didn't want out of life. My dreams of being an artist may have been fading, but that didn't mean it prepared me to resign myself to a life as *the wife* of Gregor Ivanov and nothing more. Even as an unsophisticated, immature teenager I knew I could never be the biddable accepting wife he probably wanted and expected. Someone who thought only of her husband's needs and never of her own. Someone with no identity outside of her marriage vows. My mind ranted and raved at being put into such a tiny box for the rest of my life.

He stroked my bottom lip with his thumb. "Ty milaya malyshka. To, chto ya khochu pryamo seychas, ochen' prosto."

I was almost startled to hear him speak Russian. It had been so long. Out of precaution, Yelena and I only spoke English, and we avoided the Russian neighborhoods in the cities we had been hiding out in, knowing the extensive reach of Gregor Ivanov and his family as well as my own.

I licked my lips, all too aware of his gaze focused on my mouth. He said what he wanted in this moment was very simple. I was afraid to ask but knew he would keep me here, imprisoned against this pillar all night if I didn't.

Bracing myself for him to demand sex, knowing that no matter how much I may protest, in the end, my body would probably betray me. I was no match for his strength and skill.

I exhaled on a sigh and lowered my gaze before asking, "What do you want, Gregor?"

"I want you to say you were a very bad girl."

CHAPTER 10

Samara

What?

"Say it. Tell me what a bad *malyshka* you've been," he growled.

Despite my fear of him demanding more, a rush of heat pooled between my thighs at his commanding tone and sexually charged demand.

I licked my now swollen lips before responding. A low rumble emanated from deep within his chest.

This was a command, not a request and I was in no position to refuse.

"I've… I've been a very… bad girl."

His hand slid from my jaw, over my throat and down my front. With a flick of his fingers, he undid another button. The cream lace edge of my bra peeked between the sweater folds.

"And what happens to bad girls who run away from home?"

In quick succession, he undid the two remaining buttons. Looking down, I could see the soft swells of my silk and lace covered breasts on full display.

"Please." I wasn't sure what I was begging for. I just knew I was dizzy and overwhelmed with fear and twisted lust.

He dipped four fingers into the waistband of my black dress pants and pulled me forward. With his superior height, my stomach pushed against his lower hips. I could feel the press of his thick cock as it grazed against the thin fabric of his suit pants.

"Answer me. What happens to bad girls who run away from home?"

Fuck this is getting out of control.

"I don't know!" I cried out.

I had never felt so off-balance in my life. I didn't know the rules of the game. He was in complete control of the board and all the moving pieces. All I knew was he was fucking dangerous, and I had crossed him.

Gregor pressed the brass button on my pants till it popped through the hole. Then slowly, keeping his eyes locked on mine, he lowered the zipper.

"Push them off your hips," he commanded.

My eyes filled with tears. "Just let me go, please!"

With the tip of his index finger, he caressed the nipple on my left breast through the silk of my bra. He gently circled it till it responded to his touch, forming an erect nub. Then with his finger and thumb, he grasped it and cruelly twisted.

I rose on my toes in a futile effort to escape the pain. "Stop! Stop! It hurts!"

"Then do as you are told," he ground out, anger making his voice tight.

I scrambled to push the pants over my slim hips, feeling

both relieved and vulnerable when they hit the floor. Before releasing me, Gregor placed his foot between my open legs and dragged the pants free of my feet. I now had no real protection from him, dressed only in a pair of bra and panties with the opened sweater hanging from my shoulders.

Turning my head to the side, I let out a sob as he finally released my tortured nipple.

"Samara. Baby. I'm going to need you to concentrate and listen carefully."

I bit my lip as I tried to focus on what he was saying.

His large hand spanned my lower back. I remembered how it felt to feel his hand there as we walked around the gallery. I should have realized then it was his subtle way of letting me know he was the one truly in control, the one moving my piece around the board.

Then his hand dipped lower, the tips of his fingers caressing my ass which was exposed because of my flimsy pair of lace thongs.

"Now, let's try this again. What happens to bad girls who run away?" he whispered against the delicate shell of my ear.

I sniffed. "They get punished."

"Very good, Samara."

I felt a sick moment of pride at his praise. There was just something about the way he said my name. It sounded like spiked dark chocolate on his lips.

His fingers slid to the lower curve of my ass, before traveling back up to my lower back, then down again in a slow, rhythmic movement.

"And who's going to punish you?"

This time, I knew better than to hesitate. "You are."

Gregor smiled. "That's right."

It wasn't a genuine smile. More like the triumphant smirk of predator the moment before he strikes and kills his prey.

His fingers dipped along the seam of my ass. He hooked

two fingers in the fabric of my thong and pulled. The soft silk rubbed my cunt as he stretched it taut before snapping it back into place. I swallowed a gasp as the movement sent a jolt of awareness up my spine.

I was so lost in the chaos of my mind and body that I failed to see him raise his arm. He struck with no warning. His open palm hit the smooth cheek of my ass. The sound of skin connecting with skin reverberated throughout the open loft.

I cried as the hot sting spread over my cheek. I had never been spanked before, not even as a child.

"Shhh… malyshka, don't cry. I just needed to make sure you fully understood the consequences of disobedience."

Gregor ran the back of his knuckles down my cheek before sweeping the pad of his thumb over my lower lip.

Back and forth.

Back and forth.

Like a cobra seducing its victim.

Still, I cried.

"Now, open your mouth."

His face was an indistinct blur. I swiped at my eyes to clear them of tears.

He smacked my ass again. In the same spot.

I howled in pain as I instinctively tried to move away from him. Gregor shifted his legs wider and leaned against me, pinning me between the wooden beam and his own muscular body, using the press of his cock as both a threat and a promise. His hands grabbed my thin wrists. Wrenching my arms upwards, he secured me with one hand. The other he returned to my face. Pressing his thumb against my tightly closed lips, he snarled, "Open. Your. Mouth."

I obeyed.

His thick thumb pushed between my lips. I could taste the salty tang of his skin as it slid along my tongue.

"Suck it."

Keeping my eyes trained on him, more out of fear than anything else, I hesitantly swished my tongue over his thumb.

He pulled it back, then pushed it into my mouth again.

I groaned. I knew what he wanted me to think, to feel. He was manipulating me. Taunting me. Once more there was the threatening promise of his cock as it pushed against my stomach. This was just another test. A test of my obedience. My willingness to submit to his command.

Pulling his thumb free, he wiped my saliva off along the upper swell of my breast. I could feel it cool on my skin.

"Does my malyshka understand what will happen if she doesn't do exactly as she is told?"

I nodded my head. There was no point in responding in any other way. This was his game, not mine. I was no longer the one in control.

"Good. Now go over there and open your present."

At first, I didn't understand. A present? I thought he was going to fuck me right here against this beam whether I wanted it or not, and now he's talking about presents? The shift in topic left me feeling even more confused and disoriented. I followed his gaze. On my kitchen counter was a long, rectangular white box secured with a pale pink bow.

Stepping to the side, I glanced over my shoulder to see where I was going before taking another step back, then another. Refusing to turn my back on him, I edged my way to the counter. After one more step, I could feel the cold lip of the granite countertop at my back. Keeping a wary eye on Gregor, I pulled on the box ribbon.

Slowly, the bow unraveled. I lifted the lid and set it aside. I carefully pulled back the light pink tissue paper. Inside was a dress. Holding the shoulders between my fingers, I pulled it free of its packaging. It was a 50s inspired swing dress.

Jet black taffeta with a sweetheart neckline and a thin, baby pink belt around the trim waist. Peeking out the bottom was a matching baby pink crinoline. I had only to glance at it to know it was not only my style, it was also my size.

Fear spiked through me. There could be no doubt in my mind the only way Gregor could have known my dress size and style was if he had been watching me. The question was for how long?

Gregor slid his suit sleeve back and looked at his watch. "Samara, I have no wish to be late. Please do as you're told and put on the dress so we can leave."

At least he said please, I thought sardonically.

Late? Late for what?

"Not until you tell me what the fuck is going on," I demanded. The small bit of distance from his domineering presence gave me false courage.

I didn't even have a chance to run.

Gregor reached me in two strides. Putting his hand behind my head, he fisted my hair. First, he wrenched me forward, then turned me around and forced me to bend over the low kitchen island. The dress provided a meager cushion between my naked stomach and the freezing granite top. Holding me down by my hair, Gregor spanked my ass.

One. Two. Three. Four.

The swats came in quick, brutal succession. Two on each cheek.

I screamed and kicked but could not dislodge his grip.

My skin was on fire. Every merciless touch of his palm sent shocks of pain across my whole body. This was nothing compared to the abject humiliation of being bent over and spanked like an errant child.

"What did I say about doing as you are told?"

"I will. I will. Just stop!" I begged.

Lost in my degradation, it was several moments before I

realized he had stopped. Hesitantly, I rose from the countertop, hissing as the motion sent another wave of discomfort over my now heated, sensitive skin.

"And don't let me ever hear such foul language coming from your mouth again. Cursing is a sign of coarseness, and I won't have it."

"Yes, sir," I said without even thinking as I stepped into the dress.

I gasped as the stiff crinoline scraped along my punished skin. With his warm hands on my body, I held my breath. The fabric of the dress tightened around my middle as he zipped up the back.

I turned around to face him for inspection. The pink leather ballet flats I was wearing looked nice with the dress, although I wished I had high heels on. Even with a four-inch heel, my chin would still only barely reach his shoulder, but I would feel less cowed, less dominated.

After giving me an assessing look, Gregor strode across the loft to my vanity. He returned with my bottle of Coco Mademoiselle perfume.

Mesmerized, I watched as he spritzed a small amount between my breasts. Using his other hand, he ran his fingers through the scented liquid, caressing the curve of my breast before reaching behind my ear to dab. He then repeated the gesture with my other ear. By now my skin had warmed the liquid, sending a floral cloud of jasmine and white musk to enclose us.

Just as he'd done at the gallery, Gregor placed a hand on my lower back and guided me to the door. As he picked up the keys to my apartment off the floor, I caught my reflection in the hall mirror. My tousled curls looked wild, and my lips were swollen a dark cherry red. There was a high blush of color on my cheeks, and my eyes were bright with recently shed tears. If someone didn't know any better, they would think I had just been fucked.

After motioning me over the threshold, Gregor locked the door and then pocketed my keys. Another not-so-subtle message to me about who was in charge now.

I truly was at his mercy. I didn't even have my cell phone. I had no way of talking with Yelena.

"We should be just in time for the gala," he said casually, as if we were on a proper date instead of him essentially kidnapping me.

Gala?

What the fuck is going on?

CHAPTER 11

*G*regor

IT HAD TAKEN ALL my control not to pull out my cock and fuck her hard and deep the moment I had her bent over the counter. Especially with that small pink heart tattoo on her upper right ass cheek.

Christ.

I needed to stay focused around this woman.

She may have looked innocent and sweet, but I now knew better.

She was smart as a whip and cunning.

And I'd be lying if I didn't admit I found it arousing as hell.

Damn, I loved this spirited side to her... even as I seduced it into submission.

Still, I had made the mistake of thinking her biddable once and almost lost her.

I wouldn't be making that same mistake again.

After shutting the door, I rapped my knuckles on the limo roof to signal to John, my driver for the night, to proceed. I had already given him instructions to under no circumstances lower the divider.

As the limo pulled away from the curb, I took a minute to study her, my little captured bird. She had shuffled to the opposite end of the limo and pulled her knees up to her chest. Her small ballet slipper clad feet peeking out from underneath rows and rows of pink ruffles. Since the museum gala was a formal function, I probably should have let her put on high heels, but I liked the feeling of towering over her slight form. Dominating her in every way.

She still looked younger than her years.

And vulnerable.

Fear did that to a person.

I was excellent at reading people. I knew the soft touch approach with her would never have worked. She would have seen it as a weakness. What Samara needed was a firm hand, literally.

Besides, building loyalty and trust took time and patience.

I had neither.

Fear was faster and just as effective.

I needed her to be off-balance. Needed her to not know how all the pieces were moving around the board. If she knew the complete picture, she could take advantage of the situation. Information was power. Keeping Samara fully informed was unacceptable. She would only know what I chose to tell her and no more.

I knew I was being too hard on her, but I didn't give a damn. I was punishing her for the embarrassment she had caused me and my family over the last three years. It was difficult to save face with our criminal connections when we couldn't bring two young women to heel. Fortunately, that was all over now. After tonight, word would spread that Samara Federova was in my possession… to have and to hold from this day forward till death do us part.

I flipped up the side console panel, grabbed a glass, and dropped a few ice cubes in it. Tonight's victory didn't call for cheap vodka, so I lifted the whiskey decanter and poured myself a generous portion. Savoring the warm fire as it coursed down my throat, I watched her.

How the pulse in her neck throbbed with every hesitant breath. The white of her teeth as she bit down on her full lower lip. How her fingers played with the edge of the crinoline.

The flush on her cheeks. Was it from fear or desire? Perhaps both.

"Come here," I ordered.

Samara looked at me, her beautiful green eyes wide and bright.

"Don't make me ask again," I warned, keeping my voice low and controlled.

Samara swallowed nervously, unfolded her legs, and slid along the upholstered seat towards me, stopping a few feet away.

"Closer."

I could see the hesitation in her movements as she slowly responded to my command. As her body slid further on the seat, it pushed the fabric of her skirt up higher, exposing her trim thighs. I could not help smiling when, noticing the direction of my gaze, she immediately pushed the skirt back into place.

Finally, she was within arm's length. Without giving it much thought beyond the fact that I wanted to, I snatched her around the waist and placed her on my lap.

Her small hands balled into fists as she pushed them

against my chest. One look from me and she quieted down. I liked that. Liked that we were already at the point where she would respond to non-verbal commands.

I pushed her wavy reddish-brown hair to the side and ran two fingers over her exposed shoulder, feeling her inhaled gasp as much as hearing it. The neckline of the dress was perfect on her where it gently cupped and lifted her beautiful breasts. Just enough to fill a man's hands. From my vantage point, I could see the shadow of her cleavage, smell the musk of the perfume I had placed there not moments before.

Shifting slightly, I placed my right arm securely around her waist. My left hand slipped under her dress to move up the side of her right thigh. Her skin felt warm and soft. From the determined set of her jaw, I knew she could feel the press of my hardening cock beneath her ass.

"If you promise to be a good girl, I will tell you where we are going," I offered, breaking the silence.

She didn't respond.

I squeezed her thigh. Samara's mouth opened on another gasp as alarmed eyes rose to clash with my own.

"Will you tell me if your brother has Yelena?"

"No."

"Will you at least promise me your brother won't hurt her?"

"I am not my brother's keeper, so no. Now are you going to promise to be a good girl?"

"Fine! I promise," she sputtered angrily.

"Temper, little one," I warned. I could tell she was chafing at having my bit between her teeth.

Samara tilted her head and gave me a false smile. "Fine. I promise," she said in a high falsetto voice dripping with sarcasm.

Minx.

"We are headed to the Art Institute. There is a gala celebrating the early female artists of the impressionist movement. I thought you would enjoy it."

It would also be the perfect time to parade my bride in front of some influential business associates. My plans had been delayed. It was time to get them back on track. I might as well stay in Chicago for a few meetings and events to solidify my claim on Samara before returning to D.C. to face her father. I didn't trust the man to have not tried to make other arrangements for her hand over these last few years, despite taking and spending my money. With luck, the news that I had found—and claimed—Samara would reach her father before our return to the East Coast, squashing any plans he may have made otherwise.

Plus, I had to admit, I was looking forward to walking the galleries with someone who appreciated art as much as I did. I didn't exactly associate with the type of people who liked to discuss the use of light and shadow in an artist's work. Most assumed I collected art because it was an easy way to launder huge sums of money. It suited my purposes to let them think that.

The truth was, I enjoyed looking at paintings. I was in awe of anyone who had the talent to put paint to canvas. Tonight, we'd be viewing an Impressionist exhibit, a particular favorite time period of mine. Judging by her work, I suspected the Impressionists were also influential on Samara's style as well.

I'd be lying if I didn't admit I hoped it would soften her towards me and my intentions. I may have been a monster in forcing her hand in marriage but that didn't mean I planned to make her miserable for the rest of her life. Quite the contrary.

Her cute brow furrowed. I knew I was confusing her. In order for her to be the doting bride, I needed to be the perfect fiancé. This was all just a game, and we all had our parts to play.

"You are to stay by my side at all times. It's time you started fulfilling your responsibilities as the fiancé of an Ivanov. If you try to leave, there will be consequences." I grabbed her chin and turned her face to mine. "Do I need to explain to you what those consequences will be?"

She shook her head vehemently no, breaking my grasp.

"Is that all you want from me?"

"Oh malyshka, I haven't even begun to take all that I want from you."

* * *

AFTER ENTERING THE MUSEUM, we made our way up the grand staircase and across the Alsdorf Gallery, which was filled with Himalayan and Asian art. Placing my hand on her lower back, I guided Samara to the right, into the Sculpture Court where the invitation said they would serve cocktails.

I took two glasses of champagne from a passing server and handed her one. "This is your only glass for the night, so sip it." I pretended not to see the face she pulled at my heavy-handed command.

We casually strolled among the Greek and Roman marble statues as I nodded to the occasional passing acquaintance.

"Aren't you worried someone may recognize me as Gwen Stevens?" she asked. There was a slight cheeky quality to her smile. The crowd had emboldened her, made her think she was safe from my advances, my discipline. The little one thought she had caught me in a miscalculation. How cute.

Looking to my left and right, to make sure the rest of the guests were more concerned with their own conversations, I turned my attention to Samara. Taking one step, then another, I forced her to back away. I kept stalking her till I cornered her in one of the smaller, unoccupied rooms off the main hallway displaying early American art.

Deliberately dominating her with my superior height, I leaned down.

"Failing to recognize the skill of your opponent. Rookie mistake," I teased, knowing it would get a rise out of her.

Her green eyes flashed. "Why you—"

I raised an eyebrow, practically daring her to make a scene.

Her knuckles turned white from her fierce grip on her champagne flute as I watched her master her emotions.

"I know for a fact, you do not use the same false identity twice, so no one here would have dealt with a Gwen Stevens since you haven't been in Chicago that long. I also know that you deliberately change your appearance with make-up, wigs for each new identity. So, the chances of one of these self-involved pompous asses recognizing you as the person who sold them a painting a few weeks ago is slight."

With each statement of fact, I pressed in closer till I could feel the brush of her breasts against my chest.

"How could you possibly know all that?" she asked, not even trying to hide her alarm.

I refused to answer.

Tilting my head down, I breathed in her air.

I raised my hand and brushed the back of my knuckles over the soft rise of her breast, wanting to feel her heartbeat, knowing it would be fast and erratic. My malyshka could try to hide her emotions from me, but she couldn't control her body's reaction to my presence.

Samara licked her lips as her mouth opened just slightly in invitation.

I leaned in closer but was interrupted.

"Gregor Romanovich, you bastard. I thought that was you. I heard you and your brother were in town."

A large hand clapped me on the shoulder as I turned. "Dimitri Antonovich!" I greeted him with both his first and middle name as well as was the custom in Russia.

I embraced my old friend, and we kissed on the cheeks.

"But what are you doing in Chicago, my friend? The meeting over the deal with Syria is not until next month. There is nothing I should know about, is there?"

Dimitri Kosgov and his business partner Vaska Rostov were two of the most powerful and feared arms dealers in the Western Hemisphere. They based their operations out of Chicago, so naturally he would be curious why I was here unannounced. Men of my caliber did not just show up. It rattled the other powers that be.

"Everything is going as planned for next month. I'm here on a brief trip with my fiancé. Dimitri, may I introduce, Samara Federova."

I placed a controlling hand on Samara's lower back and shot her a warning glare.

Her bottom pink lip stuck out in a pout, making me want to lean over and bite it.

Dimitri raised an eyebrow. Being the man he was, he would have heard of her abrupt disappearance and my search for her and her friend over the years. It was an embarrassment for both the Ivanovs and Federovs. All the more reason to showcase that Samara was now back at my side, where she belonged.

Dimitri extended his hand. "A pleasure to meet you, Samara."

Samara glanced down at Dimitri's heavily tattooed hand and hesitated. She shifted her stance to sidle a little closer to my side. The small, probably unconscious, move pleased me more than I would care to admit.

Dimitri was as tall and powerfully built as me, which made him equally intimidating.

Before I could reassure her, a small brunette dressed in a floral dress and Doc Martens walked up and wrapped an arm around Dimitri's forearm. "Dimitri, can't you see you're frightening her? I keep trying to tell you… you are a very scary-looking man!"

She leaned over and gave Samara a reassuring smile. "Hi! I'm Emma. Sorry if my husband came off like Caliban from *The Tempest*."

Dimitri grabbed her around the waist. Leaning down, he nipped at her ear as she giggled. "I'll show you a beast later, moya kroshka!"

Looking down, it surprised me to see Samara's cheeks flush as she stared at them with rapt attention.

My brow furrowed, and I returned my gaze to my friend and his new pretty wife.

I had heard he had made an unusual choice in bride, picking a woman who had no money or influence, who wasn't even a daughter of an important Russian family. If I remembered correctly, she was a librarian. His choice seemed foolish and short-sighted. Why not simply fuck the girl and marry someone who would better further his business interests?

One had only to look at him to know the answer.

He looked happy.

"Pozdravlyayu so svad'boy," I said as I shook Emma's hand.

Samara finally found her tongue. Taking her cue from me, she congratulated the couple on their recent marriage as well.

His new bride turned back to us. "I love your outfit, Samara. I can't wait for you to meet my friend Mary! You both have the same fabulous style."

"Thank you," answered Samara through tight, thinned lips.

It killed her to receive a compliment on the dress I had purchased for her and insisted she wear.

We both knew I had chosen perfectly.

I couldn't resist an arrogant smirk as I looked down at her. She willfully kept her head straight ahead, denying me the satisfaction of gloating. Slipping my hand more securely around her waist, I gave her a little squeeze. In response, she stamped her ballet-slippered foot down on mine.

I couldn't contain a bark of laughter. Dimitri gave me a quizzical look, but I waved his concern away. It was thrilling to know that spark of spirit I had seen in her three years ago had been flamed into a fire during her years away from me.

Looking down into her dark emerald eyes, I gave her wink, hoping it would piss her off.

It did.

Her eyes narrowed as she tried—and failed—to once more twist out of my embrace.

She really was an entertaining little spitfire.

Just then a server announced the Impressionist gallery was now open.

We followed Dimitri, Emma, and the other guests to the second floor.

Over the entrance to the Regenstein Hall was a massive banner announcing the new special exhibit, First Ladies of the Impressionists, and beneath that were portraits of Morisot, Cassatt, Gonzales, and Bracquemond. Tonight, was the gala honoring the new exhibit, while tomorrow it would open to the public. I didn't want to read into my motivation for coming, knowing deep down I chose this specific event not just because of who would be in attendance, but because I thought it would please her.

From the corner of my eye, I watched Samara swipe another glass of champagne, hoping I wouldn't notice. Soon she would realize nothing escaped my notice.

Using my hand on her lower back, I guided her to the Marie Bracquemond section of the exhibit, particularly a small self-portrait of the artist. As we stood before the painting, I asked Samara what she knew of it as I studied the burnt umber and ivory tones. The artist stared serenely back through dark, resigned eyes.

"It's a self-portrait of Marie Bracquemond. This is the only self-portrait in her collection." Samara tried to step away from me, but my hand on her waist prevented it. "I think she looks sad and beaten down by the life choices forced on her."

Surrounded by the glow of the dim gallery lighting, Samara looked luminous and beautiful as her gaze studied the painting before us, not missing a detail.

"Beautiful," I murmured softly against her sweet-smelling hair.

I could tell by her deepening blush she heard me, but she refused to look up.

Nodding to the painting, she continued, "She's not as well-known as say Cassatt or Morisot because *her husband* forbade her to pursue a career in painting despite being an artist himself. He was probably threatened by her talent. A *real* man would have encouraged her."

The little minx was baiting me.

I wondered if this was one of the reasons why she ran from me.

Had someone given her the impression I wouldn't support her art career?

She probably thinks I'm a neanderthal who wants a woman chained to a stove.

Well, I'm not.

Chained to my bed... that was different.

Making sure she could feel every inch of my body as I stood close behind her, I whispered in her ear, "*When* you are my wife, I don't care how you spend your days as long as you are in my bed with those beautiful legs spread waiting for me at night."

I could tell my honest response startled her.

"I need to use the lady's room," she announced as she quickly turned. In her haste to get away from me, she bumped into another guest, spilling the rest of her champagne.

I watched for a minute as she practically ran through the gallery. Then I followed her.

CHAPTER 12

Samara

"Excuse me. So sorry, all my fault," I said as I brushed my hand over the drops of champagne down the man's left arm before hurrying away.

In my right hand was his cell phone. A little trick Yelena and I picked up while on the run. Knowing how to get your hands on a quick cell phone that couldn't be traced back to you was an invaluable skill.

Tuscan Red.
Georgia Clay.
True Ochre.
Burnt Sienna.
Cadmium Red.

To calm myself down as I made my way through the empty galleries, I recited the names of the colors I had seen in the painting.

Burnt Orange.

Mustard Seed.
Crimson Red.
Blood Red.

Ignoring the signs for the restrooms, I hurried down the stone stairs to the first level. Motioning to the guard, I said, "Just need to use the ladies' room. The ones close to the event have lines." After his nod of approval, I made a right and went down the small stone staircase to the deserted lower level.

After hurrying inside the bathroom, I locked the door behind me.

Taking out the phone, I prayed it wasn't password protected as I hit the small, circular button. The phone lit up. It wasn't. Even as I dialed, I knew trying to call Yelena or even Nadia was hopeless. They would never answer a call on their phones from a number they didn't recognize. Especially Yelena, and most especially if she was fleeing from Damien. I prayed she got away. There was no point in both of us being dragged back to D.C. to face our fate.

Glancing back at the phone, I stared at the keypad and focused on the nine and one. The police were not an option, even I knew that. With a frustrated sigh, I wiped my prints off the phone and threw it in the garbage.

I never doubted for a moment that Gregor was a criminal. There had been whispers about Nadia's family connections since I was a child. I also knew he was dangerous. Very dangerous. Only a confident man, secure in his own power and connections, would have been bold enough to drag an unwilling woman to an event with some of the most influential people in Chicago on the guest list.

He knew I wouldn't cry out or ask for help.

He fucking knew it.

Damn him.

And damn him for my body's reaction to him. I was acting no better than the schoolgirl I was three years ago.

My cheeks heated at the memory of what he'd just whispered in my ear.

He was lying to me. He must be. He couldn't honestly think I'd believe for one moment that he would be okay with his wife having an art career? It was a lie, a manipulation, and I knew why. It was yet another tactic of his. Drawing on images of control and discipline, even safety and protection, to bend me to his will. Letting me think that while married to him, I could still have the life I wanted, that I could still have my dreams.

Damn him for doing it.

And damn me for falling for it.

As much as I hated to admit it, every time he issued a stern, heavy-handed command, my stomach flipped.

I needed to focus. I had captured the interest of a fierce opponent who already had the drop on me.

Unlocking the door, I stepped into the hall.

I instinctively ducked into the closest exhibit room when I heard voices.

It was the Thorne Miniatures Gallery.

Stepping deeper into the darkened gallery, I looked around at the light wood paneling with its neat rows of little windows. Each window looked into a tiny room, a mini diorama, and was a perfect recreation of the home furnishings and architecture from France, England, and America over the last several hundred years. Each one displayed a perfect little family in their perfect little world. If only.

"I thought I told you not to leave my side?"

I turned to see Gregor in the entranceway to the gallery. His presence immediately filled the small darkened room. The energy he exuded felt like a hand squeezing inside my chest.

"Gregor, please you need to listen to me. No good will ever come of this… of us. You need to just let me go."

Taking a few steps into the darkened room, he shrugged out of his suit jacket.

"Dammit, Gregor. Did you hear me? We have to end this… this game, you're playing. Just let me fucking leave!" I shouted as I stamped my foot. I knew I looked like an impudent child. Doing so didn't help my cause considering he already treated me like a child. My hand went back to rub my still sore ass as my cheeks heated from the memory of the humiliating spanking he gave me earlier.

"I heard you the first time," he said as he unbuttoned his cuffs and rolled up his sleeves, exposing powerful forearms.

Running a hand through my hair, I paced.

"Fuck!" I cried out in sheer frustration.

"What did I tell you about language, young lady?"

"Fuck! Fuck! Fuck!" I yelled stamping my foot again for emphasis.

Gregor's hands went to his belt buckle.

I watched in horror as he slowly unbuckled it and slid the belt free.

My jaw dropped. He wasn't serious? He couldn't mean to…to…

Gregor took a step toward me.

With a raised arm, I warned him. "Don't you dare take another step. I'll scream for the guard."

"That guard and I have an understanding. He won't be coming to your rescue."

Quickly I scanned the room, but the only exit I could see was through him.

Before I could decide what to do, Gregor lunged.

I screamed anyway.

The force of his body pushed me back against the wood

paneling so hard I could hear the glass window crack. Before I could utter a sound, his hand was at my throat.

Squeezing just hard enough to scare me, he stared down into my eyes.

There was only icy determination in the hard-silver depths of his.

Leaning down, he whispered into my ear, his low voice making his anger that much more ominous. "I warned you, malyshka. With me, there will always be consequences."

"Please," I choked out. "Just let me go."

"No."

Using his other hand to grab my upper arm, Gregor swung me around till he was behind me, his fingers still wrapped securely around my throat. We stood in front of a two-foot-wide leather padded bench in the center of the gallery.

"Kneel."

I shook my head as the tears slid down my cheeks. It scared me. For the first time in my life, I was really fucking scared. At least in my apartment, I didn't know who or what I was dealing with, confusion and the need for answers kept the panic at bay but now… now I knew only too well.

Switching his hand to my hair, Gregor twisted the curls around his fist. "It wasn't a request," he growled before forcing me to kneel on top of the bench.

Using the back of my hand, I swiped at my eyes and begged, "Please, Gregor. I promise I'll behave."

Ignoring my plea, he commanded, "Lift your dress."

I sobbed. "Don't make me, Gregor."

He snapped the belt in his hand. The sound of the leather hitting leather reverberated around the small room.

I fell down onto my forearms, burying my face as I cried.

"Now, Samara."

With one shaking hand, I reached back and grasped a fistful of fabric. I lifted it up.

"Higher. Show me that heart tattoo again."

Oh God! My tattoo. The small pink heart just above my right ass cheek. That he had seen it made my face burn hot.

Afraid to anger him further, I rose on my haunches and lifted the back of the dress with the pink crinoline in both hands before leaning back down. The layers of sheer ruffles flipped over my head, partially hiding my shame as I could feel the cold air hit my bare ass.

I jumped when Gregor put his hand on my lower back. His fingers dipped between my cheeks to grab the thin band of my thong. I could feel his knuckles rub against my skin as he made a fist.

Knowing what was coming, I braced myself.

With a yank, he wrenched my panties off.

They were just a flimsy piece of silk, but at least it was something. Now I was completely exposed.

Those same knuckles caressed my left cheek before the tip of his finger traced the heart outline of my tattoo.

Then I felt nothing.

He had removed his hand from my body.

I held my breath.

There was no sound, just tense silence.

It was worse than when he chastised me.

Then, I heard the thin hush of air before the awful sting.

Hard leather connected with soft skin.

The thin strap of his dress belt seared my ass, leaving a trail of heat and pain.

Balling my hands into fists, I buried my face between my forearms and cried.

Again, and again he punished me with his belt. My throat was hoarse from my sobs. My skin felt raw and bruised as the pain spread down my thighs and up my spine.

Humiliation at being found in this position kept me from crying out for help.

Fear kept me from trying to escape his wrath.

My body rocked forward with each swipe of the leather. My small passive way of trying to lessen the pain.

"Move your ass again, and I will flip you over onto your back, spread your legs, and whip your cunt, do you understand me?" he ground out. His harsh words came in bursts from his own exertions.

From that point forward, my agony only increased. Holding my body rigid, I absorbed each crack of his belt on my vulnerable ass, afraid to move so much as an inch.

Finally, it stopped.

Instead of his belt, I once more felt the tip of his finger. He traced the outline of my heart tattoo.

"You can barely see it. I like that you have the perfect way to tell when I have punished your ass enough. From now on, I won't stop till I see your skin blush the same dark pink as this little tattoo."

Even the slight pressure of his finger hurt.

I couldn't even think straight. I could only feel. Humiliation, pain, fear, fucked up desire, all rushed over me in dizzying waves.

I stayed where I was with my head hidden behind the pink ruffles of my crinoline. Afraid to face him. Afraid to move without permission.

His hand trailed over my ass to slip between my thighs. Two fingers caressed me.

"Are you still a virgin or has someone taken what was mine?"

Shocked, I opened my mouth but couldn't utter a sound.

"Fine, then." I could feel him step closer. The back of his hand brushed my bruised skin as he worked the fastening to his trousers. I could hear the metal clicks as he slowly lowered his zipper.

"Please, Gregor. Please don't," I cried, completely humiliated.

"Then answer me," His words were clipped and tight.

"There's been no one," I whispered against my fist.

I hissed in pain as he laid his right hand over my ass cheek. His thumb moved in small circles as he slid it closer and closer. Then the pad of this thumb brushed over my virgin asshole.

"No! No! No!" I screamed as I tried to rise back on my haunches.

Gregor responded by whipping the leather belt around my throat and arching my body back.

"If I want to fuck your ass, I'll fuck your ass because I *own* you, Samara."

He pushed me back down onto my hands and knees. The belt strap was still around my throat, secured by his left hand, which he held in a fist at the center of my back. His fingers continued to rub along the seam of my ass. A threat. He pushed a tip against my asshole again, wrenching a sob of panic from me. Then he slipped lower to the entrance of my pussy.

"This is going to hurt," he warned.

I remember him giving me a similar warning three years ago when I was perched on his lap with his hand between my thighs.

This time he used two fingers, not one, driving them deep into my body till he felt my maidenhead.

There had been no one since him. Not only was I too afraid to trust anyone, deep in my heart, I'd felt like I would have been betraying Gregor. It was crazy, of course. *He* was the reason why I was running away in the first place. Despite what he repeatedly claimed, he didn't own me. I owed no loyalty to him and yet... I couldn't bring myself to allow another man to touch me.

The belt tightened and choked off my scream as my body pitched forward from the power of his thrusting hand. He pulled free and thrust a third finger in.

Oh God, it hurt.

I was so tight and small. His entire body dominated mine, inside and out.

Something twisted and unfurled in the pit of my stomach.

The fabric of his trousers scraped against my raw skin as the ridge of his shaft pressed against me, so not for one moment did I forget the sting of my punishment or the threat that he could still use his cock to punish me further.

Deeper and deeper he pushed. Forcing my body to accept, to accept him and worse... forcing it to respond to his brutal touch. I could feel a dark rising tide of sensation. Slipping my arm beneath my kneeling body, I pressed my fingers between my thighs, teasing my clit as the thrust of his fingers quickened.

With my back arched and head tilted back, I could only breathe in short gasps as the belt tightened each time, he pushed his fingers inside of me, moving them in and out in a steady rhythm as my body clenched around him.

Bright stars formed behind my lids as the threat of death only heightened my senses.

Suddenly, he let go of the belt. Wrapping his arm around my waist from behind, he cupped my left breast and pulled me up and back. The new position tightened my inner core, sending a shock wave of sexual heat up my spine.

Gregor groaned in my ear as his hand tortured my pussy. My fingertips rubbed circles around my clit.

"Has any other man ever touched this pretty cunt of yours?"

Rolling my head back and forth on his shoulder, I shamelessly spread my knees as wide as the bench would allow and moaned. "No. No, only you, Gregor. Only you."

He leaned down and bit my bare shoulder while he once more teased my back entrance with the pad of his thumb.

I clenched. "Stop! Not there."

My body bounced up and down as he continued to push his fingers in deep into my pussy repeatedly.

The air was heavy with the scent of my sweet perfume and the musk of his cologne and the sounds of our heavy breathing.

"V odin prekrasnyy den' ya sobirayus' vtisnut' svoy chlen v etu tvoyu tuguyu kisku, poka ty ne vykriknesh' moye imya," he growled into my ear.

The guttural harshness of his Russian as he threatened to force his cock into my tight pussy one day soon sent me over the edge.

"Damn you," I sputtered as I could feel an orgasm uncoil and rise from within me. "I hate you."

I hated him with every fiber of my being for adding the ultimate degradation of forcing me to come from his assault.

"Should I make my bad girl lick my fingers?" he threatened.

Tears slid from the corners of my eyes into my hair as I imagined him once more forcing me to my knees to endure the intimate act of opening my mouth so I might taste myself on his hand.

"Please stop."

"Beg me."

"Please. I'm begging you. Please... please... please... no more."

"That's how my malyshka should always beg me."

He pinched my nipple through my dress. My orgasm was so fierce it knocked the wind out of me. The weight of my whole-body collapsed into his grasp. He released his arm, so

I might fall back onto the bench. The leather felt cool against my hot cheek.

I cried out in fear as I stretched out my arms to hold on to the bench.

As the final ripples of my orgasm still racked my body, he slid his wet fingers out of my pussy.

When he stepped away, my knees buckled and my hips shifted to the right. I curled up into the fetal position. I could feel my arousal drip out of my pussy to dry on my inner thigh.

I watched through half-closed lids as he picked up my torn thongs. Hunching down, he twisted the silk fabric into a knot which he then forced between my lips. My eyes widened in panic.

Giving my outer thigh a kiss, he then forced my knees open till my body rolled onto my back.

He rubbed his cheek against my inner thigh as he inhaled deeply.

"My turn," he growled as his left hand grasped the end of the leather belt still secured around my throat.

His tongue swept over my pussy before pushing between the lips with the tip.

I moaned around my panty gag as my fingers clawed at the leather bench.

Using his other hand, he spread me open and licked again, this time flicking my sensitive nub.

My body jolted as my hips rocked upward.

I could feel the vibrations of his groan. "This pussy is so sweet and all mine."

A man had never... touched me... let alone *licked* me down there before. It was nothing compared to using my hand. The feeling was overwhelming. I couldn't breathe. The sensations were too intense. It didn't take me long to come a second time. Digging my fingers into his hair, I pulled as my thighs clenched around his head.

Dizzy and disoriented, every limb felt both weighted down and as if I were floating at the same time.

Weakly reaching up, I pulled my panties from my mouth. I hardly recognized my own thin and raspy voice when I asked, "Now will you let me go?" My own thoughts scattered yet still focused on my one driving need to get as far away as possible from this dangerous and powerful man.

Now more than ever, I realized he would be the end of me. I didn't stand a chance against him, not when he could do things like this to my body with only the touch of his fingers and tongue!

What would happen if we ever fucked?

Gregor brushed back the hair from my tear-stained cheeks as he pulled my dress down over my hips to cover me. "No."

Then everything went black.

CHAPTER 13

*S*amara

I WOKE up in my loft.

The night before was a traumatic, fucked up blur. I can't ever remember being so overwhelmed. By the time Gregor had finished with me I was so emotionally and physically exhausted, I passed out.

That's actually not true. Why lie to myself? I passed out from oral sex.

From oral sex, not actual sex... just the touch of his mouth!

I passed out from utter sated exhaustion... from a mind-blowing orgasm.

That it came after he humiliated me and caused me pain just added to the twisted, fucked up situation I found myself in.

And the worst part is, if that man ordered me to my knees again, I'd probably have done it.

Fuck. My. Life.

I remember Gregor lifting me in his arms and carrying me out of the museum, not one guard stopped or questioned him. I can only remember little bits and pieces of the time in the limo. The only glaring thing I do recall is spending the entire time on his lap.

After that, nothing.

With a sudden thought, I lifted the sheet and looked down at my body.

I was naked.

Damn him.

Rubbing my eyes, I swung my feet off the bed. It felt like I had a hangover, even though I barely drank two glasses of champagne.

A small piece of paper caught my eye. I picked up the note.

Drink.

It was written in an aggressive, slanting penmanship. A man's hand.

Next to the note was a glass of water and two aspirin.

With a resigned sigh, I drained the glass of water, more than a little annoyed he knew I would need one.

As I stood, I noticed the curtains, which I usually forgot about, were drawn tight. My favorite big cozy sweater and a pair of yoga pants were laid out on my vanity chair.

Looking around, I quickly pulled the sweater over my head and scrambled to push my legs into the pants.

It suddenly occurred to me he might still be here.

Instinctively, I reached under my pillow for my revolver. It wasn't there. I then remembered that Gregor probably still had it.

After pulling on a pair of socks, I inspected the rest of the loft.

It was empty.

Had he left me alone?

Wasn't he worried I'd run?

On the kitchen counter was a plate with a note next to it.

Eat.

On the plate were some fresh orange slices and a croissant. There was also a glass of what looked like cranberry juice. Turning away, I headed to the coffeemaker.

On the stove was a frying pan with a note resting on the lid. I picked it up.

I mean it, Samara.

Opening the lid, I found there were scrambled eggs with cheddar cheese and some sautéed potatoes.

"What the hell?" I said out loud to no one.

Considering my refrigerator had only a half-eaten container of lo men and a single stick of butter, he would have had to have gone out for all this.

And I slept through the entire thing?

Had he slept next to me, too?

I rushed back to my bed. Falling onto the mattress with my knees, I leaned down and sniffed the pillow next to mine. It didn't smell like his cologne.

Standing, I paced.

Out of the corner of my eye, I noticed the easel in the center of my painting area was empty. The painting of the falling girl was gone; so were the stacks of my other paintings.

There was another note taped to the wooden crossbeam of the easel.

I HAVE AN UNAVOIDABLE MORNING MEETING.

Pack up the rest of your things and meet me at the below address at Noon.

And Samara, don't do anything stupid.

G -

P.S. I'm keeping the paintings.

Crumpling the note in my fist, I kicked the easel in frustration, instantly regretting it when it toppled to the side, taking another easel with it.

My front door swung open at the sound of the crash.

Two men dressed in black shirts and cargo pants with visible gun holsters strapped around their shoulders entered my loft.

I screamed and backed away. Picking up one of my paint brushes as a weapon, I waved it uselessly in front of me.

"Are you alright, Miss Federova? We heard a crash."

"Who the fuck are you?"

"Your security. Mr. Ivanov's orders. When you're ready to leave, we are to assist with your bags and take you to his home," answered one of the guards.

Well, I guess that answered my questions as to why Gregor was confident enough to leave me alone.

"I'm fine."

Both men nodded and stepped back into the hallway, closing the door—and my only exit—behind them.

Throwing the note on the floor, I walked away in a huff. What I needed was a long, hot shower. I would figure out my next move later.

Entering the bathroom, I leaned over the tub and turned the nozzle for the shower. As I straightened, I noticed yet another note on the mirror.

We will talk *about your Betty Boop tattoo later.*

. . .

My hand flew to my left hip, where just over the hip bone was a Betty Boop tattoo. She was in her classic red dress, kicking one leg into the air. Tucked into her heart-shaped garter was a tiny revolver.

Damn him.

After showering, I wrapped my hair in a towel and sat at my vanity. With my pale neck and upper chest exposed, I could see just the faintest bruise around my throat. Whether it was from his hand or his belt, I couldn't say.

With a sigh, I picked up my blush brush and tried to add some color back into my cheeks. Bright cherry red matte lipstick and my hair down with a red chiffon scarf tied around my neck completed my look.

There. Nobody'd ever know I'd spent the evening with a powerful criminal who *50 Shades of Grey*'ed me to within an inch of my life.

After throwing on a pair of cuffed jeans and a white t-shirt, I slipped on a pair of red ballet slippers, then walked into the kitchen and dumped the skillet with the eggs straight into the trash. I felt a rush of satisfaction marred by guilt, knowing I had just acted like a petulant child.

No wonder he treats you like a misbehaving little girl, I thought.

And spanks you like one, too.

I returned to my bedroom and snatched up the pink and black duffle bag lying in a corner. As I was stuffing my sparse belongings into it, I noticed the leather portfolio with my extra IDs and cash was also missing. It was going to make it hard accessing my offshore accounts without that information.

Damn him.

What was I doing?

Crossing my arms, I stubbornly stared down at the half-packed duffle bag before grabbing it and tossing it back into the corner.

There was no reason to pack anything because I wasn't going anywhere with him.

He might have me against the wall now, but there had to be a way to escape.

I had done it once, I would do it again... and this time I'd make sure he never found me.

CHAPTER 14

*G*regor

"Ya ub'yu yego golymi rukami."

Dimitri settled in the seat across from my desk as Vaska remained standing by the fireplace.

Neither blinked an eye at my threat to kill Boris Federov, my future father-in-law, with my bare hands. I should have never let that bastard live.

With my security needs and the frequency with which I traveled here, two years ago I purchased a home just outside of Chicago in the wealthy suburb of Evanston. It was preferable to a hotel. The houses were enormous and behind gates with lots of security cameras, so my own security measures would not look out of place.

After receiving Dimitri's text early this morning demanding a meeting as soon as possible, I feared it may have something to do with Samara.

I still didn't know what the fuck got into me last night.

I should have just fucked her, finally taken my long-delayed pleasure from that tight little body of hers and been done with it. But I couldn't. I wasn't even going to claim some bullshit moral code about not wanting to take her virginity on a bench at a public museum. There was just something unique about feeling her cunt clench around my fingers the moment she orgasmed and then watching her face as I brought her to a second and third orgasm with my tongue.

Her responses were so vivid and intense.

So innocent and without artifice.

Each reaction raw and unfiltered.

I had definitely made my share of women scream in the bedroom over the years but this was on a different level. To know I was the first—and only—man to touch and taste that sweet cunt of hers, the first to give her an orgasm, was a powerful emotion and awoke something primal in me.

Before, I had wanted to claim her for her family name to further my business interests.

Then, I had gotten a small taste of her spirit and beauty at my sister's party, and I had craved more but was denied when she fled.

I knew a large part of my obsessive search for her had more to do with my pride and my family name. We wouldn't let it stand that a Federov bride had run away from her Ivanov groom.

Now... now everything had changed.

If I wasn't dangerous to Samara before, I sure as fuck am now.

She had given the devil a taste of heaven.

I no longer wanted just her hand in marriage. I wanted her everything; body and soul.

I would swallow her innocence like a drug and get high off of knowing I was the one responsible for her inevitable corruption. With each lash of my belt and touch of my hand, I would watch as those striking emerald eyes of hers flashed with flecks of gold as I awakened her to the pleasure had through pain and punishment.

I would have her craving my dominance, begging for it.

Her submission would be my redemption.

My hand flexed as I imagined the feel of the back of her head. Her soft curls tangled around my fingers while I forced that beautiful mouth of hers to stretch around my cock. This time I would get to stare down into her eyes and see as the stark realization of my complete control over her crept into their jade depths.

It was all I could do to tear myself away from her this morning. I wanted to be there when those gorgeous eyes blinked open. I wanted to watch the play of emotions on her face as the events of last night came back to her. I would have savored her look of humiliation complicated by the knowledge of her complicit response, the way she clung to me as each orgasm took over her body.

Then when she tried to deny it, as I'm certain the little minx would have, I would have held her down and forced my hips between her legs and proved it to her all over again… except this time with my cock.

But these were thoughts for later.

Now seated behind my desk, staring at the steam as it rose from my coffee cup, I wondered if I could kill her father without her finding out about it.

From my little sister, I had gleaned Samara was not close with either of her parents. A fact that bore out when she did not try to contact them over the last few years. I would have known if she did. However, that didn't mean she wanted them dead.

The arrogant bastard had negotiated an even higher price for Samara's hand with the Novikoff family. Apparently at this very moment, they were completing the deal, and Boris was preparing to come to Chicago to reclaim his daughter.

Over my dead body.

Vaska stepped away from the mantel and crossed to the vacant seat in front of my desk. Unbuttoning his suit coat, he took a seat and reached for the pitcher of coffee. Pouring himself a fresh cup, he leaned back. "I don't have to tell you how dangerous such an alliance would be. The Novikoffs have increased their influence but only through significant bloodshed."

For smart men, men like us, violence was used with the finesse of a sharpened razor's edge. Often the fear of violence could be just as powerful as the deed itself and led to far fewer complications. When violence was needed, it was accomplished with precision and designed to achieve the greatest impact. That is how men like me, Dimitri, and Vaska became powerful and wealthy while still retaining a veneer of respectability. No one cared if you were dirty; they cared if the rest of the world knew you were dirty.

The Novikoff family had yet to learn this. They had the finesse of a sledgehammer and the intelligence to match. They also dealt in the lower echelons of organized crime; sex trafficking, counterfeit cigarettes and car theft. They were peasant thugs who thought they should be kings.

"Who is the intended groom?" I asked, more out of morbid curiosity than anything else.

Dimitri exchanged a look with Vaska, then answered, "Egor."

I shot out of my chair and paced to the other side of the room. Boris Federov didn't deserve a daughter as beautiful and free-spirited as Samara. Especially when the bastard had no qualms about promising her to a seventy-two-year-old degenerate.

"Apparently, as head of the family he claimed it as his right," continued Vaska with a disgusted smirk.

The statement struck a sour note with me, knowing as head of the Ivanov family, I was claiming the same right.

I didn't fucking care.

I curled my fingers into a fist, getting a sick rush as my knuckles cracked.

Samara was mine, and I dared any man to try to take her from me.

This was no longer about business—it was personal.

Dimitri rose and crossed the room to face me. "There is no winning in a war with the Novikoffs. Those idiots will bring unwanted attention to us all and possibly damage everything we've built."

I nodded.

"That being said. Fuck them. You know we've got your back, my friend. If it is a war they want, then it's a war they'll get." Dimitri smiled and clapped me on the shoulder.

I clasped his hand in solidarity, then let go with a sound of agreement. "Enough people saw us last night that word will get back to Boris and Egor that Samara is in my possession. Just to be certain, I'm taking measures to have their homes and offices bugged. I want to know what those two fucks are planning. If they're smart, they'll leave it alone and walk away."

Even as I said it, I knew it wasn't true. If Boris was bold enough to try to double cross me, there was very little hope he would just walk away as soon as he learned I had found his daughter. Even if I married her this very moment, that may not stop them. They could always find a judge on the payroll to either annul the marriage or ignore its existence completely.

I needed a more permanent solution.

"Dva medvédya v odnóy berlóge ne zhivút," Vaska said,

repeating a proverb about two bears not being able to exist in one lair.

I couldn't agree more.

Dimitri looked at his watch. "I have to go. I promised Emma I would meet her at the Newberry Library for a lecture on the role of women in Shakespeare's *Othello*."

Despite the somber mood, Vaska and I exchanged a quick look and then burst out laughing.

Dimitri smirked. "Laugh all you want, assholes. Just wait till you both get married. Let's see how keen you'll be then to let your wife sit in a lecture hall surrounded by men who want to fuck her."

Vaska rose from his seat and buttoned his suit jacket as he reached for his overcoat. "If I ever get married, I'm never letting my wife leave the house. Problem solved."

Dimitri raised an eyebrow. "Really? Perhaps I should let Mary know your views on blessed matrimony."

I'd recently learned Mary was Emma's close friend and apparently was the woman driving Vaska a little crazy according to Dimitri.

Vaska clenched his jaw. "I don't even want to talk about what that naïve, way too trusting woman did last night. She almost got herself killed. No one would blame me if I tied her to my bed and never let her loose. I'd be saving society from her antics!"

I clapped Vaska on the back. Looks like I wasn't the only man being driven to distraction by a woman.

Vaska's idea about locking my wife away had merit. Until I learned more about her father and Egor's intentions, it would be best if Samara stayed hidden behind these walls where I knew she was safe.

Waving my housekeeper, Rose, away, I escorted the men to the front door.

"By the way, I heard your brother created a commotion

near O'Hare airport last night. Apparently, he was seen carrying a blonde woman over his shoulder to his car?" said Dimitri as he shrugged into his overcoat.

They had already informed me Damien had run into *complications* securing Yelena.

"Damien is handling another concern of ours. Do I need to do any damage control?"

Dimitri shook his head. "We have taken care of it. The surveillance footage no longer exists, and the police have no interest in pursuing what they've been told was a *private* matter."

I nodded my appreciation and closed the door behind them.

Glancing at the hall grandfather clock, I realized Samara would be here soon.

My cock twitched in anticipation.

The only way I was going to keep Samara safe from her father and Novikoff's plans was by having her under my control… and the only way to do that was with a dominating hand.

It was time for another lesson in submission.

One I was certain she would find hard to swallow.

CHAPTER 15

Gregor

AN ARGUMENT in the hallway just outside my door announced her arrival.

"I'm in the house now, you don't have to keep following me!" said Samara, indignation giving her voice a deep, husky quality I liked.

My office door swung open, and Samara stormed in, head held high. The two men I'd assigned to guard her hovered on the threshold.

"Will you please tell your two *goons* to go away?" she huffed as she crossed her arms over her chest. The movement pushed her breasts up high over the scalloped neckline of her dress.

I nodded to the men who bowed their heads before closing the door behind them.

She had dressed carefully. I admired her trim waist and

the sway of her hips as she walked a few more steps into my office.

Good.

It meant I was in her head, precisely where I wanted to be.

Selfishly, I wanted her to think of me as often as possible.

I couldn't help but wonder if the crinoline underneath her vintage black with red polka dot swing dress was red or black. I would learn soon enough.

"Can I offer you some coffee?" I asked cordially, as if this were any normal morning.

I could see the play of emotions as they crossed her beautiful, expressive eyes. They really were the most startling shade of bright green. I wouldn't be surprised to learn she often used contacts when disguising herself since I cannot imagine anyone forgetting those eyes.

"No, thank you. I won't be staying," she responded primly.

"We'll agree to disagree on that point… for now."

I motioned for her to sit. The moment she chose a chair in front of me, I approached and leaned against the front of my desk. When I crossed my feet, my legs brushed her skirts. I could smell her Chanel perfume.

She immediately popped up and paced around my office. She stopped before a large bronze sculpture which was positioned in front of a pair of windows. It was of a man writhing with tortured emotion, each sinew of his muscles strained and defined.

"Szukalski," she said.

I could tell she was trying to deflect the conversation. I would indulge her, for the moment.

"Very good. Few know his work. Have you ever heard the story of how he learned anatomy for his art?"

She shook her head.

I approached.

Standing so close behind her, I could see the sunlight play off the cranberry red highlights in her warm brown hair. Art was common ground for us. She was probably unaware that I was actually a great admirer and collector of art. It was just one of the things which intrigued me about her. I was honest enough with myself to admit it would be pleasant having someone I could talk to about my passion for art.

"He was only a boy when his father was killed in a car accident. Szukalski carried his body to the morgue himself and then asked if he could be there during the autopsy. So, as he told it, he learned anatomy from his father."

She shivered.

I placed my hands on her bare arms.

She quickly shied away. "What a dreadful story."

"I could tell a far more pleasant one about the Turner hanging over the fireplace," I offered with an amused smile.

Her head turned, and she walked the few steps to stand in front of the fireplace to observe the painting. It was a classic Turner of a storm at sea.

"This is real!"

I nodded.

"You have a *real* Turner in your house?"

Again, I nodded. I stepped closer before suggestively offering, "I also have a Klimt in my bedroom. Want to see it?"

Her pretty mouth opened in shock. For most women it was jewels, for Samara it was priceless art. I could tell she was tempted by my offer to see it. After all, not many people privately owned a Klimt. Most of his work was showcased only in museums.

She paced away from me. I watched as her mouth thinned and her shoulders straightened.

"Mr. Ivanov-"

So, we were going to play that game, were we?

"Gregor," I corrected.

"Mr. Ivanov—" she stubbornly continued.

"Samara, I know what your pussy tastes like," I teased. "Perhaps you could call me by name."

I could see the movement of her slim throat as she nervously swallowed. "Gregor, I think we need to have a serious conversation about this ludicrous idea that I'm somehow obligated to marry you because of a loan you made to my father."

"No."

She continued to pace from one end of the room to the next, refusing to meet my gaze. "No? You can't just say no. I was a naïve and frightened teenager three years ago, which is why I ran, but things have changed. You can't bully me into this!"

I shook my head as I leaned against the front of my desk, arms crossed over my chest. "Samara, you and I both know that I have the power to force you... if I must."

"What are you going to do? Toss me over your shoulder and carry me down the aisle and then force me to say *I do* at the altar?"

I raised one eyebrow as she finally dared to look in my direction, letting her know that was precisely what I would do.

She paused in her frenetic pacing. Once more I watched the play of emotions cross her face. This time it was a blend of astonishment and genuine fear. "You can't honestly fucking think you'd get away with a bullshit ceremony like that?"

"Language," I warned. I did not answer her question.

She paused, hands on hips. "Of course! You're Gregor *fucking* Ivanov. You can take anything you want with no one saying shit to you."

I sighed. "Samara, I won't warn you again about your

language. If that sweet little mouth of yours utters one more foul word, I'm going to teach it a lesson."

Samara raised her arm and pointed at me. "See? That right there! Your arrogant high-handedness! Who gave you the right to dictate to me what I can and can't do?"

"No one gave me anything. I took it."

"Well, I'm taking it back! I don't have to listen to you! You don't own me!"

God, it was fun watching her hips sway as she paced in agitation. She really had a spectacular walk. Rising to my full height, I pushed away from the desk and stalked toward her. She took a few steps back. I kept forward till I pressed her against the bookcase on my far wall. With a determined hand, I reached for her skirts.

"No!" she cried out as she tried to grasp my wrist and hold her skirts down.

With one swift movement, I secured both wrists above her head, and once more, I reached for the hem of her skirt. Lifting it high, I leaned in close, my mouth only inches from hers. My fingertips shifted the soft fabric of her panties to the side as I flicked her clit.

Her red lips opened on a gasp.

"That's where you're wrong, malyshka. I do own you, and I'm going to prove it right now."

CHAPTER 16

Samara

BREAKING FREE OF HIS GRASP. I ran for the door. There was a loud buzzing sound just as I neared it. I heard the loud clack of a bolt sliding into place. Still, I tried the knob. It wouldn't budge.

"Open this…. fucking… door!"

I knew I was deliberately poking the bear, but I didn't care.

This was getting out of hand. The man was quickly strengthening his strange hold on me, and I had to leave before I fell any deeper down the rabbit hole. I didn't care that he loved art. I didn't care that he was handsome as fuck. I didn't care he made me squirm in that taboo way when he growled against my pussy. He was dangerous, and I needed to get away from him before it was too late. I would escape and never look back.

"I'll scream."

Gregor ignored me and moved over to once more lean against his desk.

"Did you hear me? I'll start screaming."

He shrugged.

"Fine! Fine! You asked for this!" I raved as I dug my cell phone out of my purse. I was bluffing, of course. I'd have to be bonkers to call the cops. The last thing I wanted was to be on their radar even as a supposed victim, but maybe Gregor didn't know that.

He didn't even bother to react.

Damn him.

I pressed the button to activate my phone. There was no service. I lifted it up. Still nothing.

"Cell phone jammer."

Of course. *Of course!* A man like Gregor would have a cell signal jammer to prevent people from recording incriminating conversations with him. Fuck him and how smart he was.

I started banging on the door. "Help! Help! Let me out!"

"Don't you want to know where Yelena is?"

My fist arrested in midair. I turned to look at Gregor. "What did you say?"

"Yelena. You *are* concerned for her welfare, aren't you?"

Slowly, I stepped away from the door.

I knew when I was beaten at my own game.

My head bowed, I whispered, "Please, Gregor. Don't hurt her because of me."

Yelena still hadn't reached out to me. I hoped she was waiting for me in Montreal, but deep down, I knew Gregor's brother Damien probably had her. If she was suffering at his hands, it was my fault. She may have angered them with her racetrack schemes, but it was definitely her helping me escape and stay on the run which made her an enemy of the powerful Ivanovs.

"You and your friend are in a great deal of danger. Her safety depends on her receiving protection from Damien. Yours depends on me and that all depends on your *cooperation*, malyshka."

His eyes were hard and uncompromising. The great Gregor Ivanov about to get his way… about to win… again.

"What do you want, Gregor?"

"Get on your knees."

I knew better than to ask if he was serious. He was. Everything was about control with Gregor. He had it and wanted me to not only know it but show him I knew it.

Tossing my purse on a nearby table, I slipped out of my heels and slowly lowered to my knees.

"Now crawl to me."

I took a deep breath. This was my punishment for disobeying Gregor. He had me trapped. I had no choice but to obey.

Leaning forward, I placed my palms before me. The Italian marble floor was cold. Inching one knee forward, I slowly crawled a few feet till I was on the plush Persian carpet. Keeping my eyes lowered, I continued to crawl. I could feel the crinoline softly scratch the back of my thighs with each shift forward. My skin was humming with awareness and the memory of his leather belt from last night.

Would he take off his belt and discipline me again?

Why did my stomach flip in anticipation at the thought?

This is so fucked up.

In my line of vision, I could see the gold leaf claw-footed legs of his back lacquered desk and a pair of polished Oxfords.

"Look up at me."

My body quaked at the command.

"Samara, don't make me ask again."

I tilted my head back. Already significantly taller than me, from my submissive position on the floor, he looked like a Roman god, all height and strength with a stony expression.

Gregor reached down and cupped my jaw. His thumb caressed my lower lip.

"I'm going to enjoy teaching this smart mouth of yours a lesson."

No!

Having a man's cock in my mouth, cutting off my air, terrified me. You had no control. *Control.* There would be no better way to teach me a lesson about who was truly in control.

Gregor smiled as if he had read my thoughts. I watched in horror as he reached for his belt buckle. The same belt from at the museum.

I shimmied back on my knees. "Please, Gregor. I don't want—"

"Move another inch back, and I'll belt your ass and then still fuck your mouth," he growled. He whipped the belt free of its loops and folded it in half, ominously holding it between his hands. "Come here."

With no choice, I shifted forward till I was prone before his spread legs.

Gregor set his belt on the desk within reach. His hands went to the fastening of his trousers.

"Push the top of your dress down. I want to see your breasts."

I slipped my arms through the cap sleeves and pushed the bodice down. With this dress, a corset was best. Refusing to give in to my initial inclination to wear my black lace corset, I deliberately put on my plain satin one. By the unholy glow in his eyes at the sight of my partially bared breasts, I could tell I could wear a sack cloth corset, and it wouldn't have mattered one bit.

Gregor pulled his erect cock free.

My eyes widened. Last night it was if I had been split in two the moment he forced three fingers into my tight pussy. How would I ever fit his cock? Even Gregor's large hand did not diminish the impact of how long and thick his shaft looked.

"Open your mouth."

I couldn't. I knew my disobedience would come at a high price, but still I just couldn't obey. I was too frightened. I couldn't allow him to shove *that* down my throat. It would kill me.

Like a viper, Gregor struck with no warning but with deadly accuracy. His arm lashed out to fist my hair at the back of my head. He pushed my body forward as he pulled down, the pressure forcing my head back.

My hands pushed at his thighs as I strained backwards.

"Please! I don't know how to… I'm not good at—"

"Open wide for me like a good girl."

There it was again. The stomach flip. There was just something about him dominating me as he called me his good girl that did it for me. There was definitely something intriguing about having someone else force your hand… having someone else in charge.

I opened my lips.

His other hand came up to grasp my head on the other side. After adjusting his feet wider, he rested the head of his cock against my lower lip.

Slowly, he pushed his hips forward. His cock pressed down on my tongue. I expected him to stop, but he kept pushing in. I gagged and pressed my palms harder against his thighs. I could feel the bulbous head at the back of my throat. I jerked my head, but his grip prevented any actual movement.

"Open your throat," he growled.

Grasping my hair, he pulled on my head, forcing me to

swallow more of his cock. Breathing heavily through my nose, I tried to quell my rising panic. My entire focus was on his cock. The musky taste. How it filled my mouth. The press of its thick length. My own labored breathing. The feel of my nails digging into the soft fabric of his suit pants. The pain in my knees as I knelt before him.

My shoulders heaved as he thrust in deeply. Spittle formed at the corners of my mouth.

Finally, he pulled back. Quickly, I sucked in a full ragged breath. Looking down, I could see my bright red lipstick smeared up the shaft.

Gregor fisted his cock. "I've wanted to see your lipstick on my cock since the moment I first met you."

This time he took a step forward. His legs straddled my hips. "Tilt your head back," he ordered.

"Please, Gregor. I don't like this," I whimpered.

Gregor stroked my cheek with the back of his knuckles. "You're not supposed to like this, malyshka. This is a punishment. Maybe next time you use this pretty mouth for ugly words and sass you will think twice."

With that, his hand flipped to grip my jaw. His blunt fingertips dug into the soft sides of my cheeks. I could feel the sharp edges of my teeth cut the inside of my mouth. With a cry, I opened my mouth wide.

With no further warning, he thrust his cock in... deep.

With my head tilted back and his stance over my hips, I was off balance. The only thing holding me steady was his grip on my head. As his thrusts increased in intensity, he pulled my head up and down, making me fuck with my own mouth.

My jaw ached. The back of my throat felt bruised. My lips swollen.

The only noise in the room were my own obscene grunts and gags.

Again he pulled free, allowing me to breathe.

"This time you're going to swallow the entire length."

I cried.

The head of his cock pressed against my lips. I turned my head to the side. Out of the corner of my eye, I watched Gregor pick up his belt. I focused on his powerful hand as it gripped the folded leather. Goose bumps rose on my arms as I remembered all too well the feel of both his hands and that leather.

"Do I need to use this?"

Dejectedly, I shook my head. "No," I whispered as I ran the back of my hand across my mouth. My skin was stained with smeared lipstick and spit.

"Good girl. Now open your mouth."

Once more he placed both his hands around the back of my head, but this time he still had the belt in his grip. As he pushed his cock past my open lips and thrust, I could feel the cold metal of the buckle bump against the back of my neck.

A threat and a warning.

"Look at me."

My eyes strained upwards, meeting his hard gaze. I could only imagine what I looked like with my lips stretched wide around his cock. My lipstick smeared around my mouth. My mascara running down my flushed cheeks.

"I'm going to push in deep. I want your nose to touch my stomach."

My eyes widened in alarm. I tried to shake my head but couldn't.

He tightened the pressure of his hands against my head. Slowly, his cock pushed ever deeper into my throat. I choked and gagged, but still he thrust forward. After an eternity, the tip of my nose touched his flat stomach. I could feel the soft skin of his balls under my chin. Gregor paused. One hand brushed the hair from my eyes.

"Good girl. You swallowed all of my cock."

I felt an absurd rush of pride at having accomplished this strange task and having pleased him.

"I'm going to come. I want you to show me my come on your tongue before you swallow."

I kept my gaze on him. His head rolled back as he began a violent burst of quick thrusts in and out of my now willing mouth.

With a roar, he came. His warm, salty come filled my mouth. As I opened my mouth dutifully to display it on my tongue, I couldn't help but choke and some of it dripped out of the corner of my mouth.

Gregor went down on his haunches. Taking his index finger, he swept up the cum and held it before my lips. Staring deep into his silver eyes, I opened my mouth and obediently sucked his finger clean.

He then rose to tower over me. With a growl, he bent low and swung his arm out. I screamed and ducked. Looking out from under my arm, I watched in shock as he swept his arm across his desktop, clearing it. Papers, pens, and his laptop crashed to the floor.

Leaning down, he clasped me around the shoulders and lifted me high. My bottom connected with the hard surface of the desk.

"Gregor—"

His hand in the center of my chest pushing me to lay back stopped all protest.

He gave me a wink. "My turn to feast."

He flipped my skirts up. My red crinoline pillowed around my waist, blocking my view of him so I had no warning when his tongue licked between my legs over the silk of my thong.

There was no hiding how aroused I was... he now knew

how turned on I was having him force his cock down my throat.

"Oh God!" I moaned.

His warm fingers wrapped around the waistband of my thong and yanked it low, then twisted and pulled on the fabric so it pushed against the seam of my ass. Then his tongue swirled and flicked my sensitive nub till my back shot off the desk as each swipe sent an electric shock up my spine.

The flat of my palms slapped against the hardwood surface as I cried out, unable to contain the force of my orgasm.

Wiping his mouth with the back of his hand, Gregor rose to lean over me. Placing a hand near my head, he gave me a wolfish smile. He bent and flicked one of my exposed nipples with his tongue. "Keep this up, malyshka, and you may never escape me," he teased.

That was what I was afraid of.

CHAPTER 17

Samara

I'M FUCKED.

That is all I could think as I stared into his eyes.

To be honest, it was too draining to think anything at all beyond that.

I wanted to hide from my own emotions. I didn't want to think about my reaction to his dominance. How I liked the way he forced me to suck his cock. No. To think about any of that right now would literally drive me insane. Better to wait till I found Yelena, and we formed an escape plan.

Until that moment, I needed to keep my shit together.

I needed to act like none of this was affecting me.

Ignoring his offered hand, I shimmied off the desk. After straightening my now hopelessly wrinkled dress, I walked back to where I had discarded my shoes... back to where I had crawled to him like a freaking harem slave.

Picking up my shoes, I asked without turning around, "Bathroom?"

"The door directly to your left."

Still without facing him, I walked through the smaller door in the left-hand corner. Like the interior of his office, he had decorated the bathroom in ebony black and gold Italian marble with accents of deep emerald green.

I could not suppress a small gasp at my reflection.

My swollen lips were covered in the smeared remains of my red lipstick. The thick black eyeliner I'd used earlier to create a dramatic cat eye was now streaming down my cheeks, which were still flushed a bright cherry red. My hair was a tangled mess of curls. The elastic band, which I'd used to secure a low ponytail before Gregor used my hair as a weapon to demand my submission, now hung limply around a single curl.

"Baby, are you alright in there?" called Gregor through the door.

"I'm fine. Sorry, the... the marble was just cold on my bare feet," I lied.

Placing my ear against the door, I listened till I heard his steps recede. I then quietly turned the latch on the knob, locking the door. Not that I thought such a small lock could keep Gregor away if he wanted in, but it gave me a false sense of security.

Grabbing one of the plush green hand towels, I ran it under some scalding water and wiped my face, then lower, trying to erase the feel of his mouth. Digging into my purse, I found my brush and ruthlessly tackled all the tangles till I was once more able to tame it back into a ponytail that hung down my back. Opening my compact, I applied a layer of powder. It wouldn't mask the deep flush on my cheeks, but at least it took away the wan appearance. After a fresh application of lipstick and a little mascara, I appeared almost calm.

I rummaged in the cabinet beneath the sink and found a bottle of mouthwash. Twisting off the cap, I pressed my lips to the plastic opening. A brief thought that Gregor's lips probably touched the same rim invaded my mind. I violently chased the thought away. Thoughts like that were for later. After wine. Lots of wine.

Taking a deep breath, I unlocked the bathroom door and emerged back into his office.

It was empty.

Spinning my head to the left, I could see the main door was open.

This was my chance to escape!

I bolted for the door.

Just as I neared the threshold, Gregor reappeared. He was holding a small tray. On it was a selection of cut vegetables, cheese, and crackers with a pot of tea.

"I had Rose put this together for you," he said as he walked into the office and placed the tray on the small table between the chairs in front of the fireplace.

His back was turned.

The door was open.

I stayed.

Damn him.

I wrinkled my nose at the offered fare. "No. Thank you."

Gregor sighed. "I thought you might say that. One of these days, I'm going to get you to eat something green and healthy."

The protective tone of his voice surprised me.

No one had really given a damn what I ate, not even my mother.

Probably why I survived on Chinese food and frozen pizza.

I was saved from having to respond by a discreet tap on the door. A large man in a suit stuck his head in. "Sir? I have the items you requested." In his hand was a McDonalds large coffee cup and a small bag.

Gregor nodded. "Thanks, Jim." He took the cup from Jim and closed the office door. Turning to me, he held out the goods. "Cafe Mocha with skim milk and extra whipped cream and an Egg McMuffin."

The dark, rich smell of espresso mingled with the scent of sweet cream. I wasn't even going to entertain the thought of refusing this gesture. I can't remember a time I'd needed the comfort of my favorite drink more.

I should have been upset and alarmed that he knew what I liked to drink, but for some reason I wasn't. It gave me a soft flutter in my stomach to think this big scary man had taken the time to learn what I liked or to care what I ate. After years on the run, unable to trust anyone but Yelena, I got used to no one knowing the real me.

Stop it, Samara! For fuck's sake, it's just coffee.

Taking the cup, I played with the sip tab as I asked, "How did you know?"

Gregor raised an eyebrow. "Same way I knew about Gwen Stevens."

"Are you going to tell me how you found out?"

Gregor took a step closer to me. He reached out to caress my cheek.

I hated my reaction to his touch.

The side of his mouth quirked up in a rare smile. "Not a chance."

I sighed. I'd expected as much. If he told me how he'd found me, then I would learn what not to do next time I ran... and there would be a next time as soon as I had the chance.

"Are you going to eat that?"

The brown McDonald's bag rested on a nearby table. The familiar scent of egg, cheese, and ham called to me, but I knew I was too nervous around Gregor to even think about eating. I shook my head.

"How about I give you a tour of the house?"

That seemed like a perfectly normal thing to ask someone… which is why I was immediately suspicious. Gregor and I didn't do normal.

I stared down at the Persian carpet that only moments earlier I had been shamelessly crawling across.

Ivory Black.

Cadmium Gold.

Alazarin Crimson.

Gregor picked up one curl and ran it over his palm and through his fingers, with only the slightest tug on my hair. It shocked me to realize I wish he'd pull harder.

What the hell is this man doing to me?

He stormed back into my life less than twenty-four hours ago and already I was practically begging him to fuck me while he pulled my hair.

Breaking into my chaotic thoughts, he said, "The real art is upstairs."

My eyebrow rose. The art was bait—a trap—and I was going to walk into it.

Not trusting myself to speak, I just nodded my assent.

Taking the now cooled mocha from my hands, he set it aside and enclosed my palm in his own.

Looking down, I marveled at how big his hand looked compared to my small pale one. The man had sexy hands. Strong and tan with a few faint scars over his knuckles hinting at his violent life. He had on an expensive-looking watch. It was chrome and black leather with an old-fashioned Roman numeral face. It suited him.

With a start, I realized this wasn't the first time I had observed his hands.

Oh, my God.

My painting.

The one from Boston. The only one I'd ever sold.

Little Girl Saved.

The man's hand clasped around her wrist, the one saving her, was Gregor's hand. Without conscious thought, I had recreated it on canvas right down to the watch.

I was sure there were deep and dark Freudian revelations to be had from this newfound knowledge, but that would have to be for later, when I was tucked into bed going over today's events in my mind.

I was just glad that wasn't one of the paintings in my loft right now. I'd hate for Gregor to know of its existence. Who knows how he'd read into it?

With a resigned step, I followed him out into the hall and up the main staircase.

It really was a stunning home.

Located in Evanston right on the shores of Lake Michigan, it was a massive crimson red brick structure with gabled windows and the outside walls covered in ivy. I'd noticed that same ivy covered the many security cameras which surveyed the parameter beyond the tall, walled-in gates.

The artwork in the entranceway was tasteful but cold.

Two pieces from Rothko's later period. The color blocks of blue and green were large and abstract, telling the visitor nothing about the personality of its owner.

Perhaps that was the way Gregor liked it?

The art showed he had money and taste but gave no other detail away about the man.

Despite the intensity of our limited encounters and our connection through Nadia and our families, I still knew very little about him while he seemed to know almost everything about me, right down to the coffee drink I liked.

It was unnerving.

The thick *Egyptian Violet* hallway carpet muffled our footsteps.

"Let me show you to your bedroom."

"My bedroom? I'm not fuc—" I stopped myself before I cursed.

I tried to pull my hand free. He only tightened his grasp. I threw my weight back and pulled harder. Finally, with a resigned sigh, he relented.

I measured my words carefully, unwilling to get another dose of his discipline for dropping the f-bomb repeatedly like I wanted to. "What do you mean, *my* bedroom?"

"It means what you think it means."

He placed a controlling hand on my lower back and pushed me through the first door on the right. At one end of the large room was a tester bed with a delicate cream lace canopy. The ash blue carpeting highlighted the golden undertones in the walnut furnishings placed around the perimeter.

In the middle of the room, there was a small pile of suitcases and boxes.

My belongings.

He must have had everything moved here after I left with the goons guarding me.

I rounded on him; claws bared.

CHAPTER 18

Samara

... BUT I STOPPED COLD.

My mouth dropped open at what he held in his hand.

My small black leather portfolio with my fake passports and access codes for my offshore accounts.

I swiped at it but he raised his arm, keeping it out of my reach.

"That's mine!"

"Tsk. Tsk. Tsk. Someone's been a very bad girl. You know it's *illegal* to possess false identification."

He was judging *me* on the criminal nature of my actions. That was rich.

"These types of off-shore accounts are notorious for their low-security. As your fiancé, I took the liberty of moving your money someplace safer."

His calm, conciliatory tone belied the evil nature of his actions.

My money was gone and so was any hope of escape.

"You bastard," I cried through clenched teeth.

I swung at him again, this time aiming for his face. He caught my arm in midair, his strong fingers wrapping around my wrist as he pulled me against him.

With no warning, his mouth descended to take possession of mine. His tongue swept between my lips and tasted and teased. My hands, which should have been pushing him away, came up to rest on his shoulders as I allowed him to plunder and take. He smelled of *Bleu de Chanel* and tasted like black coffee... and *me*.

My entire word tilted as I allowed myself to be swept under.

When I was breathless and disoriented, he set me aside. I opened my eyes to see him reach into his breast pocket for a linen handkerchief. He wiped my red lipstick off his mouth. After returning the linen to his pocket, he gave me a slow appraisal.

"You cannot win against me, Samara. The more you fight it... the *harder* it will get for you."

There was no mistaking his meaning.

I backed away, taking a few steps deeper into the room, hoping distance from him would break the seething sexual tension.

I just needed to keep reminding myself that I hated him.

Taking a deep breath, I surveyed the room. That was when I observed the Degas over the bed. It was a depiction of one of Degas' favorite subjects, ballerinas. This one showed several in the wings getting ready to go on stage.

Wanting to get a little of my own back, I tossed him a snarky smile over my shoulder. "You know this is a fake, right?"

"What?" said Gregor as he followed me into the room.

I took great pleasure in seeing the superior smile wiped off his face.

"It's a fake."

Gregor leaned his hands on the bed as he took a closer look. "You can't possibly know that for sure. You haven't even looked at the edges."

A non-invasive way to tell immediately if a painting was counterfeit was to compare the edges of the canvas, the part not seen because of the frame, with the photographed edges kept on file by whatever insurance company insured the painting. This only worked if the forger didn't also work for the insurance company.

"I know about the artist. He works out of Belgium," I said appreciatively. I had read up on the infamous forger when the gallery I worked for almost got taken in by one of his works.

Gregor's brow lowered. It was fun seeing the great Gregor Ivanov realize they had taken him in.

Gregor shook his head. "No. It can't be. This painting had impeccable provenance."

I nodded. "Yes, that would be his contact in the Ukraine. According to this article I read, no one beats her when it comes to creating a false paper trail for a painting."

Kicking off my shoes, I crawled up on the bed. Kneeling in front of the painting, I pointed to one of the ballerina's costumes. Buried in the hem of the tutu was what appeared to be an innocuous squiggle. "You see that? That is actually the forger's signature."

"Signature?"

"A lot of forgers can't resist 'signing' their work. If you know where to look, you can find their mark."

I turned to look at Gregor. I realized my position on the bed had me kneeling in front of him again. Only this time, I was eye level. I could see his platinum eyes darken as they drifted over my face and cleavage.

And just like that, all the sexual tension returned.

Gregor dipped two fingers into the bodice of my dress and pulled me closer. "I guess it's a good thing I'll soon be married to a skilled art consultant who'll protect me from forgeries from now on."

My breath hitched. Realizing where we were, I quickly scrambled off the other side of the bed. Shoving my feet back into my shoes, I walked across the room, away from his commanding presence.

"Where does this door lead?" I opened the door before he could answer.

Taking a step inside the room, I instinctively knew I was in his bedroom.

The rooms were connected.

Connected.

As in separated only by a door.

A thin piece of wood.

Ignoring the way my stomach flipped at the knowledge, I stepped further into the room.

Instead of carpeting, the floor comprised broad wooden floorboards stained a rich oxblood. Similar to his office, there were two high black-lacquered cabinets flanking the large poster bed which had rich gold velvet curtains on either side of the headboard. Leaning against one cabinet was a Gustav Klimt painting from the Block-Bauer series, the shimmering gold tones and unique style unmistakable.

In its place over the bed was the painting from my *Little Girl Lost* series. The one he had taken from my loft earlier.

Pointing, I whispered, "That's my painting."

My mind spun over what it could mean that he had hung it in such a prominent place over his bed, displacing a priceless Klimt, no less, to do it.

"It's mine now," said Gregor over my shoulder as he entered the bedroom and leaned against the doorjamb with his arms crossed over his chest.

I turned, my hands on my hips. "Do you always just take what isn't yours?"

Stalking toward me, Gregor grabbed my chin and lifted my gaze to his own. Talking low and even, his words clipped and rife with meaning, he said, "I always take what I want, and I *never* let go of what is mine."

In that moment, I couldn't decide if I was more frightened or flattered.

With an anxious glance at the enormous bed that lorded over the entire room, I escaped back into my bedroom.

Gregor sauntered after me.

Reaching around him, I made a show of slamming the door shut.

Looking at the doorknob, I said, "There's no lock. I want a—"

Gregor cut me off. "No."

"I hate you! If you think I'm going to allow you to just waltz in here whenever you like and take—"

His hand clasped me around the neck and pulled me close, cutting off my threat.

Leaning down, his lips almost touched mine. I could feel the warmth of his breath against my skin as he said with a fierce growl, "I know I'm the monster from your dreams, Samara. The beast lurking in the shadows waiting to snatch you away these past three years, but it doesn't matter, malyshka. You can profess to hate me all you want. I feel your body tremble at my touch."

Denying the raw honesty of his words, I tried to break away. Using his free hand, he pushed against my lower back, forcing me closer. I could feel the press of his cock against my stomach.

"It's not true," I spit out, trying to turn my head away, but his grip on my neck prevented it.

With a low curse, Gregor picked me up and carried me to the bed.

Tossing me onto the middle of the mattress, the heavy weight of his body quickly followed, pinning me down. My struggles were useless as he snatched my wrists and stretched my arms high over my head.

"You're lying to yourself. You and I both know if I were to flip these skirts up, I'd find you wet and ready for my cock... just like earlier." His hips ground into mine, emphasizing each word.

My cheeks flamed. I could already feel the proof between my thighs.

With his free hand, he grasped my breast and squeezed till my hips shot off the bed, rubbing against him. "Your virginity is safe from me... for now. Before I sink my cock into that sweet, tight pussy of yours, I'll make you beg for it first."

"Never," I choked out as I tossed my head from side to side.

He leaned down and bit my earlobe, before whispering darkly in my ear, "Mark my words, love. You'll scream my name."

He twisted his hips between my legs one more time before releasing me.

I curled into the fetal position on the bed as he rose to stand over me, straightening his cuffs.

He turned and headed for the door, tossing over his shoulder, "I'll leave you to unpack."

Leaning up on my hands, I pushed my now tangled hair away from my face and asked, "So I'm to be your prisoner?"

"Think of yourself as a reluctant, honored guest with fringe benefits," he taunted.

My mouth opened, and I had every intention of giving him a scathing retort when his shoulders tightened and his brows lowered.

A beast expecting a fight.

I wouldn't give him the satisfaction.

As he closed the door, I collapsed back onto the bed and cried tears of frustration and fear.

I was learning his mercurial moods, his temper, and what turned him on. At the same time, I was seeing a side of him I never would have expected. If I wasn't more on my guard, I would mistake his manipulative actions as protective and almost caring in a strange, overbearing, arrogant sort of way.

The only thing I knew for certain was Gregor was even more dangerous to me now than ever before.

CHAPTER 19

*G*regor

I WAS A FUCKING SAVAGE.

Instead of returning to my office, I walked inside my bedroom and headed straight to the connecting door.

She was crying.

I had done that.

Flattening my palm on the smooth wood, I bent my head and leaned my forehead against the door.

Fuck.

I fought the urge to go in there, take her in my arms, and promise her everything would be okay if she just trusted me. How could I expect her to trust me? I'd done nothing to earn it. Even if I marched in there right now and told her what her father was planning, explained to her that I was keeping her safe, there was no reason for her to believe me. And why should she? Her own parents had betrayed her. I'd done nothing but order her about and bully her. No wonder the girl didn't trust anyone.

Taking my anger out on a defenseless girl, and for what? Because she had wounded my pride by running from me? Embarrassed the Ivanov name?

I had truly become my father's son, and I hated myself for it.

I no longer gave a damn about my contract with her father. This wasn't about business anymore. If I were honest with myself, it hadn't been about business for a long time. Somewhere between reading her underlined passages in *Dracula*, smiling at her Cafe Mocha addiction, and appreciating her paintings, my search for her had become personal. I ached to know her as the woman she had become. She was no longer just the daughter of a Federov.

Now that I'd finally found her, she was everything I'd imagined and more. I loved her spirit and the way she challenged me, even when she feared me, and the way her eyes turned a startling green-gold when she was angry, turned on —or both—which was most of the time around me.

I turned and leaned my shoulders against the door. The painting over my bed caught my eye. I genuinely liked her work. Each canvas had an innocence and darkness which drew me in and perfectly captured Samara's essence. A beautiful, innocent soul who'd been corrupted by the evil actions of those around her. Corrupted by me.

As much as I liked this one, I liked the one I bought from that gallery in Boston better, *Little Girl Saved*. I had recognized the hand saving the little girl as my own. That was the moment I knew I was in Samara's thoughts as much as she was in mine. And in that painting, I was the one saving her… not breaking her.

I almost had her back in my arms that time. I had come so close. I remembered breaking down the girls' apartment door and finding it empty, her perfume still lingering in the air.

I almost gave up my search then and there, but I went to pick up the painting I had purchased sight unseen, the one which had led me to her. It knocked me back when I saw it. It now hung over my bed in my home in Washington D.C.

I should have just let her go… let her live her life. Now it was too late.

The only way to keep her safe from her father and the Novikoffs was to claim her as my own, as originally planned.

Even if it meant she'd hate me for it.

I may have been the devil, but at least I was the devil she knew.

CHAPTER 20

Samara

I WRAPPED my arms tightly around my middle as my stomach growled again.

Ruefully I thought of the breakfast tray Rose had brought it up to my bedroom.

I, of course, had refused it out of spite.

It was filled with healthy food and vegetables. Vegetables!

Who the hell ate vegetables for breakfast?

She told me Gregor had informed her I probably hadn't eaten something fresh and green for weeks. The fact that was true did not give him the right to dictate what I ate. Although secretly it gave me a warm feeling to know he even cared enough to think about my meals. Since my mother essentially stopped raising me when I was twelve, I had forgotten what a home cooked meal even tasted like.

Now on top of regretting not eating, I was pacing around the confines of my bedroom like a caged animal.

Exhausted, I massaged my temples; I had barely slept. My mind raced from one fanciful thought to the next all night.

I kept staring at the connecting door, knowing *he* was just on the other side. Was he in bed? Was he listening for my moments? Did the knob just turn? No? Was I disappointed or relieved? Did he sleep in pjs or naked? He probably slept naked, like a caveman. I could just imagine him stripping off his suit like he was shedding the trappings of society. He would be all tanned skin, tattoo ink, and muscle. I wondered what his tattoos looked like. The swallow on his hand was black. Would the rest be black as well or colorful? There were only a few indistinct lines on his neck, not enough to decipher an image. What kind of images would a man like Gregor have forever inked on his body? I doubt he favored cute hearts and cartoon characters like me.

I had heard him rise several hours ago.

Again, I waited, not knowing if I wanted him to knock on my door or not.

He didn't.

It had been at least an hour since I sent Rose and her breakfast tray away.

An hour of pacing and uncertainty while I hid away in my bedroom like a scolded child.

What the hell was I supposed to do?

I knew what I *wanted* to do. I *wanted* to march down the hall and straight out the front door, but there was no freaking way that was going to happen. Gregor had made that fact crystal clear yesterday.

This was ridiculous. With a huff, I pivoted and headed for the door stopping just as my hand closed over the doorknob. I released the cold knob as if it had burned me. Taking several steps backward, I fell back onto the bed.

I was a coward.

No two ways about it.

I was that scared teenage girl refusing to leave the hotel room again. For months after leaving, nothing Yelena did could convince me to leave the safety of our rooms. I saw monsters in every shadow. Finally, she started picking cities with museum collections I couldn't resist. Ironically, walking among the great paintings of long dead artists I admired became my entry back into the world of the living. It wasn't long after that she got me to paint again. We had to pay more than one fine in multiple hotels for paint spills, but it was worth it.

I was proud of how independent I had become over the last few years.

Well, at least in principle. Sure, I ate most of my meals out of a cardboard container and didn't own any furniture outside of a mattress and a second-hand vanity. And yes, I was still relying on Yelena's racetrack scheme for most of my money since my plans to become an artist hadn't quite panned out. Technically, perhaps I wasn't as independent as I would like, but I was still somewhat self-sufficient and happy with my life.

If I were completely honest, it was a little boring. Lately, it had become more and more difficult to even get motivated to paint. Once we settled down in Chicago, my life slipped into a rather predictable routine of gallery shifts, Chinese food, and staying up late watching noir films on Turner Classic Movies. It was static and a little lackluster, but I was fine with that.

That the last two days had been the most excitement I'd felt in… well… ever… had nothing to do with Gregor.

Absolutely not.

He was a beast, and I hated him.

He had ruined my life.

He was *still* ruining my life.

Yep, hated him.

Hated how dangerously sexy he looked in a suit. There was just something hot-as-hell about a man covered in ink wearing an expensive bespoke suit with a probably hundred-thousand-dollar watch on his wrist. It was just so billionaire gangster.

And I really hated that he appreciated art. It was obvious from the paintings displayed around his home. Posers, or those just investing for the tax breaks, tended to have tight, cohesive collections. Artists from the same time period or those who liked to work in the same color palette or medium.

Gregor's collection, while priceless, had no rhyme or reason. There was a small thread of Impressionism through most of the purchases, but on the whole, you could tell that most were acquired because he liked them. The sign of a true art lover. Damn him.

All of these were just trifling things when I thought about what it was like to be under his control sexually. My cheeks burned from the memory of it all. Never in my life had I ached with the need to have a man be strong and masterful enough to dominate me. It was a heady, overwhelming experience to be told I was about to be whipped with a belt like an errant child and then fucked hard. I didn't know whether to cry from the pain or relish in the all-consuming orgasm that came from completely surrendering my body into someone else's hands.

Never before had I given such control over to someone.

Hell, technically I *still* hadn't. Gregor just took it... as his right.

It was like he knew I could never—would never—say yes. My pride would never allow such a thing. So he wrenched the decision from me by force of will.

And the whole pleasure-pain kink? That was just the cherry on top.

Fuck, it was hot watching him unbuckle his belt as he told me to beg him for mercy.

I would never admit that to any living soul, including him, but *damn*.

The longer I stayed here, the further down the rabbit hole I would fall, of that at least I was certain.

I needed to get out of here and find Yelena. Although Gregor was keeping me in the dark, I had to believe that Damien wouldn't actually harm her. She was his little sister's best friend as much as I. Even though, like Gregor, there was a big age gap between us and Damien, he had still been around when we were just girls. He wouldn't be so heartless as to have forgotten that, would he? I had to remember that Yelena was even more of a survivor than me. She was probably giving Damien a run for his money at this very moment. Hopefully, she was making him wish they had never found the two of us.

Either way, I needed to find a way to escape, and that would not happen with me too scared to leave my room.

Taking a deep breath, I rose. With a determined step, I crossed to the door. My fingers had just touched the smooth metal surface of the knob when the whole door rattled from the resounding pounding of someone's fist.

"Samara?"

I jumped back, a hand to my heart.

Gregor.

"Samara, I know you are in there. Open the door."

I could practically hear his resigned sigh through the heavy wood.

My foot slid back as I eased away from the door. Glancing over my shoulder, I checked to see if the connecting door was still closed. Of course, it didn't have a lock. Maybe I could push something in front of it?

As if reading my thoughts, Gregor warned, "I'm knocking

as a courtesy, Samara. We both know I have other means to enter your room."

Having no other choice, I reached for the knob again. As I turned it, the small lock popped out with an ominous click.

The door swung open.

He was dressed all in black. With a sardonic quirk of his lips, he crossed over the threshold.

A vampire male ready to feed on my inner thoughts and desires.

Blindly reaching my arm behind me, I stumbled backward as he prowled forward. My only hope was keeping my distance. Gregor had other plans.

My hand closed around the edge of the bureau. As I shifted to move around it, Gregor sprang forward, pinning me against the wall between the bureau and bed.

Placing his hands high on either side of my head, he inhaled deeply.

Dammit. I knew how much he liked my perfume. I had put it on this morning out of habit. Now he would think I did it for him. It didn't help that I could smell the warm spicy scent of his cologne, as well. There was just something so infuriatingly sexy about a man who smelled like a campfire after a storm.

His hard gaze focused on my mouth. My tongue flicked out to wet my lips, and then the sharp edge of my teeth sank into the bottom one. The vibrations of his growl hummed across my stomach and breasts.

"Rose tells me you refused breakfast. This is unacceptable."

My chin lifted. "I wasn't hungry."

"Liar."

My eyes narrowed. "Fine. I just didn't want to eat *your* food."

The corner of his mouth lifted. I wasn't fooled. He was

amused, but only as a cat finds playing with a limping mouse amusing.

Lowering his arm, he traced the V-neck outline of my simple white t-shirt with the tip of a single finger. I clenched my stomach to keep from reacting, but nothing could stop the betraying hardening of my nipples, easily seen through the thin silk fabric of my bra.

"Your well-being is important to me, malyshka."

I snorted. "My family name is important to you, Mr. Ivanov."

Ignoring my snipe, he hooked the bottom of my neckline with his finger and tugged till the top of my bra was exposed. "Did you dream about me last night?"

My mouth opened on a gasp, but I refused to respond.

"I dreamt about you," he continued.

My breath came in quick gasps as I tried to focus on the small, gilt-framed painting of a placid lake just over his shoulder. I tried to match the colors to oil paint names, but my mind was filled only with thoughts of Gregor and his mesmerizing steel gaze.

"I laid naked in bed, thinking about the moment you'll spread those gorgeous thighs of yours and beg me to fuck you."

Turning my head to the side, I snarled through clenched teeth, "That will *never* happen."

Gregor shifted slightly, brushing his hips against mine so I could feel the threat of his hard cock caress my stomach. Leaning down, his lips skimmed my jaw as he moved to whisper in my ear. "I couldn't decide which position I want for that moment."

His words were like hands moving over my body and into my mind.

"What do you think, malyshka? Would you prefer to be on your knees? That beautiful ass pushing against my hips as

I fist your hair while I spank you till your skin glows a cherry red to match that cute heart tattoo of yours."

My teeth sunk so sharply into my bottom lip I could taste blood as I desperately tried to stifle a groan.

Relentlessly, he continued. "Or do you want to be on your back? Where you can watch as I sink my cock into that tight pussy of yours." His finger circled my left nipple, taunting me. "I must admit, I think that is my choice. I want to watch as the gold flecks in your emerald eyes gleam and catch fire the moment you feel me breach your maidenhead. The moment we both know you've become truly mine."

"Ty mozhesh' trakhnut' moye telo, no ya nikogda ne stanu tvoim." I spat out the threat as if it were poison.

His hand closed over my jaw, forcing my head forward. I could tell me taunting him in our own mother tongue that he could fuck my body, but I'd never be truly his had angered him, had broken through that icy, false veneer of civility in which he cloaked himself.

With his free hand, he reached down to clasp the buckle of his leather belt. "Eto vash sposob prosit' menya nakazat' vas?"

Tears pricked my eyes. "No, I don't want to be punished."

"Then I suggest you start being a good girl. It is dangerous to anger me this way, malyshka."

He shifted his hand off his belt and raised it to caress my lips. "Now use this pretty mouth to say you're sorry."

My body shook as it responded to the physical threat his mere presence caused. "I'm…" I swallowed past the dryness in my throat. "I'm sorry, Gregor."

"Good girl." He stepped back and adjusted the cuffs on his shirt. "Now I get to reward you with your surprise."

Shivering, I wrapped my arms tightly around my stomach. It was terrifying how a usually pleasant phrase could sound so ominous when uttered by this dark and mercurial man. "Thank you, but I don't want any surprises."

He chuckled. "When are you going to learn that very little about your life from now on is about what you want...." One eyebrow quirked up. "Unless it's me."

Stretching out his arm, he held his hand palm up to me. I stared down at his hands. The dark ink lines of some mostly unseen tattoo wrapped around his wrist and disappeared under his watchband and up his sleeve.

"Come with me, Samara."

CHAPTER 21

Samara

Gregor headed straight down a hallway dotted with lesser known artists' landscapes, till he came to a massive set of glass French doors.

As we crossed the threshold, I could tell we were inside a rooftop conservatory. The walls and ceiling were all glass. It looked as though all the plants had been recently removed and the cement floor scrubbed clean. Despite their efforts, you could still see the watery brown circles where large planters used to rest. In place of the plants were stacks of rolled canvases, several easels and four long workbenches filled with every imaginable paintbrush, paints, drawing paper, and pencils.

Walking past Gregor, I surveyed the room.

"The roof has automated blinds which are reactivated by heat and light. You can reprogram them if you want to keep the light streaming in."

The bright morning sunlight streaked down from the glass ceiling of the open and airy room. Its tall windows let even more light in while offering a stunning view of the battleship grey waters of Lake Michigan.

It was amazing.

It was like Gregor had consulted with a painter to find out what their dream studio would look like and followed every bit of advice right down to the smallest detail.

He had even had his staff hang up all the completed paintings he had moved from my apartment. They looked beautiful against the exposed brick wall. I stared at the various canvases of pretty girls in pink ruffled dresses staring down fierce thunderstorms or shadowy beasts. My Lost Girl series.

In awe, I ran my fingers over the beautiful stainless-steel topped workman's bench. All of my brushes had been carefully cleaned and displayed in clear mason jars.

I didn't even hear him leave.

I only turned when I heard the quiet catch of the door latch as he closed it behind him. Instead of being offended, I was even more touched. He hadn't made me grovel or thank him. He hadn't even leveraged my obvious delight of having access to such an unbelievable painter's studio for future sexual favors. I didn't trust anyone to do something for nothing. It couldn't be possible that Gregor did all this just to be kind to me? Could it?

Mentally shaking the confusing emotions off, I picked up a bright white canvas roll and spread it out on a nearby open table. This is what I needed. This is what helped my chaotic world make sense. Picking up a jar of Gesso, I unscrewed the lid and scooped a generous amount into a plastic bowl. Tightening the red bandana scarf around my ponytail, I got to work preparing my canvas.

* * *

I TESTED the canvas to see if the layer of Gesso I had spread to prime it was dry. Seeing that it was, I stretched the canvas over the frame and tacked it down. The familiar rhythmic banging of the hammer soothed me. Lifting the newly stretched canvas, I placed it on the easel and surveyed my work.

Since I didn't know how long Gregor was going to keep me prisoner in his house, or when I'd get an opportunity to escape, I decided the hopefully tight timeframe would make using my usual oil paints extremely problematic. They took too long to dry. I was going to use acrylic instead.

Reaching for my favorite wooden palette, I prepared and mixed the different colors I would need to start the background. Gently pulling the glob of paint in one direction then swirling in the different pigments, I slowly created the colors building from light into dark.

Then, I painted.

At once I slipped into the comforting embrace of my own little world. Where I was in control of everything. Where every brushstroke, every swipe of color, was my decision.

* * *

I HAD BEEN PAINTING for hours and didn't even notice when Gregor entered the studio. When I moved away from the easel to mix more paint, I noticed him leaning against the door.

"How long have you been there?"

"Long enough to know you bite your lip when you paint," he replied as he went into the hallway and returned with a small tray. "I come bearing gifts."

"McDonalds?"

That earned me a smirk. "No. Roast chicken with sage fondant potatoes and a winter green salad," he responded as he placed the tray on a small table that stood in front of a row of the windows with the view of the lake. He then dragged two crates to either side of it.

I wrinkled my nose at the super fancy sounding fare. "I would rather have a cheeseburger and fries."

"I know but Rose worked all morning on this special lunch for you, and her feelings would be hurt if you didn't eat it, especially after you turned your little nose up at her breakfast tray."

I huffed good-naturedly. "Blackmail.".

Gregor walked over to the painting. "You're making fast progress. An impressionist work?"

He surveyed the hectic brushstrokes in various shades of purple and green, with shadows of grey and white to create the illusion of light. It was odd. I should feel nervous with him looking at my work. Like most artists, I had a rather thin skin when it came to criticism, so I rarely let anyone see my work unfinished. Not that many had clamored to. My parents never gave a damn about my *hobby*. Yelena and Nadia had always been enthusiastic and supportive, but with Gregor it was… different. For one thing, the man actually knew about art. All this should have had me scrambling to hide the painting under a tarp, and yet I found myself eager to hear his opinion.

I nodded as I also assessed my work. "I decided to work with acrylic instead of oils like the true impressionists would have used. By adding a drying agent over a thickening agent, I will achieve the same texturized look. Plus, there is virtually no drying time."

"Smart. This will look beautiful in our study in Washington. I know just the place. Near a window so it will catch the morning light, and I'll have a view of it from my desk."

There I went, tumbling down the rabbit hole again as a feeling of pride rushed over me. I needed to focus on his presumptive phrasing that *my* painting would hang in *his* other home. Not all the gushy, warm emotions which rose at the thought of him already planning on hanging a simple painting of mine in a place of honor in his home. My own parents had never done me that honor.

Shrugging, I tamped down my true feelings. "Whatever. It's just a throwaway practice piece."

Ignoring my defensive comment, Gregor gestured for me to sit and eat.

"Do you always do that?" he asked casually as I lifted the lid off my lunch plate.

"Do what?" I asked evasively as I paid way more attention than was necessary to unrolling my napkin.

"Downplay your talent," he said, his voice dark and gravely. "I will not push you… for now. But just know that I know you're lying. You're a talented artist, Samara. Each of your paintings mean something to you. I know it, even if you won't admit it."

My cheeks flamed. In many ways, what he was saying now was far more intimate and soul-seeing than any of his previous scandalous comments about having sex with me, which made every word he uttered that much more dangerous.

We settled into an uneasy ceasefire as I cut into the roasted chicken Rose had made for me.

After rolling a cherry tomato around my plate for a few moments, I finally worked up the courage to ask him, "How do you know so much about art?"

"Why? Do I not seem like the type of person who can appreciate high culture?" He snatched the same tomato off my plate and ate it with a wink.

"I'm serious."

He nodded toward my plate. "Take a bite of salad, and I'll answer."

Spearing a single leafy green with the prongs of my fork, I raised it to my mouth and ate it with a flourish and a cheeky smile.

"Cheater."

"You didn't say how big of a bite. Now answer my question."

Without quite realizing it, I held my breath for his answer. I needed to know. Was his interest in art just a ploy, part of his scheme to get me to relax my guard under his control, or was it a glimpse into the real him?

Gregor thought for a moment as he finished chewing his bite. "My life is filled with darkness and destruction. I see the worst of human nature in all its disgusting glory on a daily basis. Art reminds me that humans are capable of creating beauty. It shows me there is some higher power out there, trying to balance the scales. I am in awe of anyone who can take a piece of canvas or wood and some globs of paint and create something that gives you a glimpse into the human mind and soul."

I was speechless, struck by the raw honesty and intensity of his response. Somehow, I expected some machismo speech where he denied it. This man continued to confuse and intrigue me.

Clearing my throat, I risked raising my eyes to his, knowing the danger of looking deep into that cold, hypnotic gaze. "Beauty will save the world."

He nodded. "Dostoevsky's *The Idiot*. One of my favorite books."

"Mine is *Dracula*." I wasn't sure why I offered that. We were having as close to a normal conversation as I believed either of us were capable of, and I didn't want to ruin it.

"I know."

My arm stopped halfway to my mouth with a piece of roasted chicken speared on my fork's prongs. "How do you know that?"

"Same way I know you can't cook worth a damn."

"What? I certainly can to cook—"

"You cannot. I doubt you could even boil water."

"So? What does—"

"By all your underlined passages in the copies you've left behind over the last three years, I also know your favorite book is *Dracula* because you're drawn to the vampire's dark soul. Tempted by it." His voice was low and suggestive.

I blinked. This was cutting a little too close to the bone.

"Your red lips and dresses come from your love of film noir. Your favorite film is *In a Lonely Place* with Humphrey Bogart."

Dropping my fork, I folded the napkin on my lap into a tiny square. "So, you've learned a few random things about me, that doesn't prove—"

His silver gaze focused on me. Reaching over, he stroked my cheek with the back of his knuckles before tucking a long curl behind my ear.

"It proves that you are not just a family name to me. I will admit that was the case at one time but hasn't been so from the first moment I had you in my arms."

I shook my head. "You were just playing games with me then as now," I accused as we both remembered his Russian roulette trick.

This whole conservation had taken a disturbing turn. After years of false identities and playing pretend, it was intoxicating to believe that someone out there knew me... the real me.

"I'm not playing a game, Samara. This is far too important to me."

"I don't believe you."

"You'll just have to show me a little faith," he whispered as he continued to play with a lock of my hair.

"Faith, that faculty which enables us to believe things which we know to be untrue," I responded, quoting from *Dracula*.

"There are darknesses in life and there are lights, and you are one of the lights, the light of all lights."

My heart skipped a beat as he quoted it in return. And damn him for quoting one of my favorite passages in the book.

"Whether or not you want to acknowledge it, you are in danger, Samara. You don't get to choose who saves you. You don't get the hero; you get the monster. Nothing and no one is going to harm you on my watch. You are mine now, which means your problems are mine to solve."

The crazy thing was, he meant it. All I'd have to do is say the word, and *he* would swoop in and fix everything as if it were no more than a scrape on my knee.

I searched his face but couldn't read his expression beyond an earnest offer of help.

Once more I was struck by the same dizzying sense of being off-balance around him.

I had to remind myself that fixing my problems was just another element of control. Control I wasn't sure I wanted him to have - no matter how intoxicating the idea might be. He kept alluding to some kind of danger. I refused to take the bait. It was just a ploy, a game, a threat of something going bump in the night so I would run into his arms seeking protection.

Brushing off my fingers, I got up and returned to stand before the painting. "I need to get back to work."

Though he didn't say a word, I could feel his disappointment.

"Very well. One last surprise before I go."

Again, he went out into the hallway and returned with a McCafe cup in his hand.

"A mocha!"

The moment I reached for it, he held it high out of my reach.

"What do you say?" he asked playfully.

Giving him a coquettish look, I sing-songed, "Thank you." And gave him a spontaneous kiss on the cheek, which surprised the both of us.

He handed me my still warm mocha and then gave me a slap on the ass as I turned back to my painting.

Once again, I had survived a round of Russian roulette with Gregor. The problem was, according to the laws of probability theory… I was running out of chances.

CHAPTER 22

Gregor

SHE FEELS SOMETHING FOR ME. She may hate herself for it, but it's there.

I knew if I had reached for my belt and bent her over the closest chair, I probably could have gotten an admission out of her, but that was not how I wanted to play this. I was in it for the long haul with Samara, and in order for that to work, she had to start trusting me. I wanted her to come to the understanding on her own that I was the man who would keep her protected.

It would not happen overnight. Someone like Samara didn't trust easily. She was also far too independent to willingly hand the reins over to someone else.

I wasn't a patient man but I would be for a prize like Samara. I also didn't trust easily, but I knew from the moment I laid eyes on her that she was the woman for me.

And I had absolutely no intention of letting her go, even if she never learned to trust me fully.

I would just have to keep proving her wrong.

* * *

SHE REALLY LOOKED adorable when she painted. Faded jeans, a little V-neck t-shirt splattered with paint, her hair up in a messy bun, and the cute way she bit her lower lip when she was concentrating.

It was late. She had already worked through dinner and into much of the night. I knew from my surveillance of her that she liked to work late into the night but that was going to change. I had spent most of the day away from her, dealing with the escalating situation with her father and the Novikoffs, and now craved her touch.

"Time's up, malyshka. You can start on it again tomorrow."

"I just wanted to finish her necklace. Just a few more hours," she said without even looking up from her task.

"No."

That got her attention.

"Listen, just because I'm a prisoner in your house doesn't give you the right—"

I stormed over to her, careful to avoid paint splatters in my bare feet since I had changed out of my suit and was now also in a pair of loose-fitting jeans and an old long-sleeved t-shirt.

Without saying another word, I reached my hand around the back of her neck and pulled her in for a kiss. I took complete possession of her mouth, bending her body into mine. It was a reminder of who was really in charge.

After I had her breathless, I pulled away. "Yes, it does."

With that, I picked her up in my arms and carried her out

of the studio and down the hall to the master bathroom in my suite.

Setting her down, I turned to start the shower stream. Some of the best money I ever spent was on installing a large marble shower with multiple jets at varying heights. Adjusting the water so it was hot but not too hot for her delicate skin, I turned my attention back to my adorable little artist.

"Arms up," I commanded.

She kept her arms tightly wrapped around her middle. "You're crazy if you think I'm getting in that shower with you!"

Placing a hand at her lower back, I pulled her forward till our bodies met. Skimming my lips over hers, I taunted, "I've already told you I won't fuck you till you beg for it. What's the matter, malyshka? Worried you'll start screaming my name the moment you see my cock?"

"You wish," she spat out, rising to the challenge.

Staring down into her eyes, I lifted the t-shirt over her head. I loved her eyes.

Next, I pulled the red bandana out of her hair. Her soft brown curls tumbled down past her shoulders. It was the perfect length, just long enough to wrap my fist in it.

My knuckles skimmed her stomach as I reached for the buttons of her jeans. Her quick inhale at my touch was like music.

"Step out of them."

Kicking off her converse sneakers, she then stepped out of her jeans and panties. I reached around to unhook her silk and lace bra. Unable to resist, I leaned down to flick one dark pink nipple with my tongue. Placing my hands under her arms, I lifted her into the shower. As I undressed, I watched as the water caressed her body, making it slick and warm. By the time I stepped in to join her, my cock was already long and hard.

Her beautiful eyes skimmed over my chest and arms, careful not to slip lower. I knew she was taking in the chaotic burst of colorful tattoos which stretched across my collarbone, over my shoulders and down both arms. People could only see a hint of the amount of ink I possessed with the suits I wore.

She couldn't mask the warring emotions of desire and fear in her gaze.

"Gregor...." she started.

I placed a finger over her lips. "Stop overthinking. Just let me take care of you. You have my word; I'll only take this as far as you want."

I placed the soap between my hands and rubbed till I had a nice full lather. "Close your eyes."

The first thing I wanted to do was wash off her makeup. She looked beautiful with her liquid black eyeliner and red lipstick but I wanted to see her fresh-faced. Gently, I moved the tips of my fingers over her cheeks and eyes, memorizing the feel of each delicate feature. When I was done, I titled her head back into the jet stream to wash off the suds. Her eyes were bright with unmistakable need when she opened them again.

Taking up the soap, I lathered my hands again and started on the soft slope of her shoulders before moving down her arms, then over her flat stomach and the gentle swell of her hip. Her gaze stayed on mine as I moved my hand around to her lower back. My hand dipped over the curve of her ass. My middle finger slipped along the seam, applying subtle pressure. The tip circled the puckered ridge of her asshole. I watched as awareness flared in her eyes. Her pretty mouth opened on a gasp. I pushed in just to the first knuckle, a subtle reminder of what I still intended to do to her.

Her small hand reached up to grasp my cock, which was pressed against her stomach. My head fell back as I let out a throaty groan.

This is the first time she's touching me willingly.

The silky grasp of her hand moved up and down my heavy shaft. I clutched at her shoulders. It was then she shifted and moved to her knees.

Her sweet, innocent face looked up at me as she opened her mouth. The wide head of my cock disappeared between her lips.

"Fuck, malyshka," I groaned.

She released my cock and looked up at me with an impish smile. "No cursing."

She then licked the tip before sinking her mouth around my cock again. I pushed my hand through the wet strands of her hair, as I gripped the back of her head. As she moved forward, I pulled her even closer, challenging her to swallow me deeper for longer. Her hands gripped my thighs as I watched my thick shaft disappear down her tight throat.

With a growl, I pulled her up by her shoulders and pushed her against the now warm marble wall of the shower.

Placing my hands around her narrow waist, I lifted her high. "Put your legs around me," I growled, my voice harsh with need.

Shifting my hips, I pressed the head of my cock against her heat. Using every ounce of restraint I possessed, I forced myself to not enter her. The hot water beat against my back as I leaned into her soft curves. Reaching between our two bodies, I fisted my shaft. Using the head to tease her clit, I pumped my hand up and down the heavy length of my cock, imagining my tight grip was the clasp of her sweet cunt.

The need to enter her in one violent thrust clawed at my insides, but I ruthlessly forced it down.

I could feel her fingernails dig into my shoulders as her head rolled from side to side.

I ran my open mouth along the slim column of her throat, wanting to taste her pulse.

Her beautiful mouth moaned as the tip of my cock swiped over her clit again and again. Applying just enough pressure to tease, but not enough to get her off.

Rising on my toes, I pumped my hand harder until I felt my balls tighten. I threw my head back, relishing in the wave of pleasure that coursed through my veins the moment I released my seed onto her wet stomach. Knowing soon, I would do so deep inside her body.

Unwrapping her legs, I let her slowly touch the ground, but only for a moment. I immediately lifted her into my arms and carried her out of the shower. Not caring about our wet bodies, I walked into the bedroom and placed her in the middle of my bed.

Standing over her slight form, I could read every emotion on her adorable face.

"I know what you want, but you're going to have to ask me for it."

Samara buried her face in the pillows. "I can't," came her muffled response.

"Then I guess I will just get dressed," I teased.

Her lower lip popped out as she flashed me a glare.

I shook my head. "You'll have to ask me."

Stubbornly, she turned her head away.

"Another minute, and I'll make you beg for it instead of just asking," I warned her.

I watched as pride warred with desire in the golden green depths of her eyes.

Kneeling up, her legs slightly open so I could peek at the soft curls hiding her pussy, she whispered, "I want you to—"

She stopped. I knew she was warring with herself, with her body. "—make me come," she finished in a rush.

We both knew that wasn't what she really wanted.

"Only if you put your face down with your ass in the air," I commanded.

It surprised me when she did as she was told.

Kneeling behind her on the bed, I raised my hand, waiting for just a moment till a shiver of anticipation coursed down her spine. Then my hand came down on her right cheek with a resounding smack. Samara yelped and pitched forward, but quickly righted herself. I smacked the same cheek again and again before switching to the left one.

Over and over my skin connected with hers till her ass glowed a pretty pink.

Pausing to let the pain sensations heighten her awareness of her body and my touch, I traced the outline of her cute heart tattoo. My playful spanking had not given her skin quite the same pink blush, but it was close.

Leaning down, I placed my hands on her inner thighs and forced her legs open wider. Once I had her in position, I began to lick and lave at her exposed cunt. My hands ran over her hot skin, squeezing and massaging it to keep the delightful sting going. Samara squealed and whimpered. Right when I knew she was close, I placed a thumb at her tiny puckered entrance and pushed. Her body arched as her head flew back on a moan. Pushing my thumb in deep, I softly scraped the edge of my teeth against her clit.

Samara screamed her release before pitching forward.

Laying down by her side, I caressed her back in long, soothing caresses, now and then giving her bottom a playful swat.

Leaning down, I whispered into her ear, "Admit it, malyshka. That wasn't *all* you wanted."

CHAPTER 23

Samara

I MAY HAVE FOUND a way to escape.

After last night... I had no choice.

I needed to get the fuck away from Gregor Ivanov before he drew me in any deeper.

I couldn't believe I had willingly sucked his cock.

I had gone down on my knees like some wanton begging at his feet.

The man truly was Dracula incarnate. An evil seductive master able to manipulate and hypnotize me into doing the most out of character things.

On my knees.

Sucking his cock.

My cheeks burned with the memory.

I don't know what came over me. He was just there, looking sexy as hell with all those muscles and tattoos. And in that forceful way he was kissing me with his hands on my lower back. And then there was the way he was looking at me. That hard steel gaze just boring into my soul, making me feel like all he wanted on this earth was to devour me.

I didn't even grab my clothes. I just ran out of his room buck naked into my own room.

His knowing laugh haunted my dreams last night.

In our battle of wills, Gregor was winning and what was worse... he fucking knew it.

I needed to get out of here now before it was truly too late.

Rose told me he would be out of the house in meetings for much of the day before offering me a real tour of the house. There were two things I noticed. First, there were no physical guards patrolling the house and grounds. Second, he left the keys to the multiple cars housed in the connecting garage in an unlocked cabinet by the door.

Careful not to give my true intentions away, I quizzed Rose whether she was the only staff.

"Usually there are security guards and assistants clamoring about the place, but this wasn't a planned trip. Mr. Ivanov sort of popped in unannounced, so now Jim is scrambling to get the guards back from other assignments. Those two who helped with your things yesterday couldn't stay, unfortunately," she clamored on as she bustled from one room to the next.

Mistaking why I asked, she then assured me I was perfectly safe by helpfully pointing out where all the security cameras were located. The unmanned security cameras.

I still had some money in my purse and my Gwen IDs. If I borrowed one of Gregor's cars, I could be halfway to the Canadian border before he even knew I was gone. Hopefully, with any luck, Yelena was there waiting for me. I had checked my phone throughout the night and there was still no word from her.

When I returned to my room, there was a large box wrapped in a thick pink ribbon on the bed.

Quickly looking to the connecting door, I assured myself it was still closed.

Tiptoeing to the door, I pressed my ear against the surface and listened.

All was quiet.

Biting my lip, I crossed back to the bed.

On top of the box was a note. I immediately recognized Gregor's slanted handwriting.

Do me the honor of having dinner with me tonight, 7pm.

G -

I FLIPPED the heavy cardstock over, but there was nothing on the back. He wasn't exactly ordering me to dinner, but still…

I had half a mind to request a tray be sent to my room like last night.

After my mortifying experience with Gregor, I had been determined to once more go hungry.

Fortunately, an hour after our interlude, there was a discreet tap on my door.

When I'd opened it, there was a dinner tray resting on a small table to the side. Poking my head out, I'd looked both ways, but the hallway had been deserted. It was a simple meal of lemon chicken with rice and broccoli, but it tasted like heaven to me. I was starting to get used to eating off a plate and not out of a cardboard container.

Pulling on the pink ribbon, I loosened the bow and slipped open the lid. I pushed the cream tissue paper aside and gasped. Just like the last time, it was another fifties-inspired vintage gown. This one was an off-the-shoulder, A-line in a beautiful warm gold. There were matching shoes and underthings nestled in the box under the dress.

Well… a girl did have to eat.

CHAPTER 24

Samara

I WAS SLIPPING my feet into the kitten heels as I pulled the dress up over my waist when there was a knock on the connecting door. Without waiting for my response, it swung open.

Holding the dress up over my breasts, I spun around.

Oh. My. God.

I forgot my anger at him arrogantly just barging into my pretty prison cell the moment I saw him.

He was dressed in an expertly tailored tuxedo that highlighted his broad shoulders. His jet-black hair was slightly damp, which made it curl at the ends more than usual. His dark grey eyes practically glowed silver in the soft lighting of the bedroom. He looked like a gorgeously dangerous Bond villain.

Without saying a word, he motioned with his finger for me to turn around.

Like a transfixed doll, I obeyed.

I sucked in a breath when his warm fingers caressed my back. A tremor ran over my body, as he slowly zipped up the back of the dress. Leaning down, he placed a kiss on my bare shoulder, before whispering in my ear, "Ty vyglyadish' prekrasno."

My cheeks flushed the moment he called me beautiful.

I tried to turn back but his warm hands stopped me. Something cold and heavy touched my collar bone before sliding upward to clamp around my throat. My fingertips skimmed across metal and stone.

Spinning around, I pushed my hair away and reached for the clasp. I didn't want to even see the necklace. I knew what it stood for, and I wanted no part of it.

Gregor snatched my wrists and shifted them down, imprisoning them in one large hand as he pressed against my lower back.

Placing his finger under my chin, he tilted my head back. "I mean it, and I'm a bastard for not saying it sooner. You are without a doubt the most beautiful woman I've ever laid eyes on, Samara."

My heart lurched before reality crashed in, shattering the fantasy.

I narrowed my gaze.

Gregor chuckled. "Those eyes of yours give you away every time, malyshka. I can see you don't trust what I'm saying. I'll just have to prove it to you."

"I won't be around long enough for that. I don't want jewelry from you. I don't want *anything* from you."

I jerked my arms, but he held fast. It was dangerous being this close to him. Feeling the heat from his body, the brush of hard muscle, the familiar scent of his cologne… It was too easy to focus on the man and not who he really was—an Ivanov, a threat to my freedom.

He inhaled deeply before responding. "Careful, malyshka. I'm not a patient or forgiving man. I'm allowing you liberties to give you time to adjust to your fate, but you'd be foolish to test me too far."

I swallowed. The heavy press of the necklace felt like a tightening leash around my throat.

He ran the back of his hand down my cheek. I shivered in response. Whether it was from fear or in response to his touch, I couldn't say. Both reactions seemed always to be intertwined, locked in some twisted, macabre dance.

"Now, be a good girl and thank me properly for your gift."

What did he mean by *properly*?

I clenched my thighs together, hating my body's reaction to the prospect of him just tossing me on the bed and climbing on top of me. Hating what a fucking turn on it was to imagine his heavily tattooed and muscled arms holding me down while he forced my legs open. It was wrong on every conceivable level.

This man was my enemy.

A savage bent on destroying my life.

So why did I crave his touch?

The tension in the room was so thick I could barely breathe. My eyes flickered over to the bed again, which loomed only a few feet away. The corner of his mouth lifted. Damn him. He knew the direction of my thoughts as if I had blurted them out loud.

My tongue flicked out to wet my dry lips. His hard gaze zeroed in on my mouth.

Would he kiss me? I clenched my abdomen muscles, bracing myself. My mind was too chaotic to even discern if I wanted him to or not—knowing where it would lead, if he did.

Paralyzed, I stayed trapped within his embrace, my rapid heartbeat pounding in my ears.

Casting my gaze downward, I choked out, "Thank you for my gift, Gregor."

"You're welcome, Samara. Shall we?" He gave me a wink before offering his arm.

After a moment's hesitation, I slipped my shaking hand around his sleeve to clasp him just below the elbow.

I forced myself to concentrate on breathing and putting one foot in front of the other rather than on the dangerous man at my side. As we walked down the hallway, I glimpsed us in a gilt-framed mirror. A string of large emerald cut diamonds set in platinum circled my neck. Jewelry was one of the few things my mother ever taught me. There wasn't a doubt in my mind I was currently wearing over a million dollars in diamonds.

Unfortunately, I knew it wasn't a gift. It wasn't even really a necklace… it was a collar.

As we reached the entryway, I expected him to open the front door. Instead, he turned right to lead me into the dining room.

At my confused look, he shrugged then answered, "Safer. Besides, this way I get you all to myself."

Safer?

He was still worried I'd bolt at any moment.

He should be… because I would.

As he led me around the large, polished mahogany table to my seat, I noticed a small envelope propped up against my empty wine glass. I barely noticed when he pulled out my chair and then tucked it behind my knees. The moment I was seated, I snatched the card up. I recognized Yelena's handwriting on the front. Tearing into it, I read then re-read the contents.

S‍amara,

Time to stop running.
Going to Canada will have to wait.
I'm with Damien right now.
I'll see you very soon.
Tell Gregor I hope he's well.
- Yelena

CLOSING THE NOTE, I glanced at Gregor who was watching me closely. He lifted the bottle of red wine at his elbow and poured me a glass.

"I figured you wouldn't trust a text but you would trust a handwritten note."

He was right. I wouldn't have trusted a text.

Folding the note in half, I took a sip of wine to wet my dry mouth. "I'm assuming you've already read it."

He didn't even look ashamed of the fact. Picking up his glass, he nodded before taking a swallow.

We watched each other closely. Two opponents squaring off.

Still, I couldn't tell if he realized her note was complete bullshit or not. Yelena, Nadia, and I had a code. We had used it since we were in grade school to protect the notes we passed in class. If the first line started with a consonant, then it meant the opposite. What she was really telling me was that our escape plan was still in play. She was heading to Montreal, and soon.

I should have been elated.

Yelena was safe.

I had a plan of escape.

And yet....

I peeked at Gregor from under my eyelashes. The man both infuriated and terrified me but there was something else there. He was just so big and strong and handsome.

When he took me in his arms, the whole world just disappeared. It was hard not to be drawn into his dark energy, to submit to his will. It was everything I had been afraid of three years ago before I ran. This feeling of losing all sense of identity and self when around him. Now that it was happening, I was too caught up in his seductive web to care.

I was beginning to crave his attention, his touch. It was like a drug. When he turned that dark gaze on me and pulled me into his arms, I forgot to breathe. There was no denying the electric charge between the two of us. It was like nothing I had ever experienced before in my life—this compelling connection to him. As if despite all the bad blood and anger, he was destined to claim me. Despite everything, I was destined to be his bride.

I gave myself a mental shake. *Stop it.* That was just what he wanted me to think and believe. *Don't buy into his charm.* He was still the same monster who'd been haunting my dreams and lurking in every shadow these last three years.

You are just a means to an end for him.

Collateral on a loan.

A family name.

Nothing more.

Rose entered and placed two plates in front of us before silently leaving.

The meal looked delicious: Oscar Filet Mignon. The lump crabmeat on top of the filet was covered in a buttery béarnaise sauce with some poured over the steamed asparagus as well. Picking up my fork and knife, I cut a small piece off the filet. I placed it between my lips, but then had to reach for my wine glass to wash it down. It tasted like sawdust in my mouth. Extreme nerves would do that to a person.

"So, you have a big decision on your hands," said Gregor, breaking the silence.

I started.

Had the man read my mind?

I wouldn't put it past him.

It was infuriating how he seemed to know what I was thinking before I knew my own mind. He had proven he definitely knew what my body wanted despite my repeated attempts at denial.

My hands shook so badly I had to bury them in my lap. Refusing to meet his gaze, I licked my lips and concentrated on the plate before me. "What do you mean?"

I crushed my arms against my side to try to stop my body from quaking.

"Georgetown would be a solid choice and is in the top fifty in the nation, but I have to be honest, based on my research and your unique style, I think George Washington's program would suit you better."

I blinked. My mind couldn't quite process what he was saying. "I... I... don't understand."

Gregor finished chewing his bite of steak before responding. "Art programs. Once we return to D.C., I assume you will want to enroll for the Spring semester."

He reached for a dinner roll. I watched him tear the delicate bread in half with his enormous hands. A small puff of steam wafted up as the dining room filled with a comforting warm yeasty scent.

I picked up my knife, closing my fist around the handle.

Gregor paused as he raised a piece of bread to his mouth. His gaze shifted from my hand to my face.

"You don't think I'm dumb enough to think you'd let me pursue a degree in art *if* I agreed to marry you?"

Gregor picked up his own knife. He raised an eyebrow in challenge. "I think the word you're looking for is *when* not *if*. And you're correct—I don't want you to pursue an art degree."

I smirked. I knew it.

He smirked back. "I'd expect you to pursue *both* an art and business degree so you are better prepared to run your own gallery one day."

My mouth dropped.

Recovering myself, I raised my chin in defiance. "You're lying."

Gregor leaned in close. "Try me, malyshka. I don't lie. That's for cowards and the powerless of which I'm neither. How about you and I come to an agreement? Before you say *I do*, I'll not only support whatever college you choose in the D.C. area, I'll pay all four years of tuition in advance."

I released my grip on the knife. "Why? Why would you do that?"

His gaze moved from my breasts to my lips to my eyes. "Because it's something *my wife* wants, and I plan on giving her *everything* she wants."

I swallowed. His double meaning was clear. I clenched my thighs under the table.

Jesus, just a look from this man could get me wet.

I shook my head. "No. It would be far too expensive. I couldn't possibly accept, especially not after you loaned my father money."

His gaze hardened, and he clenched his jaw. It seemed my father and him were not on good terms. While I wasn't surprised, my father often rubbed people the wrong way, it was probably because he hadn't paid all the money back yet. Since it was in Gregor's possession anyway, maybe the money I had in my offshore account would cover the rest?

Yelena's trick at the racetrack was scary effective, but we were careful not to abuse it and to spread our bets between live racetracks and online betting to reduce our chances of getting caught. Even so, I had about fifty thousand dollars saved.

The silence stretched.

"Speaking of your loan to my father, how much was it for?" I kept my eyes trained on my plate as I forced myself to take another bite.

Gregor put down his utensils and wiped the corner of his mouth with a linen napkin. Rising from the table, he crossed to a long sideboard where there was a silver tray with crystal decanters. Picking up a double old-fashioned glass, he poured himself two fingers of vodka and turned to face me.

"Is this really how you want to spend our first dinner together?"

"I was, after all, put up as collateral. I think it's a reasonable thing to ask."

I refused to acknowledge that Gregor still thought he was going to take possession of that collateral. One battle at a time.

Gregor returned to his seat. He took a swallow of vodka, then responded. "Fifteen million."

My fork made a terrible clatter against the gold-rimmed porcelain plate when I dropped it.

"Fifteen million?" I repeated, incredulous. *Fifteen million.*

Gregor leaned back in his chair and nodded.

"And... and how much has he paid back so far?"

My stomach twisted. Although I wanted to deny it, I was afraid I already knew the answer.

Gregor inhaled, clearly reluctant to speak about this. "Samara...."

"How much?"

"None of it."

"None of it?"

He shook his head.

I swallowed, trying to force all the poisonous revelations down my throat. "You keep saying I'm in danger. Is my father why?"

He slowly nodded, his hard gaze watching me, missing nothing.

"Are you going to tell me what kind of danger?"

"No."

"Why not? I have a right to know!"

"You have a right to know that I am handling it and nothing more."

"Maybe there isn't any real danger? Maybe you're lying and the danger is just you?"

His lips lifted at the corner. "I never said I wasn't also a danger to you."

The room spun.

I tried to focus on the plate before me.

Chromium Oxide - the color of the asparagus.

Nickel Yellow - the color of the béarnaise sauce.

Quinacridone Magenta - the color of the wine.

Gregor shook his head as he watched me intently with those mercurial eyes of his.

I reached for my wineglass and drained it.

Gregor picked up the bottle and poured me a second glass, but only halfway.

Dear God.

I had assumed my father had done the honorable thing and returned the money after I fled. No wonder this man pursued me with such a vengeance over the last three years. It was retribution, pure and simple. My father cheated him, and he was making me pay for it one way or another.

Even with Yelena's racetrack scam, I could never hope to pay him back and buy my freedom from him.

Clawing at the diamond necklace at my throat, I tried to force air into my lungs as I stumbled out of my chair.

Gregor rose and raised his arm toward me. "Samara…."

I shook my head violently as I backed away from him. "No wonder you hate me! My father fucked you over."

His brows creased. "I never said I hated you, Samara, and watch your language."

"Fuck my language! You do hate me! Of course, you do! You must!"

I rounded the long dining room table putting distance between me and Gregor.

He followed.

"This isn't about your father or our families or about the damn money. I don't give a shit about the money. This is about us," he yelled as he quickened his pace.

Panicking, I pulled out one of the chairs and thrust it in his way. "There is no us! There is nothing between us. We are only bound by blood money."

Gregor reached down and flipped the chair on its side, sending it skidding across the hardwood floor.

I screamed and turned to run.

His hand wrapped around my upper arm. I was propelled backwards till I slammed against the wall. Gregor quickly followed, placing his forearms on either side of my head, caging me in.

"I don't ever want to hear you say that again. Do you understand me, malyshka?"

I was breathing heavily. My breasts brushed against his chest with each inhalation. I could feel my nipples tighten against the silk fabric of my strapless bra.

Still, I dared to challenge him. Why not? The damned have nothing to lose.

"Say what? The truth?" I viciously spit out. "You're just the monster who's been chasing me. Nothing more."

Reaching down, he raised the hem of my dress. His hand became a fiery brand on my thigh.

"No! Stop!"

He ignored my protest. Wedging his knee between my thighs, he forced my legs open. His fingers sought out my core, caressing me through the thin fabric of my panties. He leaned down to nuzzle my neck just below my ear.

I bit my lip to stifle a groan.

He shifted his hips so I could feel the hard press of his cock against my inner thigh. "You're lying to yourself and to me. Does that feel like *nothing* to you?"

I rolled my head from side to side. "*Lust* fueled by hatred and revenge. Every kiss taken by force."

He raised his arm and slammed his fist against the wall, making me cry out. He then clasped his hands over my jaw to cradle my face. His gaze bore into my own before it traveled to my mouth. It looked as if he were going to say something but instead, he turned away with an animalistic growl.

I stayed plastered against the wall, afraid to move.

Gregor turned back to me, his eyes dark and cold as steel. "So be it, Samara. I'll show you just what a monster I can be."

A terrified scream tore through my body as he tossed me over his shoulder and carried me up the dark staircase to his bedroom.

CHAPTER 25

*G*regor

I WAS DONE PLAYING the gentleman.

I should have known better than to go against my nature. I was after all my father's son.

Carrying her writhing form over my shoulder, I violently kicked the bedroom door open.

"Let me go!" Samara screamed.

Storming over to the bed, I flipped her onto it. Her body bounced twice before she scrambled onto her knees.

She pushed the tangled curls off her face, her cheeks flushed with indignation and fear as she raged, "How dare you?"

I chuckled as I slipped out of my dinner jacket. "Baby, I'm about to dare a whole fucking lot more."

Wrenching one of her high heels off her foot, she threw the shoe at me. I easily ducked, as I twisted the platinum and black diamond cuff link off my left cuff and tossed it onto the bureau top.

"You can go to hell!" She threw the other shoe at me but it fell short, tumbling off the side of the bed.

Twisting off the second cuff, I kicked off my shoes. "Only if I can take you with me."

Shifting backwards, she climbed off my massive bed and stilled her emerald gaze, surveying the distance between the bed and door.

Loosening the knot to my tie, I pulled it from my collar. "You'll never make it," I growled.

I watched as her body tensed seconds before springing into motion. She launched herself toward the connecting door. Lunging, I caught her around her slim middle. Her nails scratched at my forearm through the thin linen of my shirt.

"Stop!" she shrieked.

Placing her back on her feet, I twisted my fingers into her hair and ruthlessly pulled, snapping her head back.

"Never," I savagely vowed before claiming her unwilling mouth.

My head twisted to the side the moment her sharp teeth sunk into my bottom lip. I ran the tip of my tongue over the wound; the tang of blood only spurred me on.

Placing my large hand under her jaw, I squeezed till she let out a small whimper. "Bite me again, and I will whip you with my belt till you bleed."

"Please, Gregor. Just let me go," she begged.

In answer, I dragged her by her hair over to the bed, only releasing my grasp when I had her caged in between the bed and the wall.

"Snimay odezhdu," I ordered.

Her eyes, already wide with fear, teared up as I ordered

her to take off her clothes. Her body trembled but didn't move to obey.

"A teper', prezhde chem ya sdernu s tebya odezhdu." My voice was more vicious bark than anything else.

At my threat to tear them off her body, she finally obeyed.

Her arms reached back, but I could see she was shaking too badly to work the zipper. Grabbing her by the shoulders, I spun her around and lowered the zipper. Remembering how this evening started, had I really thought it would end any other way?

Not giving her a chance to, I pulled the garment down till it pooled at her feet. Reaching for the corset style strapless bra, I snapped the small metal hooks and tore it off her body, then caressing my knuckles up the center of her back.

Her shoulders rose as her back arched. Samara swung around, her arms covering her breasts, andher eyes narrowed. "You promised you wouldn't take my virginity by force."

"Trust me, malyshka, I won't have to use force."

Her arm lashed out to strike me. Wrapping my fingers around her tiny wrist before she could make contact, I pulled till her body slammed against my own. Leaning down, I inhaled the citrus and jasmine perfume scent of her warm skin just below her ear. "Fight me all you want, Samara. This is happening."

Dragging her back onto the bed, I straddled her squirming form as I raised her arms high over her head and knotted my silk tie around her wrists, then secured them to the newel post in the center of the headboard.

Climbing off the bed, I slowly unbuttoned my shirt as I surveyed her beautiful body, now on display. The swell of her hips, the gentle curve of her breasts, the creamy ivory of her skin, my diamonds glinting around her throat… everything was perfection.

"I hate you," she seethed, even as her gaze stayed riveted on the opening of my shirt and the tattoos it exposed.

"No. You don't. And we both know it." I slipped the shirt off my shoulders and tossed it over a nearby chair.

Keeping my gaze steady on hers, I reached down to unbuckle my belt. As I pulled the long black leather strap through the belt loops, her thighs clenched together. Folding the belt in half, I yanked till the flat ends slapped together, renting the silence with a harsh snap.

Samara's hips shot off the bed as she groaned.

There was nothing—absolutely nothing—good I had done in my whole wretched life to deserve such an amazingly sensual woman, but I didn't give a damn. The fact that no other man but myself had ever touched her sent a shot of primal white-hot need straight to my already throbbing cock.

She was my possession... untouched and pure.

The only innocent thing in my twisted fucked up life.

She was mine and no one—not her father, not the Novikoffs, *no one*—was taking her from me.

Wrapping the leather belt around my fist, I left the final length dangling. Reaching over her form, I trailed the soft leather over one erect nipple. She inhaled sharply. I caressed her flat belly with the end of the belt. As I neared her sweet pussy, her hips twisted to the side, denying me. Raising my arm, I unraveled more of the belt from around my fist and slapped it against her ass.

Samara cried out.

As a large, dark pink mark appeared on her pale skin, I commanded, "Open your legs."

She whimpered. "Please, Gregor. Don't do this."

"Open. Your. Legs."

Her knees shifted open, but only slightly.

"Wider. I want to see what I paid for all those years ago."

"Fuck you," she seethed through clenched teeth.

"Well chosen turn of phrase, baby girl."

Flattening my hand against her knee, I forced her legs open wide before whipping the end of my belt against her inner thigh. She screamed and strained against the binds around her wrists. Fighting my restraining hand, she tried to twist her hips and close her legs but to no avail. I slashed the leather against her other thigh.

"Consider that your only warning. Close your legs again without permission, and the punishment will be much harsher."

Tears streamed down her flushed cheeks. "I'll never forgive you for this."

Her words were a knife to my gut, but they wouldn't change anything. It was past time I claimed her for my own. It was selfish and cruel, but there were reasons beyond my own needs. This was the only way I could keep her safe. Every moment she remained an unmarried virgin, she was in danger.

"It's not your forgiveness I want."

I crawled onto the bed between her now open knees. Grinding my hips against her core, I balanced the rest of my weight on my right forearm near her head.

A shaft of moonlight from the window crossed over the bed and highlighted her beautiful emerald eyes. One day, maybe those eyes would look on me with love, but not tonight. For now, I would settle for lust.

Lifting my left arm, I ran the tips of my two middle fingers along the cold diamonds which now encircled her neck, stopping at the base of her throat. I gently caressed her skin and could feel the flutter of her rapid pulse. Leaning down, I ran my lips along her jaw, relishing in her sharp inhale and how her body tensed. She was fighting her response to me.

Flicking my tongue against her earlobe, I whispered, "Give in to me, malyshka."

Tears wet her eyelashes, turning them a deep sooty black. A single tear escaped and slid down the high crest of her cheekbone. I pressed my lips along the salty trail, knowing this wasn't the first or last time I would make her cry.

Her lips trembled. "I can't."

Cupping the gentle weight of her breast in my palm, I opened my mouth and breathed warm air over her pebbled nipple. "Soznatel'nym vkusom togo, ot chego otkazyvayesh'sya. YA proshchayu grabezh tvoy, vor nezhnyy, Khotya ty ukral vsyu moyu bednost'," I murmured in a low, dark tone, punctuating each phrase with a sweep of my tongue over the cherry nub.

Her hips ground against my own. The press of her pelvic bone against my painfully hard cock almost made me lose my resolve. With a growl, I skimmed my teeth over her nipple before switching to the right one as I continued with the honeyed words I'd hope were soothing her fears. "I vse zhe, lyubov' znayet, eto bol'shaya pechal'. Snosit' lyubov' - zlo, chem izvestnuyu ranu nenavisti. Pokhotlivaya blagodat', v kotoroy vse plokho proyavlyayetsya, Ubey menya zlost'yu; no my ne dolzhny byt' vragami."

Samara moaned as her head tossed from side to side.

Skimming my hand over her flat belly, I pressed my warm palm against her sex. Since I knew her Russian was not as good as my own, I repeated Shakespeare's Sonnet Number Forty in English as I teased her entrance with the tip of my finger. "By willful taste of what thyself refusest. I do forgive thy robbery, gentle thief, Although thou steal thee all my poverty."

I never understood poetry until this moment. There was something about having the most extraordinary creature in your arms that made everyday language seem impotent and wholly inadequate. Unique women, like Samara, were the reason why men stared at stars, scratched words on paper, and wondered at the mysteries of the universe.

I pushed my first finger into the base, feeling the tight wet clasp of her body. Her body was ready and willing if her mind was not. Slipping out, I pulled her nipple deep into my mouth at the same moment I thrust two fingers inside her untried cunt.

Samara groaned as she pulled on the binds around her wrists.

She was almost there.

Shifting, I moved over her body till my shoulders were nestled between her thighs. The sweet musk of her body nearly drove me over the edge. Thank God I still had my suit pants on as a feeble barrier. If my naked cock were pressed against her right now, there would be no stopping me. Looking down at the colorful tattoo of Betty Boop low on her hip, I couldn't resist giving it a quick sweep of my tongue.

Training my gaze up her body, I took in every creamy inch of her ivory skin, which shimmered from a faint sheen of sweat.

"Look at me, Samara," I growled.

She tilted her head back, pressing deeper into the pillows, avoiding my gaze.

Sliding my arm over her hip, I captured her nipple between my thumb and forefinger and squeezed.

"Ow! Stop! It hurts!" She tried to twist away from the pain, but my shoulders between her legs prevented it.

"Obey me, and I'll stop."

Her wide gaze trained on me as her chest rose and fell with her rapid, frightened breath.

"Good girl."

Holding her gaze, I opened my mouth and extended my

tongue. I could feel her body tense as she held her breath, mesmerized by the lascivious gesture, knowing my intent. Giving her no quarter, I swept the tip over her engorged clit.

"Oh God," she moaned.

"And yet, love knows, it is a greater grief," I whispered as I continued to recite the sonnet, letting my warm breath caress her before once more flicking the tight bundle of nerves. "To bear love's wrong than hate's known injury. Lascivious grace, in whom all ill well shows." I wrapped my lips over my teeth and gently bit down till she cried out from pleasurable pain. *"Kill me with spites; yet we must not be foes."*

As I swirled my tongue around her clit, I pushed a third finger into her narrow passage. Pumping them in and out as I twisted my wrist, I prepared her for the girth of my cock.

"Come for me, baby."

Her body bucked and thrashed as much as her binds and my body would allow.

Increasing the pressure of my tongue, I forced my fingers in deep just as I swept her dark puckered hole with the pad of my thumb. Samara screamed her release. I lapped at her sweet cream as I relished in the glorious sound of her surrender. I had won the battle, but not the war. Victory would come after her complete surrender.

"Say it. Say it for me, malyshka," I commanded as I settled my weight on top of her.

Her eyes squeezed shut, she jerked on her wrists.

Leaning up, I pulled on the end of my silk tie, releasing her wrists.

I hated to admit it, but I held my breath, waiting and watching to see what she would do.

Curled into claws, her fingers drove into my hair, fisting the short wavy length as her legs wrapped around my hips. Air left my body in a rush as I reached between us to lower the zipper of my trousers and lower them past my hips. My heavily engorged cock sprang free. I fisted the length and ran my hand up and down the length a few times to ease the building tension, knowing if let off the leash, I would fuck her like an animal without a hint of mercy.

Leaning my hips up, I rubbed the head of my cock against her now sensitive clit. "Say it," I growled, my restraint slipping.

She opened her eyes and stared at me. Even in the dim moonlight, I could see the glint of the flecks of gold nestled within her emerald depths. "Take me, Gregor."

"Louder," I commanded as I released my cock and reached over our bodies to snatch a small black velvet case from the nightstand. I flipped open the lid with one hand and pulled out a platinum, diamond and emerald engagement ring. I had been carrying this ring around with me for three years. Tonight, I would finally put it on her finger where it belonged. While diamond engagement rings were not the tradition in my culture, they were a sign of ownership in America, and I needed every man who ever laid eyes on her to know… she was taken. Although my concession to our new country would only go so far; she would wear it on her right hand not left.

"Take me," she cried out as I wrapped my strong fingers around her right wrist.

"Who do you belong to, malyshka?"

Her gaze dropped.

With my free hand, I grasped her jaw and forced her gaze back to mine. "Say it. Who do you belong to?"

"You, Gregor. It's always been you."

I slid the ring onto her finger. Spanning her hips with both my hands, I positioned my cock at her tight entrance and viciously thrust into the hilt, feeling the feeble resistance of her maidenhead stretch and surrender as I claimed her.

Samara screamed. Curling her small hands into fists, she

pounded ineffectively on my chest. I was undeterred. Ruthlessly thrusting in deep, I could feel the slick coating of her arousal mixed with blood, easing my cock with each stroke.

"Stop! It hurts!" she begged.

"It's too late, baby," I rasped against her cheek as my hips drove into her body.

My entire body strained not to hurt her with the ferocity of my need. In the three years I'd search for her, I'd barely looked at it let alone touched another woman. There was no satisfaction to be found in any else's arms. She had become my all-consuming obsession, my dark religion. Finally sinking into her tight passage was like finding God.

Her hands pushed at my shoulders. My back bowed as I groaned the moment her impossibly still tight cunt spasmed around my shaft. Swinging her right arm wide, Samara slapped me across the face.

Sliding my fingertips over my cheek, I could feel the sting of blood. The ring had turned on her finger, facing the palm so the sharp edge of the multiple diamond settings had torn at my skin.

I smiled. "Blood for blood."

Snatching both her wrists, I stretched them high over her head. Subduing her with the oppressive weight of my body, I pounded into her soft flesh. Our bodies rocked back and forth on the silk coverlet as the bed frame squeaked and groaned.

"Oh God! Oh God! Gregor!"

She continued to scream my name over and over.

Her inner muscles rippled over my shaft. I knew the rhythm of my thrusts were bringing her to another orgasm. I held back till her body tensed. The moment her back bowed and her lips opened on a long keening moan, I slipped the reins.

"Fuck!" she cried out as her legs wrapped tightly around my hips.

I thrust several more times before I released my seed deep within her body. If there was a God, it would take root and bind this amazing creature to me forever.

With a growled curse of my own, I collapsed to the side of her, pulling her body against my side. My hand reached down to cup her behind the knee to stretch her leg over my hips, needing to feel the wet heat of her cunt pressed against my skin. Still breathing heavy, I kissed her forehead.

"You're mine now, Samara. There's no turning back."

A tremor swept over her body. Whether it was a chill or fear, I didn't question.

Pulling on a corner of the coverlet, I swept it high to cover our naked forms.

With my arm wrapped tight around her shoulder, I picked up her right hand, which had been resting on my chest. I lifted it high till the ring on her finger caught the moonlight. The diamond glimmered as it caught the meager light, and a primal wave of possessiveness sunk its sharp claws into my soul.

"Mine."

CHAPTER 26

Samara

My head rested against his chest. I could feel the vibrations of his steady heartbeat but couldn't hear it. There was nothing but an ungodly rushing sound in my ears, as if I were underwater. My body was both numb and sore at the same time.

Afraid to stir, I stayed unnaturally still, waiting, for what I didn't know.

Finally, Gregor moved. Sliding out from beneath my bent leg, he kicked off his wrinkled suit trousers and padded naked across the room to his walk-in closet attached to the bathroom. Like his chest and arms, his back was covered in colorful tattoos, one blending into the next. A twisted kaleidoscope of religious symbols and macabre images. Beneath all the color was nothing but hard muscle. Closing my eyes, I tried to block out the overwhelming memory of his heavy body pressing mine into the bed.

He returned wearing a worn pair of grey sweatpants low on his hips. Crossing to the bed, he pushed a lock of hair away from my cheek. In his hand was a wet washcloth.

"Lean back."

My cheeks heated. Reaching for the washcloth, I protested, "I can do it."

He shifted his arm away from my grasp and raised an eyebrow.

Resigned, I fell back onto the pillows. A cool rush of air kissed my heated skin as he pulled the gold satin coverlet away. My arms crossed over my breasts and my knees bent up.

His large hand slid down my thigh, then applied pressure till I opened my legs. Turning my head to the side, I bit my lip and squeezed my eyes tight as waves of mortification rolled over me. Using the soft washcloth, he caressed me between my legs and over my inner thighs. Wiping away all traces of blood and our mutual arousal. Returning to the bathroom, he discarded the washcloth and crossed once more to the bed.

Running his knuckles over my cheek, he said, "I'll be right back. Don't move."

I swallowed but said nothing.

Waiting till I heard his retreating steps down the hall, I lifted my arm and stared at the ring on my right hand. It was massive. The center princess cut diamond had to be at least ten carats. Two five carat, step-cut emeralds flanked it on either side of its platinum setting. The ring befitted the wife of a powerfully rich man.

The future Mrs. Gregor Ivanova.

Oh God. What had I done?

Panicking, I tried to pull the ring off my finger. It wouldn't budge. The diamond setting scratched my fingers on either side as I twisted and pulled in vain. My pale skin turned bright red and bruised, but the ring would not slide off.

I had to stop when I heard Gregor's step outside the bedroom.

In one hand he carried two glasses half-filled with a clear liquid and a bottle tucked under his arm. In the other was a small, gold-rimmed plate stacked high with delicate pink swirls—Zefir pastries, my favorite Russian pastry.

He extended his arm, and I took one of the glasses.

"Thought you could use a drink," he said with a twist of his lips.

Without pausing, I tossed back the vodka. The harsh liquor burned a path down my throat to settle uncomfortably in my empty stomach. My eyes watered as I tightened my lips and swallowed my coughs, not wanting to give him the satisfaction.

"Careful, little one, you haven't eaten nearly enough to swill vodka like that."

Defiantly, I snatched the second glass from his grasp and downed it before he could object.

Picking up one of the meringue cookies, he ordered, "Eat."

Taking it from his hand, I gratefully bit into the chewy cookie, hoping the sweetness would dull the gasoline fumes from the vodka. As I chewed, my eyes wandered over his hips, to the outline of his still semi-erect cock as it pressed against the cotton of his sweatpants.

Jesus. I couldn't believe that *thing* fit inside of me.

"And it will fit again and again and again."

My jaw fell as I raised my alarmed gaze, knowing he had read my illicit thoughts.

The bastard winked.

Tearing at the coverlet, I tossed it around my shoulders and slid off the bed. "I… I… have to use the bathroom."

Gregor nodded towards his closet. "Through the closet to the left."

"No!"

He raised an eyebrow.

"Uh… no… I'd rather use my own," I stammered as I tripped over the trailing blanket and backed away from him.

"You have two minutes."

I nodded and turned, practically lunging for the doorknob of the connecting door. As I swung it open, Gregor repeated, "Two minutes, Samara. Don't make me come and get you."

Without turning, I nodded and crossed the threshold into my darkened bedroom.

Dragging the heavy coverlet, I walked past the bureau and searched the darkness for the white, molding outline of the bathroom doorway. Reaching out my hand, I swiped the light switch up.

Without warning, a large hand wrapped around my throat and yanked me backward.

My frightened scream was cut off when a second hand slapped across my mouth.

"Shut the fuck up, bitch."

I recoiled as my vodka-filled stomach clenched at the stench from the man's fetid breath.

Gregor stormed into the room.

Breathing heavily through his nose, his fists clenched as his sides, he looked like the devil incarnate. I had only thought I had seen him angry in the past. It was nothing like now. He looked ready to tear the limbs off my captor.

Clawing at the hand around my throat, I tried to kick out, but the blanket tangled around my ankles. A sharp sting against my throat stilled all my struggles.

Gregor's face paled as his gaze focused on my neck.

A trickle of blood itched as it dripped from the fresh wound.

Gregor's hard gaze returned to my captor's. "I was going to kill you but spare your family. Now everyone you love will die."

I could feel the man's head turn as he spit on the carpet. "Fuck you, Ivanov."

The devil you know. The devil you know. The devil you know.

My frenetic mind just kept repeating the phrase. Gregor was the devil I knew, and now I desperately wanted to stay with him. Lifting my gaze, I silently pleaded with him.

Don't let him take me.

Once again, like a mesmerist, Gregor read my mind. "No one is taking you from me, malyshka."

There was the sound of splintering wood and broken glass from somewhere downstairs. Oh God, there must be more of them. My captor laughed, his rank hot breath making me want to vomit.

"There's four of us and only one of you, Ivanov. We're taking the bitch."

Gregor took a step toward us.

The knife at my throat shifted. I hissed as another sharp sting of pain sent a shock up my spine.

The man cackled. "There's nothing you can—"

"Am I interrupting?"

The dirty hand over my mouth muffled my scream as my captor swung wide.

In the doorway stood the man I met at the museum gala. Dimitri, that was his name. He was leaning against the doorjamb eating one of the pink Zefir cookies. Completely oblivious to the blood splattered across his white button-down shirt and tie. "Correction. There *were* four of you. Now there's just you."

Gregor grabbed him by the hair and ripped his head back.

The man abruptly released me. I fell to the floor, scrambling to cover my nakedness with the discarded blanket at my feet. As I turned, I watched Gregor cock his bent arm back before punching the man in the throat.

My captor's eyes bulged, and he grasped his neck. As he stumbled backward, Dimitri raised his leg and kicked him back into the center of the room. Gregor twisted his hand in the front of the man's shirt and held him steady as he punched him again. This time in the mouth. Dark crimson blood spewed from the man's mouth as he tried to scream for help.

No one came.

Gregor struck him again and again.

There was a sickening crack as the man's jaw shifted to an obscene angle before falling slack.

The man's face was beaten to a bloody pulp as he laid curled on his side on the floor. His body twitched before blood-stained air bubbles foamed at the corner of his mouth. There was a strange gurgling sound, then the lifeless body pitched forward.

Gregor stood over him, breathing heavily as his arms stayed raised, fists clenched.

Dimitri broke the tense silence. "Vaska is loading the other three in the van. We'll take them to the usual place."

Gregor nodded. "I'll meet you there."

Dimitri's gaze slid to my prone form as I huddled on the floor against the bed frame.

"Take your time. We'll wait to start."

He turned and left, leaving me alone with Gregor.

Gregor bent down on his haunches in front of me. He reached out his arm. I cried out and scuttled backwards on my ass till my back hit the wall. My horrified gaze shifted from his furrowed brow to his blood-stained hands.

In fact, he was covered in blood. Streaks of it crisscrossed his chest, and there was even a bloody handprint on his sweatpants from when my captor desperately reached out to try and stop the beating.

"Don't do that again," he warned.

This time when he reached for me, I stayed frozen in place. With a gentleness which belied the savagery I had just witnessed, he brushed my hair aside and inspected the cut on my neck. I bit my lip as even his light touch caused a painful, sharp sting.

Cursing under his breath, Gregor gathered me into his arms. As he rose, I grasped the edge of the blanket tighter over my chest. He had taken two steps toward the connecting door when Jim appeared. He looked disheveled and out of breath. His shirt was torn and his left eye swollen shut.

"Boss, I—"

Gregor didn't take his eyes off me. "I don't want to hear it. Put that piece of shit in the back of the Range Rover and wait for further instructions."

"Yes, Boss."

Gregor carried me into his bedroom and through the closet to the bathroom, where he placed me on the green marble counter between the double sinks. As the shock of what I'I'd just witnessed started to settle in, I wrapped the blanket tighter over my shoulders. Gregor then pushed the blanket down till it barely covered my breasts. When I reached to pull it up again, his warning glare stopped me.

Placing a finger under my chin, he tilted my head back. I hissed as the dried blood pulled at the wound, making it sting and itch.

He got a fresh washcloth and ran it under some warm water. "It's just a scratch. It won't scar." He placed the cloth over the cut, and after the warmth penetrated the dried blood, he swiped it clean.

Turning back to the sink, he ran his hands under the faucet. Swirls of red-tinged water circled the basin before slipping down the drain. If I hadn't just witnessed the brutality, it would have reminded me of cleaning my paint brushes.

"Next time, bend your knees. Your attacker won't expect it. Then pivot and slam him in the kidneys"—he gestured to a spot on his side—"right here with your elbows. If you do it right, your attacker will let go and bend over in pain. That's when you grab them by the back of the head and slam their face down on your raised knee. That will break their nose and give you a chance to escape."

Next time?
NEXT TIME!

What the fuck had happened to my life?

I was an artist, or at least trying to be one. I wanted to create beauty, not be a part of destruction and violence. My reluctant attraction to Gregor and surprise at his more cultured side had blinded me to the reasons why I ran in the first place.

I didn't belong in his world.

When I didn't respond, he placed his warm hands on my jaw and looked into my eyes. "You're safe. I'm going to make sure no one harms you ever again. Do you understand me, Samara?"

Looking down at the blood covering his chest, I shook violently. Gregor followed my gaze and cursed. Snatching up the wet washcloth, he ran it over his chest as he exited the bathroom.

I stayed put on the counter.

Afraid to move.

Afraid to speak.

Afraid to think.

After the muted sounds of rustling fabric, Gregor entered the bathroom dressed in a pair of jeans and a dark grey sweater. He pushed the sleeves up his forearms before resting his hands on the counter on either side of my hips. "I need to handle a few things. I want you to be a good girl and stay in our room. Jim will keep guard."

His voice had such a casual tone, as if he were telling me he was just popping over to the store for bread and milk, instead of basically letting me know he was about to go bury four bodies.

My knuckles were white against the gold fabric of the bed coverlet as I continued to clasp it to my chest. His ring shone brightly under the stark bathroom light.

Mrs. Gregor Ivanova, mafia wife.

Was this now my life?

My entire being rebelled at the prospect.

"Samara?"

My throat seized shut as I licked my dry lips. I couldn't meet his gaze.

"Everything is going to be okay, malyshka."

Everything was *not* going to be okay.

Swallowing past the sick lump in my throat, I finally spoke. "Who was that man?"

"No one you need to be concerned about."

I blinked. Was he serious? "How could I not be concerned? He just tried to kill me!"

Gregor nodded sagely. "And he paid the price for that, as will his family and cohorts."

"Gregor, what the fuck is going on?"

"Language."

"Language! Really? You're going to lecture me about my language at a time like this? You know what? You can go fuc—"

Switching his hand to the back of my neck, he pulled me close to claim my mouth. His tongue swept in to take possession as his other hand ruthlessly shoved the blanket aside so he could cup my breast. Shifting his hips, he wedged himself between my legs. His hard cock pressed against my still sore pussy. Whimpering, I tried to pull away, but he fisted his fingers into my hair and twisted, keeping me still and under his control.

His mouth tasted of vodka and violence.

The moment he released me, I sucked in a desperate breath. Before I had a chance to fight him off, he swept me back into his arms and carried me into the bedroom. Placing me on the bed, he stormed back into the closet and returned with a fresh blanket. My body spun and twisted as he pulled the old, soiled one free. Draping the soft down over me, he tucked it in along my sides as if I were a little girl being soothed after a nightmare.

"Samara, the only way this marriage is going to work is if you learn to question less and obey more."

I opened my mouth to object.

He placed his fingers over my lips. "Before you even attempt to deny it, let me assure you... we are getting married as soon as possible. Nothing has changed, especially after tonight, and no, I'm not referring to the intrusion."

My cheeks flamed. He had promised that in the end I would beg him to fuck me, and damn him he was right, but just because I surrendered to him in bed didn't mean I was ready to surrender the rest of my life.

Gregor leaned over and kissed me on the forehead. "Try to get some sleep."

I listened to the muted voices on the other side of the door. The deeper, angrier one was definitely Gregor. The other must be Jim, trying to apologize again for the security lapse. After a short heated exchange, heavy footsteps headed off down the hallway.

Still, I waited… holding my breath.

After several minutes, headlights glowed through the gauzy bedroom window curtains as a car pulled around the circular drive and sped away.

I waited a few more tense minutes till I was certain Gregor was gone, before tossing the covers aside and rising.

CHAPTER 27

*S*amara

CROSSING INTO MY BEDROOM, I avoided the bloodstain on the carpet and ran to the closet.

I changed into a black t-shirt and yoga pants with black sneakers and checked my purse for what little cash I still had and my Gwen Stevens IDs. He'd be able to trace them, of course, but hopefully I'd be across the border, already have a new ID, and be in the wind before he caught up to me.

Placing my ear to the outer door, I listened for any sound of movement. There was none. Still, I knew Jim must be there.

Taking the lamp off the bureau, I unplugged it and ripped off the shade before hoisting the heavy glass and metal base over my head. Standing just to the right of the door, I inhaled deeply before letting out a loud scream.

Jim came bursting through the door.

The moment he did, I slammed the lamp down onto this

skull. He crumpled to the floor without so much as a whimper. Tossing the lamp aside, I whispered a quick apology to his prone form.

Creeping over to my bedroom door, I peeked my head out and surveyed the hallway.

It was quiet and still.

Careful to avoid any squeaks in the floorboards I had noticed earlier on my tour, I made my way down to the main floor and into the kitchen where there was a door to the garage. Rose had shown it to me earlier, bragging about her boss' taste in luxury cars.

I surveyed my options.

Escalade

Porsche 911

Audi A4

Cadillac CTS

BMW 3 Series

I decided on the Audi. It was less flashy than the others. I didn't want to stick out on the road. Going to the key box, I selected the one with the Audi key chain. After opening the car door, I placed the car in neutral then went to the side wall and pressed the automatic garage door button. Immediately, I dove into the backseat of the Audi and hid just in case someone came to investigate. A bead of sweat slid from between my shoulder blades down to my lower back as I tensely waited.

The evening remained still and calm. No cry of alarm.

Getting out of the car, I circled around to the back and pushed. The hardest part was just getting it rolling. It didn't budge. I turned around and pushed with my back, bending my knees to use all my weight. Finally, the car inched forward. Then it rolled. Thank God he had a smooth asphalt driveway and not a gravel one.

I pushed the car till it was a few lengths away from the gate at the end of the drive.

Getting behind the wheel, I found the gate remote and pressed the button. The gate silently slid open on greased rails. Once more, I got out to push the car. By the time it was through the gate, I was sweaty and exhausted. This had taken way longer than I thought it would, and my heart raced at the idea Gregor could return home at any moment.

I turned the ignition on, and the car hummed to life, then I drove out of the cul-de-sac as I fiddled to put the air conditioning on blast.

I finally allowed myself to breathe.

CHAPTER 28

Gregor

AFTER PULLING into the dimly lit warehouse loading dock, I flipped open the glove compartment and pulled out my pair of brass knuckles. They were actually made of a heavy iron. Swiping the pad of my thumb over the faded image of Lenin imposed over a laurel wreath crest, I thought of my father. Cast back in 1927, the weapon had been smuggled out of Russia by a long-forgotten family member when they stowed away to America. My family, my father especially, thought it was amusingly ironic to use a tool of the Bolshevik revolution to inflict violence, command, respect and restore our own wealth.

He gave them to me on my thirteenth birthday.

I had wanted a BMX bike.

Looking down at the deep, black etching of 1917 and

1927 on either side of the four finger holes, I shook my head. Like father, like son.

Although perhaps not entirely.

While he used them to instill fear, I used them to inflict the maximum amount of pain with the fewest punches to save my hands.

I may have been a criminal, but I wasn't a thug.

I took no pride in walking around with bruised and cut knuckles to showcase the violence of my business. I had no need for such a superficial display. If I were handling myself correctly, a man should have been terrified regardless of whether I looked like I could throw and take a punch.

Against my own wishes, I honored my father and the Ivanov name by taking on the mantle of the family business, but I took no pleasure in it. Probably why I so often sought escape through acquiring art or reading one of Shakespeare's tragedies. My soul needed to be reminded there was culture and beauty in the world, even though my daily actions sought to destroy it.

Perhaps that was why I clasped on to Samara so tightly. There were other marriageable females with family names of equal reputation and standing, but they didn't compare to her. Samara had an artist's creative soul, but with a dark edge. She knew the only way to truly appreciate beauty was to experience pain and ugliness. It was clear in her chosen art subjects, in every stroke of her brush.

I knew bringing her into my world would expose her to even deeper levels of darkness and foolishly dispelled any unease by assuring myself it would make her a better artist, and I did truly believe that. Yet, that didn't mean I ever wanted her to experience that darkness firsthand.

As her husband in all but name, it was my duty to protect her.

I failed her tonight.

Never again.

Haunted by the look of disgust and terror in Samara's eyes when she saw the blood on my shirt from earlier, I pulled my sweater over my head and tossed it back onto the passenger seat before stepping out of the car. Slipping the brass knuckles into my back pocket, I slammed the door shut and made my way in the dark to the back storage room where I knew I'd find Vaska and Dimitri.

They were both standing over a crate of guns. Three men —looking worse for the wear—were tied up and gagged with duct tape on the cold, cement floor.

I slapped Vaska on the shoulder in greeting.

"What is this?" I asked with a nod in the direction of the guns.

Dimitri lifted the Russian sniper rifle. "Knock offs those piece of shit Petrov brothers tried to palm off on us."

Dimitri tossed the useless chunk of metal and plastic back into the crate. We all turned to stare at the tied up men.

Rolling my shoulders in preparation, I offered, "I just want to say—"

Vaska cut me off as he handed me a flask. "No need to thank us, Gregor."

I took a swig and choked. Swiping the back of my hand across my mouth, I shook my head as I handed the flask back to Vaska. "You're still drinking that Moskovskaya shit?"

It should have been illegal to call that swill vodka. It tasted like gasoline poured through a dirty sock.

Vaska laughed, then took a swig before replacing it in his coat pocket. "You and Dimitri are too soft with your fancy tastes."

Ignoring the familiar jibe, I asked, "How did it happen?"

Vaska shrugged. "I was having a steam at Red Square." He nodded in the captive's direction with the swollen right eye.

"That idiot bragged about fucking over the great Gregor Ivanov. I tried calling to warn you..."

"I was busy." While always being aware that my life choices may have put Samara in danger, it never occurred to me that my obsession for her would put us *both* in danger. There was no denying the woman was a distraction... now a dangerous one. I was so focused on her I had neglected to secure the house as well as I should have by bringing in extra men to patrol the grounds and monitor the security cameras. If it hadn't been for Dimitri and Vaska interceding, I may have lost her. "I thank you, my friend."

Vaska shrugged again. "This was not a problem. Although I am sorry about the damage to your side door... and your dining room table... and your—"

I smirked. "A small price to pay."

With the pleasantries over, it was time to get down to business. Vaska shrugged out of his coat as Dimitri loosened his already blood-stained tie. Reaching into my back pocket, I pulled out my brass knuckles and slipped my fingers through the four holes, testing the familiar weight.

The captives attempted to scream past their gags as they shifted and shuffled along the floor.

It would do them no good. They were dead the moment they accepted the job to kidnap my bride.

Flexing my fist, I approached them. I recognized the first man. It was Pavel Rasskovich, a flunky for the Novikoffs. "Your comrade is already dead. How painfully you die and whether your loved ones die as well will depend on you."

I tore the duct tape off the mouth of the closest perpetrator. "Who sent you? Egor or Boris?"

Before I proceeded, I needed to know if it was her father, Egor Novikoff, or both who set this into motion.

The man sneered. "Fuck you. I'm not telling you—"

Raising my knee, I used the heel of my boot to kick the

man in the mouth. His head snapped back, and blood poured from his lips. He choked and retched as several teeth fell onto the cement.

I gave the man another kick, and he fell sideways as he continued to choke to death slowly on his own blood.

Twisting my left hand into the shirt of the second man, I wrenched him to his feet. Before removing his gag, I drew back my arm, curving it to lessen the jarring impact because of the brass knuckles. I struck out, breaking his nose with one punch. Allowing his body to fall as it absorbed the impact of my blow, I leaned over him and watched him struggle for breath as his nostrils filled with blood. When his eyes rolled back into his head, I finally removed the duct tape. He sucked in a ragged breath.

Leaning down on my haunches, I wiped off the blood on the iron bands around my fingers on my jeans. "Now that I have your attention. I want to know who sent you? Was it Federov or Novikoff?"

Turning his head to the side, the man blew air through his nose, splattering the ground with flecks of crimson before answering. His Russian accent had the thick, unmistakable twang of a newly arrived Muscovite, just like the man who'd held a knife to Samara. "We don't know who hired us."

I shook my head. "Wrong answer."

Rising, I took a few steps back. As soon as I was clear, Dimitri fired a single bullet. Killing him.

The third and final man shook his head furiously as he tried to scurry backwards on his ass away from us.

"Well, this is just sad," quipped Vaska.

"What do you expect from a Muscovite?" responded Dimitri.

"Aren't the Petrovs from Moscow?" Vaska asked.

"Exactly." Dimitri pointed his handgun at the man, who froze in place.

Approaching the man, I leaned down and ripped off the duct tape. The man immediately began crying and ranting in Russian about how they had just arrived in the United States and heard on the street someone was offering big money to anyone who could capture Samara Federova. He didn't know who or how they would have even collected the money once they secured her.

Chances are these three idiots would never have been able to collect and would have wound up killing Samara after doing God knows what to her.

He continued to sob and plead. "Pozhaluysta! Ne ubivay menya! My ne znali, chto ona tvoy zhenikh. My by nikogda ne proyavili neuvazheniye k imeni Ivanov."

The fact he claimed they had no idea she was my fiancé and that they never would have dared to disrespect me was of little consequence to me. What was done was done. A man like me didn't get and keep a reputation like mine by being understanding or forgiving. Taking the gun from Dimitri, I shot the man in the head, then turned away and forgot him before his body even hit the floor.

"It looks like you have a problem, my friend," Dimitri remarked.

I nodded. It didn't make sense. I had both Boris and Egor under surveillance. Both their offices, phones, and cars were all bugged. Neither man spoke on the matter of Samara. Her name had yet to even be mentioned. Admittedly, it had lured me into a false sense of security. It had me thinking I had a little extra time to convince Samara to marry me willingly. It had me believing that perhaps in this one instance I didn't have to live in the shadow of my father's legacy.

That was obviously over now.

"What are you going to do?" asked Dimitri as I reluctantly accepted the offered flask from Vaska once more and took a swig.

"I'm not going to get any answers here. I need to return to D.C. immediately." I took out my phone and texted my pilot to get the plane ready, not caring that it was 1:30 in the morning. He was paid very well to be available at all hours. I then texted Damien, letting him know my change of plans.

"And Samara?"

I finished texting a judge in D.C. who I had firmly in my pocket before answering, "If all goes to plan by this time tomorrow, she will be Mrs. Gregor Ivanova… whether she likes it or not."

CHAPTER 29

*S*amara

AT JUST AFTER TWO AM, Lake Shore Drive was practically deserted.

I looked in my rearview mirror to see the lit up Chicago skyline behind me and the crashing surf of Lake Michigan to my right. As I did so, my chaotic thoughts switched to Gregor, despite my best efforts to avoid thinking of him.

I stared at my grip on the black leather steering wheel where the diamond and emerald engagement ring glinted accusingly on my finger. In my haste, I had forgotten to take it and the diamond collar he had clasped around my throat off.

Had he noticed my absence yet?

My inner thighs tightened at the thought of what kind of punishment Gregor would have devised if he had caught me sneaking out of his house.

His punishments tended to be very creative, fucking with both my mind and body.

I knew why he did it; he liked to be in control. He was like those men who revel in the challenge of taming a wild creature.

The task master.

The disciplinarian.

The protector.

What I still couldn't grasp is why I liked it. True, there was something intoxicating about a powerful man stepping up and taking everything off my shoulders. It was frightening to think how the idea of his protection made me feel safe and not as alone.

It wasn't just frightening.

It was dangerous.

And I had almost fallen for it.

I had almost fallen for *him*.

Fallen for the way his sexy, gravelly voice quoted *Dracula* and Shakespeare. For the way he talked about Impressionist art as if he loved it almost as much as I did. For the way his eyes seemed to devour me whenever we were together. For the intense way he focused on me and my needs... even the kinky needs I didn't know I had. For the powerful way he took control.

I actually almost said yes to marrying him. Yes to it all.

I would have been trapped in a loveless marriage like my parents.

Caught up in his world of violence, blood, and destruction... completely under his control.

I still couldn't get the image of Gregor covered in that man's blood out of my mind.

I was lost in my thoughts when I noticed a car approaching at a very high rate of speed. Probably a drunk driver. At this time of night, I needed to be careful, since the main people on the road were drunks and cops. As a precaution, I switched to the right lane to give the car a little extra room.

At a glance, I could see it was a black Range Rover, but the windows were tinted so I couldn't get a look at the driver. In my rearview mirror, I watched as the SUV passed a slower moving car. It was now barreling toward me.

Like a high-stakes game of chess, in an instant I analyzed the possibilities.

One, it was a drunk fucking around, and I was letting my nerves get the best of me.

Two, it was Gregor.

The SUV quickly gained ground.

I held my breath, allowing it to get closer and closer. waiting till I could get a view of the license plate. I didn't remember all the details from Gregor's Range Rover, but I remembered it started with an A3 and a... *Fuck!*

I slammed my foot on the gas.

The Audi surged forward.

It was Gregor.

Keeping a firm grip on the steering wheel, I maneuvered the different curves and bends as the road followed the Lake Michigan shoreline.

I had no plan. My only thought was escape.

The Range Rover picked up speed.

I swerved around a slower moving car and increased my speed. Hazarding a glance in my rearview mirror, I watched as Gregor made the same quick maneuver.

I had to get off the drive. It was going to be too easy for him to run me off the road into one of the deserted parking lots which lined the different parks along the route. I was coming up on Irving Park Road. No. That exit was no good. It was always jammed up at the intersection right off the drive, no matter what time of night. The area was too saturated with bars and restaurants.

In my side mirror, I could see Gregor maneuver from behind me to the lane next to mine. He was getting ready to force me off the road.

I slowed the car down to throw him off. As he adjusted his own speed, I hit the gas again, shooting past him. His car switched back into gear, and I could see the Wilson exit approach. It was perfect. A less popular, somewhat dark exit straight into Wilson Park. It was unlikely any cars would be on the ramp.

At the last possible minute, I pulled the car to the right, exiting at a high rate of speed. I could hear the screech of his brakes but didn't dare take the time to look. Keeping my grip on the steering wheel, I struggled to maintain control of the car as I forced it into a right turn. The moment the car recovered, I went left. Straight through the park.

Finally, I dared a look.

The road behind me was empty.

There was no doubt he saw me turn onto Wilson, but maybe I got lucky, and he assumed I couldn't make the sharp turn onto Simonds in time. If my strategy worked, perhaps he would assume I went right to head back into the safe anonymity of downtown.

Just as I turned onto Lawrence, I could see the distinctive narrow headlights of his Range Rover turn onto Simonds.

Damn.

The Lawrence exit led straight into Uptown. Another popular area that would be active with people as the bars closed and kicked everyone out. There would also be cops.

It was a risk I would have to take.

With Gregor quickly gaining, I made one turn after another, zigzagging through the narrow one-way streets in an attempt to lose him.

Finally, a car emerged from an alley, blocking his path.

I made a few quick turns and was gone.

I needed to get on the highway and get to O'Hare as quickly as possible. Driving to Canada was no longer an option since Gregor would probably report the car stolen once he realized I'd lost him.

I would hop on the first plane leaving the city, no matter the destination. Once I was in the air, I would send a message to Gregor telling him at what airport parking lot he could find his car. Maybe that would help lessen the possibility of him coming after me this time.

Too nervous to slow down, I continued to race around the small streets of Uptown, when I saw it.

Blue lights.

Trying to outrun a cop would be beyond stupid since he could easily call in backup and box me in.

With no other option, I pulled over.

Leaning over, I searched through the glove box for the registration as I waited for the cop to emerge from his vehicle. I then reached into my bag for my fake I.D. Hopefully, he just wrote the ticket and didn't try to run Gwen Stevens through the system.

Some of my aliases were deep. Social security numbers, high school transcripts, paystubs, social media accounts. Others were very shallow, a quick fake I.D. to leave town without being traced.

My Gwen Stevens alias was very, very shallow. If the cop ran the name, he would come up with nothing and immediately become suspicious.

Taking a deep breath, I repeated in my head.

I'm Gwen Stevens. Gwen Stevens. Gwen.

Rolling down the window, I greeted the officer with a smile. "Good evening, officer. Did I do something wrong?"

"License and registration, ma'am."

"Absolutely. I have them both here."

"Ma'am. Are you aware your speed exceeded the posted limit by twenty miles per hour? You failed to bring your vehicle to a complete and full stop at that last intersection."

I twirled one thick curl over my right shoulder and gave him an innocent, slightly teary-eyed look. "I know, officer. I'm so sorry. This is my boyfriend's car, and I'm just nerv—"

"Ma'am, I am not finished. Do not interrupt me."

So, I guess flirting won't help me.

"You used an alley as a through street and failed to yield to a right of way vehicle."

I remained silent.

"Remain here, ma'am."

The officer walked back to his vehicle.

Stay calm. He rattled off mostly minor violations. At least he said nothing about reckless driving. I hunched down in my seat as headlights approached. A small blue Camry slowly passed. I let out the breath I was holding.

I kept an eye out for Gregor's car. I had pulled over on a small side street, so my odds were good he wouldn't find me.

The cop was taking forever.

As I waited, I checked outgoing flights at O'Hare on my phone. The earliest was at four-thirty am to Los Angeles. It would have to do. I would fly to LA, then double back to Montreal.

Finally, I heard the cop's car door close and then his approach.

"Ma'am, I'm going to need you to step out of the vehicle."

"What is the problem, officer?"

"Ma'am, please step out of the vehicle," repeated the cop as he opened the driver's side door for me.

Not wanting to cause a scene, I got out of the car.

"Please place your hands on the hood of the vehicle. Do you have any sharp objects or illegal items in your pockets?"

"I don't have any pockets. These are yoga pants. Are you arresting me?" I asked as I placed my hands on the warm metal hood.

"Ma'am. You have the right to remain silent."

I turned around to confront him. "What the hell? I'm getting arrested for a few traffic tickets? This is ridiculous!"

"Ma'am, please resume the position."

I turned back around.

"Your vehicle matches the description of a vehicle which engaged in a reckless, high-speed drag race on Lake Shore Drive. You are being arrested on suspicion of—"

"Wait. Wait! This is not happening," I argued as I turned back to face the officer.

"Ma'am. Please resume the position."

"Stop calling me ma'am!" I shouted. This whole thing was getting out of control. I wasn't worried about getting arrested. They wouldn't have my real name, and my fingerprints had never been on file. I was worried about getting caged up and Gregor finding out. A man like him had to have just as many, if not more well-placed contacts in the Chicago police force as he did in D.C.. They would no doubt contact the registered owner of the vehicle. I would be a sitting duck.

This is bad. Really bad.

At my outburst, the cop grabbed me by the shoulders and slammed my head down onto the hood of the car. He wrenched my arms behind me, I could hear the clatter of metal as the first cuff encircled my wrist.

Okay, this is way worse.

"Can I be of any assistance, officer?"

Gregor.

"This is a police matter, sir. Please return to your vehicle," said the officer as he clicked the second cuff tightly into place.

"Officer Freidman? Perhaps you don't remember me,"

said Gregor in that calmly controlled voice I knew meant he was angry. Very angry.

"Mr. Ivanov?" responded the officer. He dragged me with him as he went to shake Gregor's hand. "I'm sorry I didn't recognize you at first. Mr. Ivanov, I want to thank you for that union construction job you got my brother. It was a real lifesaver. If there is anything I can ever do to repay you, you just say the word."

"Actually, Friedman, there is something you can do."

I could practically hear the charming smile through his words.

"I need you to release this female into my custody."

Oh God.

"Why do you—"

"No questions asked," finished Gregor. His tone said what he didn't have to. Gregor could take away his brother's job as easily as he gave it. Would a cop risk that over a traffic stop?

I shifted my aching shoulders as the stress of waiting for the cop's response coupled with the uncomfortable position of being slung over a car hood with my arms handcuffed behind my back.

The cop turned and approached me. Without saying a word, he lifted me off the hood of the car into a standing position by my cuffs.

With Gregor back-lit by the headlights of his car, I couldn't read his expression. Did I really need to see his face to know he was pissed?

So was I to be arrested or face Gregor's fury?

I held my breath, still not sure which scenario was worse for me.

No, I knew.

Going with Gregor would be much, much worse.

Now that I was back under his control, I could see the transformation to his demeanor. There was a play of light in his eyes, a shift from slate grey to a deeper, darker, almost black grey. Transitioning from the look of someone haunted to someone who hunts.

His calm demeanor with a sheen of sophistication was a ruse which hid his true darker nature.

The very dark nature which drew my twisted heart to him, always giving me that wicked sensation I was playing with fire. And I had a feeling was about to get badly burned.

I watched out of the corner of my eye as the cop leaned down and fumbled with his keys, searching for the one to the cuffs.

He's going to give me to Gregor!

"No," Gregor said. "Leave the cuffs on."

CHAPTER 30

Gregor

Power meant control.

That was my mantra.

It shaped every action of my life.

When I returned and found her gone, I was powerless and the lack of control tested my sanity.

Samara had become necessary to my existence. It was that simple.

She was mine.

And I kept what was mine.

You did not build a powerful criminal empire by being weak when it came to going after and keeping what you wanted. I still couldn't believe she had left our bed to disappear in the middle of the night like that. I had honestly thought we had gotten past the idea she would return to the life she had before I reclaimed her. Sure, I hadn't given her much choice in the matter but that wasn't the point.

Whether or not she realized it, she needed me.

I was her only protection from her father and the Novikoffs.

They had come after her once. They would come after her again.

A dark wave of possessive fury overtook me at just the thought of what would have happened if her father or Egor had succeeded tonight. She did not understand the danger she was putting herself in, but by the end of tonight, she would if I had to strip her ass raw with my belt.

If Samara thought I was overbearing and controlling this past week, she was in for a rude awakening. *Actions have consequences.*

My malyshka was about to learn her harshest lesson yet.

I thought I had made it clear to her I was in charge from now on.

Apparently, she hadn't gotten the message.

I would just have to make sure I made myself *painfully* clear from this point forward.

I reached my hand down to my belt. The edge of my thumb caressed the smooth leather as thoughts of tying Samara to a bed and giving her a belt lashing only partially appeased me.

I knew that if she had chosen to run, I might never find her again. Damien was good, but I doubted even his abilities in being able to track down someone with Samara's skills again. No matter. I intended on clipping her wings, and soon. I wasn't waiting any longer. The arrangements were already being made.

By this time tomorrow, Samara would be my wife... whether she liked it or not.

"Are you fucking kidding me with this?" she shouted as

soon as the cop drove off, bringing me back to the present situation and her imminent punishment.

"Little one, I have already made myself clear on how I feel about that pretty mouth of yours uttering such vulgar words. Do I need to remind you of the punishment again?"

I watched her beautiful face turn pale.

"I was only borrowing your car," she lied as she refused to meet my eyes.

I took a step forward. She instinctively stepped back. This angered me even more.

Would I be forever chasing after her?

She needed to recognize that her situation had changed. I was in her life now, and I had absolutely no intention of leaving. The sooner she accepted that fact, the easier everything would be.

With both hands, I reached out and grabbed her upper arms, snatching her body to mine. With her arms secured behind her back, her full breasts were pressed against my chest. The V-neck of her t-shirt exposed the upper swells of creamy skin. A low growl rumbled from deep in my throat.

All I could think was mine.

Mine.

I was a decisive man in business and in life. When I saw something I wanted, I took it. No regrets. And there was no mistaking that I wanted Samara. All of her. No other man would ever touch her again as far as I was concerned.

She struggled within my grasp, inflaming me more as her hips brushed my already erect cock.

"Let me go!"

"No."

"Will you stop saying that? All I ever hear from you is no," she complained, stamping her small foot into the dirt like the petulant child I planned to treat her as.

I placed a finger under her chin and forced her to meet

my gaze. "That's because you keep asking the wrong questions."

With our bodies pressed close, I could feel as well as hear her short gasp.

"Uncuff me," she demanded.

"No."

With that, I bent low and placed a shoulder against her stomach. With little effort, I lifted her slight weight high and carried her back to my car.

Samara cried out. A swift slap to her ass silenced her immediately.

Without any ceremony, I deposited her into the back seat of my Range Rover. Sitting her upright on the passenger side, I reached over to buckle her in tight. As I closed the door and headed toward the Audi, I called Jim, who had suffered more from a bruised ego than the bashing she gave him on the head.

"I found her. Grab the extra set of Audi keys and come pick up the car on the corner of Broadway and Bryn Mawr," I instructed as I grabbed the keys out of the ignition and Samara's purse before locking the door and returning to the Range Rover.

* * *

We drove back in silence.

Samara stubbornly kept her face averted as she stared out at the dark sky over Lake Michigan.

The house was dark and quiet when I pressed the button to open the outside gate. I had chosen to only wake up Jim when I realized Samara was missing. Rose was used to late night comings and goings of myself and associates, so she was unlikely to be alarmed by the sound of us entering the house at three in the morning.

I marched Samara out of the garage and through the dark entryway up the main staircase. Walking past her door, I went straight to my room.

"I'm exhausted. I would prefer to go to my *own* room, if you please," she said primly.

"You've been told before. Bad girls who run away from home in the middle of the night earn severe punishments, not a quiet night in bed," I growled in response.

Samara pulled away from me as we crossed the threshold into my bedroom. As she turned, I could tell she was ready for a fight.

Good, so was I.

"Stop saying things like that."

"Like what?" I asked as I pulled the sweater I had tossed on over my head.

I watched as her eyes darted over my naked chest. She probably didn't even realize the tip of her cute pink tongue darted out to wet her lower lip.

"Like… like I'm some little girl you can… can spank!"

Closing the distance between us, I grabbed her around the waist. "As far as I'm concerned, I'm already your husband, and I have every intention of punishing that impertinent ass of yours," I warned I, reaching down to grasp her ass with both my hands and squeezing.

As her mouth opened on a shocked gasp, my own descended. I took her mouth with all the pent-up rage and possession I felt. Claiming her tongue as my own. Biting that plump lower lip. Rubbing the underside of my tongue along the sharp edge of her teeth. Remembering how this same mouth felt wrapped around my cock.

"Say it," I commanded as I pressed my lips to her vulnerable throat. "I want to hear you beg me for mercy."

Lifting her head up and away, she broke our kiss. Her

hard green gaze met my own. "To quote your favorite word, no."

I smiled.

I loved it when she taunted me into playing rough.

Grabbing her by the hair, I dragged her over to my bed. I tossed her slight weight into the center onto her stomach. Leaping onto the bed, I straddled her hips. As she screamed and thrashed, I reached for the silk cord that held back thick velvet curtains on either side of the headboard. With swift efficiency, I secured a simple slip knot around her throat, then wrapped the cord around the center post of the headboard.

She stilled.

Moving off her body, I walked to the foot of the bed and watched as she tried the knot around her throat. Every time she moved too sharply, it tightened, cutting off her air.

Grabbing her flailing legs by the ankles, I took off her sneakers. My fingers then gripped the soft band of her yoga pants and removed them and her panties in one smooth motion.

There it was, one of my favorite things about her. The small heart tattoo on her ass. It embodied her spirit of sass and innocence and beckoned to me like a heart-shaped bullseye. Unable to resist, I gave her a single smack on her ass.

Her whole body bowed.

"I'm going to scream this house down," she threatened through clenched teeth as those beautiful emerald eyes flashed daggers at me.

Within her line of view, I slowly unbuckled my belt. I wanted there to be no doubt what was going to happen next.

Samara's face crumpled. "Don't do this. I'm sorry I tried to run. I promise I won't do it again."

Whipping the thick leather through my jean belt loops, I

folded it in half between my hands. "I'm going to make sure of it."

Her mouth snapped shut as she lowered her eyes.

Her half naked form was prone and vulnerable. The black blanket I had placed over her earlier highlighted her luminously pale skin.

Taking a step back, I raised my arm high.

Samara let out a scream as the thick leather came down across her naked backside. I waited till the first red welt appeared on her white cheeks before raising my arm again. Careful to avoid her straining, still cuffed hands, I belted her ass again and again. Each time, an angry red stripe would appear either on her cheeks or her upper thighs.

Samara cried out in anguish with each strike.

"Beg me," I commanded.

"Please stop!"

I hit her with my belt again, this time on the delicate curve just below her ass where her thighs began.

Samara's body curled into a fetal position as she fell to her side. The rope around her neck grew taunt. Immediately, she laid back down on her stomach like a good girl.

The room was once more filled with the sound of leather against skin and her shrieks of pain.

"I'm sorry! I'm sorry!" she cried in desperation.

My belt fell across her reddened cheeks several more times.

"Please! I'm sorry!"

Finally, her precious heart tattoo disappeared as her skin burned a furious red.

Lowering my hands to the fastening of my jeans, I growled, "Your punishment isn't over, malyshka."

Her only response was a disheartened sniffle as she wiped her cheeks on the coverlet.

"I'm going to fuck your ass now."

Her pussy would still be too sore from earlier tonight. If I weren't such a savage, I would leave her alone, hoping a good belt whipping would suffice, but I *was* a savage, and I had every intention of teaching my future wife the harsh lesson she richly deserved.

Samara's wide eyes turned to me. "Please, Gregor. I… I don't want to do that. It's going to hurt."

"It's supposed to hurt."

Opening the flap of my jeans, I pulled my painfully swollen cock out. Fisting the hard length, I placed one knee on the bed and leaned toward her. "Suck it."

Samara pleaded with me instead. "Please, don't do this."

"Suck my cock."

Samara buried her face in the bedcovers.

Grabbing her hair, I wrenched her head back. She cried out.

"Suck my cock now, or I fuck your ass dry."

With a sob, she opened her shaking lips.

I thrust my hips forward, watching as she gagged on the length.

"Get it good and wet."

Unable to breathe through her nose because of her tears, she continued to choke and sputter as I forced my shaft past her lips. I could feel her tongue swipe the underside and had to rein back my impulse to fill her mouth with cum.

After a few more moments, I pulled free and walked to the foot of the bed.

The mattress dipped as I knelt between her open legs. I placed both palms on her ass cheeks, relishing in the heat radiating off her skin. Samara hissed in response to my touch.

Using the heels of my hands, I pried her cheeks apart.

Samara whimpered and tried to clench them back together. That earned her a hard slap on the right cheek.

Once more, I opened her ass cheeks wide, knowing the humiliation this was causing. Leaning down, I gently blew on her small puckered hole, watching as it twitched and winked from the cool touch of air. Next, I placed my tongue on her small opening. Wetting the soft ridges with the tip of my tongue.

Her entire body quaked in response. I knew she was fighting her embarrassment with her obvious arousal. I could see the lips of her cunt were slick with it. Leaning up on my knees, I pressed the head of my cock against her asshole.

I could hear Samara suck in her breath as she braced herself for the pain we both knew was coming.

Pushing my hips forward, I pressed my shaft against her flesh. I watched as the small ridges became smooth from the pressure. The delicate pink skin turned white as the head of my cock opened her hole wider and wider.

"Ow! Ow! Ow!" Samara whimpered. Her hands, which rested just above the curve of her ass, curled helplessly into fists.

My cock slowly pushed in till the ridge of the head was swallowed by her body. At this point, I grabbed hold of her hips.

"Who do you belong too, malyshka?"

"You," came the muffled, obedient response.

With that, I ruthlessly thrust forward. Driving into her tight body with all my might till my balls slapped against her cunt. Pulling back, I pistoned into her tight warmth again. Her body gripped my cock like a fist just as it fought each intrusion of my shaft. I could feel the twitch and stretch of her inner muscles as she struggled to accommodate my girth. Looking down, I relished in the sight of her tiny puckered hole, stretched taut as the wide base of my cock forced it open.

Samara begged and pleaded for me to stop.

My response was to force her hips up higher, so I could plunge into her with even more ferocity.

The feel of her punished skin against my stomach drove me to near insanity as I tried to possess her body in every way imaginable.

Grabbing the silk cord from around her neck, I pulled it over her head. Then I thrust my fingers into her mouth like a bit. As far as I was concerned what I was doing did not differ from breaking in a wild, untamed animal. Pulling back on her jaw, I could feel her teeth sink into my fingers. The edge of pain only spurred me on. Her smooth back was slick with sweat and bowed, her hips forced to meet my thrusts.

Finally, I released her mouth, only to grab her beautiful hair. Twisting its long length around my fist, I kept her body in the curved position as I used my other hand to fondle her breast and pinch her nipple.

"Oh God," she moaned as pain turned to pleasure. Her body vibrated and hummed with the intensity of her release.

Taking pity on her, I drove into her body a few more times before loosening the reins on my own desire and letting my release crash over me like a dark wave.

My cock jerked inside her tight back passage as I pumped warm come into her body.

Breathing heavily, I reached into the bedside table and withdrew a pair of handcuff keys. I uncuffed her, then rolled her slack body onto her back.

"Pull your knees up high," I ordered.

My mouth latched onto her clit, now swollen with need.

Samara's hips bucked. Lifting my head, I breathed against her sweet cunt. "Be a good girl, and I will make you come a second time."

It took only a few flicks of my tongue before her body clenched with her own release.

Rising on my knees, I moved up to the head of the bed and collapsed beside her prone body.

Now that I had taken all my fear and adrenaline out on her pretty little body, my white hot rage returned. She had deliberately put herself in danger. In fact, she chose to leave *my* bed to face that danger alone.

Unacceptable.

"You don't understand," she whimpered against my chest as she tried to justify why she snuck away like a thief in the night.

I tightened my grip around her waist as I pressed her harder against my shoulder.

"I understand perfectly. You disobeyed me."

"It's not like that. I had no choice. I don't belong in your world."

"You always have a choice. And choices have consequences."

There was an unmistakable dark threat to my words.

The shiver that coursed through her body proved she understood.

Fisting her hair, I pulled her head back and cupped her jaw. I wanted to look deep into those beautiful, changeable emerald eyes of hers to make sure she understood every word I was about to say.

"Listen very carefully, malyshka, because I don't want there to be any more confusion. You are mine, and I protect what is mine. Never… ever… run from me again. Do you understand me?"

Samara nodded. "I promise. I won't."

She was lying.

CHAPTER 31

*S*amara

LIKE IN BED, when Gregor took control... *he took complete control.*

He awoke me hours later. I was surprised to see it was already dusk.

Ordering me to dress, he made several phone calls in swift succession. I overheard one which seemed to be Gregor giving instructions to have a plane gassed and ready. A private plane?

My objections fell on deaf ears.

"You have two options, Samara," growled Gregor, "You can either walk onto the plane or be carried, but either way you are getting on that plane."

He was right. It was time to stop running. I wasn't sure how I felt about Gregor, but I knew I would never sort it out until I confronted my parents, because based on last night's attempted kidnapping, things had gotten way out of hand. As much as I hated the thought, it was time to return home.

As we entered the small metal door to the massive hangar, my jaw dropped. When he said we would take his plane back to Washington, I envisioned a grueling bumpy ride on some little Samara, single-engine four seater.

"What the fuck, Gregor!"

"Language, Samara!" he scolded as he grabbed my hand and led me toward the descended staircase. I knew better than to even ask about customs or having to show my ID knowing a man of Gregor's resources would probably bypass such pedestrian necessities.

The plane was at least one hundred feet long. It was white with two crossing sabers emblazoned on the tail in gold, part of Gregor's family crest. If I wasn't mistaken, this was a Global 5000. It had a crazy security system with integrated cameras in the forward belly, quad, and even in the stabilizer fin. Some casino had sent one to pick us up when Yelena had hit big on some well-placed track bets. That was when we learned we needed to keep a lower profile.

I ducked my head as we crossed the threshold. The interior was gorgeous. Four oxblood leather club seats took up most of the space. In the front galley there was a polished bronze bubinga bar stocked with crystal decanters filled with deep amber liquids.

"Seriously. Just how wealthy are you?" I asked as I tried to remember how much this plane probably cost. I mean, there was money and then there was *money*. Gregor apparently had *money*.

At the back of the plane was a massive king-size bed covered in black and gold satin.

I met Gregor's knowing gaze and blushed.

He led me past the club chairs to the bed.

I resisted, although the thought of someone witnessing Gregor fucking me senseless gave me a voyeuristic thrill.

Gregor stroked his knuckles down my cheek. "You're mine. And I don't share."

The pure unadulterated masculine arrogance of his statement made my heart skip.

A little embarrassed by my reaction to his declaration, I looked back to the bed and the various size packages heaped on top.

"What is all this?"

"Clothes for you," he said nonchalantly as he opened his laptop.

I surveyed the signature orange Hermes bag and the glossy black Coco Chanel bags. There was even one from Louis Vuitton.

"How? Why?" I stuttered.

"I knew you would need something to wear for what I had planned, so I arranged for a personal shopper to drop those off."

I wanted to ask how wearing designer clothes fit into his plan of us returning to Washington to reason with my father, but the tone of his voice warned me not to.

I opened the largest box from Chanel. With a delicate touch, I peeled away the tissue paper and gasped. Lifting the dress by the shoulders, I pulled it free from the box. It was a vintage Chanel dress in champagne silk. The surplice v-neckline was trimmed in small white pearls. It looked like a dress Audrey Hepburn would have worn in a movie wedding scene.

"Gregor? You can't mean for me to wear this?"

"I do. It's part of the plan," he said without looking up. "Everything you need is there."

Peeking inside the rest of the boxes, I found lingerie, a purse, and shoes. The large black garment bag next to my packages looked to contain a Giorgio Armani suit for Gregor.

"What exactly is this plan?"

Gregor closed his laptop and approached me. Without saying a word, he lifted me in his arms.

"Gregor! What are you doing?"

He took a few steps and deposited me in one of the club chairs. He then reached for the seat buckle and latched me in tightly. He gave me a quick peck on the lips. "Be a good girl and sit still for take-off. After that, get dressed without asking me any more questions."

I crossed my arms over my chest with a petulant huff.

Just to tweak me further, Gregor teased, "You're just going to have to trust me, malyshka."

* * *

TWO HOURS LATER, I peered out the small oval window through the midnight blue evening sky to see the orange and white runway lights of Reagan International Airport.

After our takeoff, Gregor had personally supervised undressing and redressing me with a pleasurable interlude in between.

Good lord, what that man could do with his tongue.

Feeling more than a little overdressed, I waited as the plane taxied into Gregor's private hangar.

ThenI unbuckled my seatbelt and searched around for my purse as I prepared to disembark.

"Not just yet, baby. We are waiting for a guest first," said Gregor as he rose from his seat and moved to the bar. He poured himself a vodka and me a glass of chilled wine.

"Gregor. Do we have time for this? I want to see Nadia."

"We're making time. And trust me, you're going to want a drink."

Perplexed by his secretive mood, I took the offered glass.

Shortly after, there was a knock on the plane door. The pilot opened the hatch and an older man in a dark suit entered.

"Gregor," he said in warm greeting as he crossed down the aisle to shake Gregor's hand.

"Judge Matthews. Thank you for accommodating me on such short notice."

The judge shrugged. "It's incredibly irregular, but after that little mishap you extracted me from last year, how could I refuse the chance to return a favor?"

Gregor put his arm around my shoulders as he eased me forward. There was no mistaking the tension in my body.

"Samara. I'd like you to meet a friend of mine. Judge John Matthews."

I nodded my head. "Your honor."

The judge reached for my hand. "Well, I certainly understand your haste now, Gregor. She is stunning. If I were thirty years younger..."

"We are in a hurry, Judge," interrupted Gregor.

"Of course! Let me just get the marriage paperwork signed, and we will get to it."

Marriage!

I took a step back... then another.

Marriage!

Gregor moved his dark gaze to me.

I shook my head.

He took a step forward.

I held up my hand in a useless effort to hold him at bay as I continued to back up as far as the plane would allow. All too soon, my back bumped against the wall of the plane.

"Samara. Listen to me."

I just shook my head.

Marriage.

I knew that was his aim, but never in a million years did I think he would pull a stunt like this. I thought I would have more time to convince him we would never suit. I figured he would want a church wedding and all the pomp and circumstance. I thought I had months… weeks… not minutes.

"You've lost your mind," I rasped. My voice sounded strange to my ears. High-pitched and strained.

Gregor nodded. "Quite possibly."

"You can't actually think I'd say yes to this?"

"I wasn't planning on giving you a choice in the matter."

What the fuck?

"That's not how these things work. You kind of need my permission," I snapped as panic set in.

"Let's just say that Judge Matthews isn't one to stand on a little formality like the bride's agreement."

I stared at Gregor. His shoulders were set, his jaw firm. Arrogant and confident. *Holy shit!* He really meant this.

"No! No! I won't do this."

Gregor leaned close, resting both hands against the wall on either side of my head. Nudging my hair aside with his nose, he whispered into my ear, "Do I have to remind you I will never take no as an answer from you?"

I gasped.

Gregor ran a knuckle down the front of my dress to circle the barest outline of my nipple through the delicate satin.

"If necessary, I will strip you out of this dress and spank that beautiful ass of yours red right in front of the Judge. I couldn't care less if you are married in satin or your bare skin," he threatened.

"You would, wouldn't you?" I asked him, my eyes wide with shock.

"In a heartbeat," he growled.

"This is insane," I breathed as I shook my hands in a lame effort to quiet the frenetic pace of my heart.

"Trust me, malyshka. I'm doing this to protect you."

God, when he purred those strong, protective words to me, I almost believe him.

In a daze, he took my hand and led me back to the Judge.

Someone handed me a pen; I didn't even know who. I tried to read the official-looking document. There were our names, neatly scrawled in permanent ink.

Samara Federova

Gregor Romanovich Ivanov

I turned to Gregor. In a last ditch effort to slow this speeding train, I asked, "What about my friends?"

"We will have a full ceremony later. Sign," he ordered.

With a sigh, I signed my name. My signature looked delicate and shaky next to the thick slant of Gregor's confident one.

As the pilot stood witness, the Judge began with the ceremony. I leaned heavily on Gregor as I stood by his side.

I wasn't even listening.

It was all just a dull white noise.

"Samara?"

"Samara?"

Everyone was looking at me expectantly.

I quaked.

I couldn't do this. This was insane.

"I can't do this. I don—"

Gregor grabbed me by the shoulders and turned my body to face him. His dark gray eyes pierced my own, trapping me with the intensity of his gaze. Without taking his eyes off me, he said, "She does."

He didn't even wait for the judge to finish the ceremony.

Gregor claimed my lips in a fierce kiss full of possession and promise. His tongue swept into my mouth, swirling and capturing my own. Taking by force what was now his right.

Setting me aside, he shook the judge's and pilot's hands.

We immediately disembarked to find Jim waiting inside the hangar. Gregor handed him our signed marriage certificate. "See that gets filed first thing and send out a press release. Make sure it is in all the morning papers. I don't want there to be any doubt. Samara Ivanova is now under my complete protection."

Samara Ivanova.

Samara Ivanova was Gregor Ivanov's wife and under his protection.

But who was going to protect me from Gregor?

CHAPTER 32

*S*amara

SEVERAL SCARY MEN in black fatigues holding even scarier automatic rifles greeted us as we disembarked. One man stepped forward with authority, and I recognized Mikhail Volkov, head of security for the Ivanov family. I wondered if Nadia still had a crush on him. I hoped not. I wouldn't want her to share my same fate.

Parked inside the private hangar was a small motorcade of black SUVs. Gregor quickly rushed me into the backseat of the closest one. Before I could even buckle my seatbelt, the car lurched forward.

So, this was my life now?

Surrounded by guards?

Under constant surveillance?

I sat in silence staring at the engagement ring on my finger as Gregor received a status report from Mikhail on the various additional security measures that had been taken since they attacked me.

We raced through the familiar streets of Washington D.C. and then Alexandria, Virginia. Through the window, I could see several tourists stop and stare. A few even took photographs, assuming some big politician or celebrity was behind the tinted glass. Soon we were in Fairfax. A sign announced we had just entered the grounds of George Washington's former Mount Vernon Estate. We passed several large homes before stopping before an impressive wrought-iron gate that was at least one story high and attached to a solid, two-story brick wall.

After the driver punched in a security code, the automatic gate slowly slid open. I cast a nervous glance at Gregor, but he was still talking with Mikhail who was in the passenger seat, though he'd turned around to face us in the back. He must have seen my expression, because without pausing or looking in my direction, he reached over and placed his warm hand over my chilled ones and gave them a reassuring squeeze. It was an oddly affectionate, couple-like thing to do, and I was even more oddly pleased and comforted by the gesture.

As the car rolled down a wide, tree-lined driveway, I tilted my head to look out through the front windshield. When the house came into view, I couldn't stifle my gasp.

It was gorgeous and massive.

A white clapboard, Palladian-style home with a grey slate roof, it must have been at least four stories high with large arched windows every few feet. Behind it, I could see the gentle rolling waters of the Potomac River. The house was set on a slight hill just above its banks.

As we pulled into the circular drive, beautiful evergreen wreaths with scarlet ribbons were visible on the front door and side windows. There were also tiny electric candles in each window. While American Christmas had passed several weeks ago, I realized with a start that Russian Christmas was tomorrow.

"Whose house is this?" I whispered to Gregor.

His lips stretched into a rare smile while his eyes shone with pride. "Mine."

"*This* is your house?"

"What? Did you think I lived in some villain's fortress underground?" he teased.

My nose wrinkled as my lips twisted into a grimace. "Sort of."

Gregor shook his head as he reached to unbuckle my seatbelt. "Let me show you inside."

As we exited the car, the double front doors swung open. A tall, rather severe looking woman with a tight bun in her hair and pinched lips greeted us. "Welcome home, Mr. Ivanov."

"Thank you, Matilda."

Too busy staring at the spiral staircase that dominated the entranceway, as it spun around an elaborate crystal chandelier and seemed to head straight up into the heavens, I didn't notice when Gregor moved to sweep me into his arms.

"What are you doing?"

"I'm carrying my bride over the threshold."

I blushed. I could almost believe this was a proper marriage.

Striding to the base of the staircase, Gregor tossed over his shoulder, "We don't wish to be disturbed, Matilda."

"Yes, sir."

I clung to his neck as he easily carried me up a dizzying three flights of stairs. The glossy white painted wood panels and dark wood of the staircase gave way to rich cranberry walls cluttered with English fox hunt and landscape paintings in burnt mahogany frames. An open loft space took up most of the upper floor, dotted by a pair of chocolate leather sofas and a few scattered upholstered barrel chairs .

Gregor headed straight for another pair of double doors. Turning, he pushed them open with his back. Like the rest of the house, the bedroom was decorated in the cozy, colonial style which favored bold colors set off by thick white crown molding and dark wood furniture.

As he swung me around, my mouth dropped. The high ceiling allowed for a wall of tall arched windows which looked out onto the Potomac. The sky was a fiery orange and pink as the sun set, sending shafts of shimmering light over the blue-grey surface of the river.

When he finally placed me on my feet again, the first thing that caught my eye was the enormous four-poster bed. Just as my still reeling mind was about to conjure up all the kinky things Gregor probably had planned for us, I saw it.

I could feel Gregor's eyes on me as I approached it. Grasping the cool railing at the bottom of the bed, I just stared. The bright emerald green of her dress shone brightly against the white wall backdrop. I stared at the firm masculine hand, Gregor's hand.

My painting.

Little Girl Saved.

The one someone had purchased in Boston.

The only painting of my own I had ever sold.

Hung in a place of honor over his bed.

Of course, I knew he had hung my other painting over his bed in Chicago, but I had just assumed that was to taunt me, to prove his control not only over me but my belongings and my artwork.

This… this was different.

I sold that painting close to two years ago.

"It was you. The buyer in Boston." It wasn't a question, more a statement of fact. I kept turned away from him, my face averted. He had an uncanny way of reading my every thought, and in this moment, I didn't want the intrusion. My emotions were too raw.

There was a slight shuffling of clothing and the scrape of a boot on the hardwood floor as he stepped behind me. My stomach fluttered, and shoulders tensed slightly, anticipating his powerful arms wrapping around me. He didn't disappoint. His arms caressed my sides as he flattened his palms against my stomach and eased me back to lean into him.

"Yes," he said simply.

No. No. This wasn't happening. He would not pull me in to believing this had some deeper meaning.

I broke free of his arms and paced across the room.

Gesturing frantically at the painting, I asked, "Why? Why do you have that?"

"Because I have all your paintings."

"What do you mean *all* my paintings?"

"The ones you stuffed into your closet at your parents' house. The ones you left behind in your art locker at school. The one from the gallery in Boston and the ones from Chicago."

My eyes widened as he ticked off all the different groupings of my paintings he had collected over the last three years.

I ran my hands through my hair as I paced again. "I don't understand."

Gregor crossed the room and tried to reach for my arm. I shrugged him off and backed away. He refused to relent, stalking me till I was trapped against the wall.

My eyes filled with tears as I slowly shook my head. "Please, don't do this. Don't do this to me. Don't make me think… make me believe…." I couldn't even force myself to form the words.

Gregor's hands enclosed my jaw as the pads of his thumbs

caressed my cheeks. "Force you to believe what, Samara? I want to hear you say it."

I tried to shake my head, but his grip on my face prevented me. I reached up to clasp my small hands around his wrists. "No. I won't."

"Would it be so terrible?" His gaze burned a dark molten steel as it searched mine. He leaned in. Instead of claiming my mouth as usual, his lips skimmed over mine, caressing. The tip of his tongue flicked out to taste my tears.

I could barely choke out the words. "Don't do this."

His body leaned into mine, pressing me harder against the wall. "Do what? Say that I love you? That I've been collecting your paintings to feel close to you?"

"Stop," I begged, but his lips muffled my protest.

I turned my head to the side. He then bit my earlobe as he rasped, "Admit it, Samara. You love me too."

I groaned. "I don't. I can't. I can't!"

"You can't what? Admit you've fallen in love with a monster?" His hips ground against mine, punctuating each word. "Admit you love the feel of my hands on you? Admit that despite three years apart you never let another man touch you?" He kissed the column of my neck. His hands wrapped around to my lower back and pulled me forward.

I inhaled the familiar spicy scent of his *Bleu de Chanel* cologne as my fingers clawed at his shirt, unsure of whether I was trying to pull him closer or push him away. "You can't love me. You barely know me. This is all just a game... a sick, twisted game."

"God dammit, malyshka," he growled.

Placing his hands on my ass, he lifted me against his body and swung around. Taking three long strides, he flung me back. I sunk into the deep, downy softness of the navy blue coverlet on his bed. His hard body quickly followed, pinning me down. Before I could protest, his mouth claimed mine, his tongue sweeping in to devour me. The inside of my lips pressed painfully against the sharp edge of my teeth as the five o'clock shadow along his jaw scraped my sensitive skin. Each bite of pain only enhanced my awareness of him.

Pushing his fingers into my tangled waves, he curled his hands into fists as he held me captive. "Listen very carefully, you beautiful wild creature. I love you. For the last time, this is not a fucking game to me." His gaze flicked down to the thin line of dried blood still visible on my neck from last night's attack. "If I had lost you last night, I wouldn't have gone on living. You are my salvation. I need to see the beauty in the world through your eyes or there is no point. Don't you understand? You are the only light in my unrelentingly dark world."

I couldn't breathe. The enormity of what he was saying overwhelmed me. To be loved with such a savage violence and with such completion felt as if I were submerged in dark stormy waters and yet could still see the shafts of sunlight glimmering on the waves, cutting through the gloom.

"YA lyublyu tebya," I cried, repeating in English, "I love you."

The moment I blurted out the words, I realized they were true. It made little sense. It was beyond crazy to even think it possible. The man terrified me. He could be overbearing and controlling and the shadowy nature of his business scared the hell out of me but he was also incredibly intelligent and cultured and thoughtful. He was also just so powerful and sexy. He made a girl just want to curl up in those big, tattooed arms of his and never let go.

"YA lyublyu tebya, malyshka."

Holding me around my waist, he flipped till I was straddling him. Reaching under my champagne silk skirts, his fingers slipped past my thong to caress my already wet pussy. My head rolled back as he pushed one long finger deep inside of me. With a moan, I ground my hips against the hard ridge of his cock.

"Unbuckle my belt," he ordered.

My fingers clawed at the leather strap as I rushed to push it through the metal buckle. Once it was free, I slipped open his trousers' button and lowered the zipper. Reaching inside, my hand wrapped around the hot, hard length of his shaft.

Gregor's hips rose. "Fuck, baby. Yes, squeeze me tighter. Jesus, you'll be the death of me."

Rising onto my knees, I tried to position the tip of his cock, but my panties kept getting in the way.

With a sexy as fuck growl, Gregor twisted his hand around the fabric and pulled, tearing them off me. I placed the large bulbous head at my slick entrance. Pressing down slightly till the heavy ridge slipped inside. I bit my lip, adjusting to the feel of him, waiting for him to take over and thrust.

Gregor stayed still. "Not this time. I want *you* to fuck *me*. You're in control."

I braced my palms against his flat stomach and held my breath as I slowly lowered myself onto his rigid cock, Only releasing my breath in a rush when he was fully seated inside of me. From this position, I could feel every thick inch. Closing my eyes, I gloried in the slight sting of pain as my body strained to accept him.

Tearing at his shirt, I lifted it high so my hands could explore his warm tattooed skin as I lifted onto my knees again then lowered my body onto him.

Again, I paused.

His cock felt good, but something was wrong… off.

Gregor reached up. The pad of his thumb caressed my lower lip. I sucked it into my mouth, swirling my tongue around the tip, tasting the salty tang of his skin. "What's the matter, baby girl?"

Releasing his thumb, I grasped his hand and lowered it till he was cupping my breast. He gently rolled my erect nipple between his fingers through the fabric of my dress.

My cheeks flamed. "Gregor, I need... I... I need..." I stammered to a halt.

His lips twisted into a knowing grin. "Say it."

"Don't make me."

He bounced his hips up once, and a sharp moan escaped my lips. "You know the rules. I won't do it unless you say it."

"Oh God. Fine! This is too... gentle. I need you to fuck me, Gregor. Make it hurt!" I blurted out in a rush.

His large hands wrapped around my hips. "Thought you'd never ask."

Lifting me high, he tossed me to the side of him. As I was about to flip onto my back, he commanded, "No. Stay on your knees."

He shifted off the bed and stood at the edge. Grasping my hips again, he pulled me toward him. Next thing I heard was the rending of fabric as he tore the thin silk of my dress right up the back. The useless dress pooled beneath me. The next sound had me biting my lip and shifting my hips in dark anticipation. It was the sound of leather sliding against fabric.

He had taken off his belt.

My entire body jerked when he snapped the leather ends together, sending a deafening crack resounding across the bedroom.

His hand twisted in my hair, wrenching my head back. "Have you been a bad girl?"

"Oh God, yes! Yes. I've been very bad," I groaned as memories of him saying just that when he first found me in Chicago and my illicit kinky reaction to the taunt came crashing over me.

The first strike of leather had me crying out as I pitched forward. He yanked me back by my hair.

Yes! This is what I wanted… what I needed from him.

Pleasurable pain.

Him in control.

Using me.

Owning me.

His cock thrust in deep at the same time he struck my ass a second time with his belt. As he pounded into my body, he tossed the belt aside and used the palm of his hand, making my skin sting and burn with every touch. My body rocked back and forth with the power of his thrusts. Reaching between my legs, I swirled the pad of my finger over my clit as the pressure of my release built and built like waves crashing over me. As my climax peaked, I fell forward, unable to stay on my knees. His hands pressed into my lower back as he continued to thrust several more times before filling me with his hot seed.

Gregor collapsed next to me. His breathing harsh and heavy, he pulled me into his arms, my head resting against his chest. HE stroked my hair as he growled against my forehead, "Say it."

I smiled. I knew what he wanted to hear. "I love you… husband."

CHAPTER 33

Samara

IT WAS late into the evening when we finally ventured downstairs looking for something to eat. I was dressed in Gregor's rumpled light blue dress shirt and he in his even more wrinkled grey trousers.

I cried out in delight when I saw the twinkling white lights and bright red star of the spruce tree he had set up in the center of his spacious living room.

"You have a yolka tree?"

"Of course, every year."

Circling around its evergreen branches, I inhaled the sweet scent of the forest. The living room looked more like a wood-paneled library with its inlaid bookcases filled with maroon and gold leather volumes and its black marble fireplace. Like the bedroom several stories above, the high ceilings allowed for sweeping arched windows. Since it was so late, the darkness outside only provided a backdrop for the twinkling tree lights to be reflected on the panes of glass.

Gregor padded barefoot into the room and joined me on the Persian rug where I was sitting cross-legged between the unlit fire and the tree. He handed me a heavy, earthenware bowl filled with sweet smelling porridge. As I looked down, I could see golden drizzles of honey and plump pieces of dried fruit and nuts.

"What's this?"

"It's sočivo."

I sounded out the Russian word. "Soh-chiva?"

He nodded.

I inspected the dish. "You didn't sneak any vegetable in here, did you?"

His eyebrows raised. "No. I promise. Your mother never made sočivo for Christmas Eve? It's tradition."

I shook my head. "My parents were usually out at some party on Christmas Eve, and my mother never bothered herself about cooking or honoring any traditions. I usually just heated a pizza and watched holiday movies."

It's why my Russian was barely adequate, and I didn't know any real traditions from the mother country. My parents never really behaved as if we were a genuine family. Especially after their actions several years ago and their failure to even bother looking for me, I doubted they even loved me.

"By yourself?"

I shrugged. "It's fine."

Holidays were usually pretty lonely for me. Gregor and Nadia's family usually returned to St. Petersburg for two weeks, and Yelena spent the time off from school with her mother's side of the family, grateful to get away from her abusive father, so they typically left me alone. These last few years, most of the time, Yelena and I were too busy moving from city to city to remember to celebrate.

"No. It's not. Give me that."

I hugged the bowl close to my middle. "Why? No! I haven't even tried it yet."

"You will, but we are going to do this the right way."

Gregor stood and held out his hands to me. After raising me to my feet, he lifted me into his arms.

"Where are we going?" I laughed.

"To the bedroom."

As much as I thrilled at another round of kinky sex with Gregor, the demands of my stomach objected. "But I'm starving."

Carrying me up the three flights of stairs again, he made a sharp left just before the bedroom doors. We were inside a mostly empty large dressing room. They had emptied all the designer bags from the plane, and the contents now hung on padded hangers nearby.

Setting me down gently, he nodded toward the ivory dress with the black lace trimming.

"Get dressed. Meet me downstairs."

"Seriously?"

"Yes, seriously," he tossed over his shoulder.

About twenty minutes later, I heard Christmas carols as I reached the bottom of the stairs. Crossing the main entryway into the living room, I smelled the pleasant acrid scent of a wood burning fire before seeing the glow of the orange and yellow flames. As I crossed to it, Gregor emerged from the kitchen, once more carrying a tray with the two bowls of traditional porridge and two clear glass mugs filled with a steaming purple liquid I knew to be сбитень, a warm drink with honey, preserves and spices. This time he was wearing a striking black suit with a crimson silk tie.

Setting the tray down, he handed me a mug. I inhaled the richly sweet cinnamon scent.

"Merry Christmas, Mrs. Ivanova," he toasted as he clinked my glass and gave me a wink.

"Merry Christmas, Mr. Ivanov."

After taking a sip, he set the mug down and reached into his suit pocket. Clasping my right hand inside his own, he slipped a bright silver wedding band onto my finger, which fit snugly against my engagement ring. Just then, Bing Crosby's *I'll Be Home For Christmas* began to play.

Gregor took me into his arms and danced me around the yolka tree as it softly snowed outside.

Everything felt warm and cozy and safe. For the first time in my life, I felt loved. Perhaps I could allow myself to believe this was all real and that maybe, just maybe, as crazy and outlandish as it sounded, I had found a home with Gregor.

Too bad wishes on Christmas Eve were like those pretty snowflakes… fragile and fleeting.

CHAPTER 34

Samara

GREGOR KISSED ME AWAKE.

I groaned and turned onto my stomach, burying my head under the pillow.

He lifted the pillow. "Wake up, malyshka, and give your husband a proper kiss goodbye."

Peeking out from the pillow, I opened one eye. "Where are you going?"

"I have some business to attend to."

Business.

My stomach twisted.

Already, the bright light of morning was shining its awful beams onto the realities of our life together. The truth I desperately tried to suspend forever last night when I told him I loved him.

The reality of his dangerous criminal life. One he would probably never really share the details of with me. I would always be the pretty wife waiting for him at home while he attended to business.

Mrs. Gregor Ivanova, mafia wife.

It was strange to think when I first learned of the arranged marriage, my concern was that my whole identity would be swallowed up by bigger-than-life, powerful Gregor and his lifestyle. Now my worry was that I'd be kept too much away from his lifestyle. I didn't want to be a part of it as much as I didn't want to be kept in the dark. He was treating me like a child. Protecting me from the ugly details. He said I was in danger, and he was protecting me, and the attack the other night was proof, but he refused to say more.

Why couldn't love just exist in a vacuum?

Why did reality always have to crash the party?

He was dressed as always in an impeccably tailored suit with a probably impossibly expensive watch strapped to his wrist. If it weren't for the scary tattoos, you'd think he was waltzing into a boardroom on Wall Street later today.

"I have to go, and you have your surprise waiting for you outside."

"You know I hate surprises."

Gregor chuckled. "No one really hates surprises. They just hate bad surprises. Mine are good."

I lifted myself up onto my elbows and raised an eyebrow at him,. my sardonic look reminding him of his idea of a *good surprise* in our not so recent past.

Gregor slapped me on the ass. Reading my thoughts as always, he taunted unapologetically, "Think what you want, but I definitely enjoyed those surprises."

I threw my pillow at him, which he easily dodged.

"So, I guess you don't want to visit with Nadia today, after all."

I sprung out of bed. "Nadia! I can see Nadia today?"

"Yes, if you promise to be a good girl."

I wrapped my arms around his neck and gave him a hug and a kiss on the cheek before racing to find something to wear in my dressing room. The rest of our luggage had arrived, and Matilda must have unpacked it early this morning. I would have to remember to thank her.

Gregor called out another goodbye, which I barely answered as I struggled to pull on a pair of jeans while also slipping my feet into patent leather flats.

Less than ten minutes later, I was climbing into the backseat of a sleek black SUV and being spirited away.

* * *

"Oh my God, you're here!" shrieked Nadia as she launched herself into my arms the second I opened the little shop door.

I hugged her close before taking a step back. Eyeing her up and down, I shook my head and laughed. She hadn't changed a bit. Still wearing her strawberry blonde hair in a messy bun and baby doll dresses with Doc Martens. "You know Yelena is going to die when she sees that you haven't given up those boots yet."

Nadia twisted her foot, showing off her signature pink Doc Martens with silver laces. "She will when she learns that this is actually my fourth pair. You should see the purple ones with the black stars!"

"Nadia, you haven't changed a bit! I've missed you so much!" I gave her another hug.

Snatching up both my hands she pulled me further into her cute shop but stopped. Her mouth opened in shock. She was staring at my wedding rings. Her blue eyes filled with tears. "So it's true. I'm so sorry, Samara. I know you didn't want this."

"It's okay. Really. Things have… changed."

"You and my brother?"

I nodded. How could I put into words for her what I was still struggling to understand myself? My love for him was still too new to be completely trusted.

"So, we're officially sisters?" she asked, her voice raising an octave in her excitement.

I nodded again.

She shrieked a second time and gave me another hug.

"My beast of a brother wouldn't tell me any details, just that you were married and that I would see you soon. Was it a nice wedding? Was Yelena there? Where is Yelena?"

I held up my arms in mock surrender. "I promise I will tell all, but first I need coffee. I only just woke up."

Nadia winked. "Got you covered. I grabbed McDonald's on my way to open the store. It's in the back."

"You're an angel." As we headed to the back area, I stopped her. "So, this is your store?"

Nadia beamed with pride. "Yep! It's a little small, but I love it. Against both of my brothers' wishes, I live in a cute little apartment above."

The shop was adorably cozy. There were little table displays with vintage typewriters and all sorts of earrings, necklaces and bracelets made out of the keys. There were scarves, figurines and cute stuffed animals. It was the perfect, unique gift shop. I picked up one of the necklaces. It said *true love* in old typewriter keys. "Did you make these?"

Nadia nodded. Back in high school, she was forever making jewelry out of beads and string. It was nice to see she had turned her favorite hobby into a business.

"After you and Yelena left, I spent more and more time perfecting my craft. I got my associate's degree in business management while taking different classes on jewelry making." She waved her arms about. "And here we are! My own little corner of the world. My family owns the building, so that helps, but I still pay rent and the shop is actually successful."

"It's all so wonderful, Nadia! I'm so proud of you."

Picking up my hands again, she led me to the back. "You know. The shop next door is available. I think it would make a perfect art gallery. Oh! We could also display some of your work in here! Maybe even break down that wall and have them connect!" Nadia talked a constant stream as she sat me on a stool to the side of her wooden workbench. She handed me one of the McCafe mochas as she unpacked two hash browns and two Egg McMuffins.

As I unwrapped the still warm breakfast sandwich and took a bite, I settled back and thought about what she was saying. It sounded nice—really nice. Even before Yelena and I ran, what I wanted most in the world was a place where I could paint and feel as if I were a part of something, part of a family. And now the idea that I could have a gallery of my own attached to one of my best friend's shops was almost too good to be true. All we needed was for Yelena to return and everything would actually start to feel back to normal.

Nadia ripped the top off a hash brown and, before popping it into her mouth, asked. "Do you know where Yelena is?"

I shook my head. "Have you heard from her?"

"No. I've been answering all calls on my cell phone just in case. I can't tell you how many robocalls in Chinese I've gotten."

"Best case scenario, she's in Montreal and will find a way to reach out soon. Worst, and sorry about this, she's with your brother Damien."

Nadia rolled her eyes. "Damien is a pain in the ass, but he won't actually hurt Yelena."

I nodded as I also ripped the crispy, greasy top off my hash brown and then tossed the rest aside. "It's the only thing that has kept me sane throughout this whole fucked up situation."

"I mean. I love my brothers. And really they act like big, scary grizzly bears, but deep down they are just teddy bears... mean-looking, tattooed teddy bears... but still teddy bears. Don't get me wrong. I'm still very angry at them for the whole marriage mess and what's going on with Yelena, but their intentions are good, if not their methods."

I blushed. I'd finally realized just that about Gregor.

"Yes. Your brother Gregor certainly growls and shouts an awful lot, but I have to admit, he does have his sweet side."

Nadia reached up and grabbed a section of hair and started to twirl it. Ever since she was little, that was always a sign she was nervous or lying about something.

"Okay, out with it. What do you know?"

Nadia played with the foam holder around her mocha. "I'm feeling a little guilty because I'm not supposed to know what I know, but I know *a lot.*"

I leaned in closer. "Spill it."

"I overheard Mikhail talking to Gregor a few nights ago about setting up some wiretaps and surveillance on your father and a man named Egor Novikoff."

"Egor Novikoff? I know him. He's one of father's old friends. Why was Gregor spying on him?"

Nadia twirled her hair faster. I reached up and grabbed her hand to stop it.

She sighed. "I'm not certain, but it sounded like your father might have also arranged a marriage between you and Egor."

"Between me and Egor? That's not possible. The man is a fucking hundred years old!"

"I know! Mikhail and Gregor were pretty angry about it. They were both cursing up a storm, and you know how much Gregor hates cursing."

I shifted in my seat, practically feeling the sting of his belt from the multiple times I'd cursed in front of him. "Yes. I'm well aware."

Nadia shrugged. "Gregor's always been a bit sensitive about being seen as only a Russian thug, so I think it's why he doesn't like to curse."

I nodded. That made sense. The man went out of his way to smash any stereotypes someone might have about a man in his line of *business*. Pushing aside my half eaten McMuffin, I rested my arms on the table and told Nadia about the knife attack two nights ago.

She covered her mouth in shock. "Oh my God, Samara! You could have been killed or worse!"

Brushing my hair aside, I showed her the minor scratch. "I know it looks small, but it stung at the time and definitely scared the crap out of me."

Nadia's eyes went wide. "Did Gregor just completely flip out?"

I lifted my right hand and wiggled my fingers, showing off my wedding rings. "What do you think?"

Nadia grimaced. "You are happy though, right?"

I thought about it for a minute. "I think it's too soon to say if I'm truly happy. I will say that I'm not unhappy, and I'm starting to think about the future, which isn't something I've allowed myself to do in a very long time."

"Do you think... maybe given time... you could learn to love Gregor? I know he can be terribly controlling about getting his way, but he really can be sweet, and I know I said you shouldn't marry him before but I was being kind of hard on him... and...."

I leapt up and wrapped my arms around Nadia's shoulders. "I don't need time to know I already love him."

Nadia gave me a kiss on the cheek. "I'm so happy for you

both, and once Gregor meets with your father today, everything should be all cleared up."

"Wait, what?"

"I thought you knew? Gregor is confronting your father at this moment about the whole mess."

"Your brother! He is driving me crazy! Of course, why wouldn't he tell me he's meeting with my father. He's only my father. I guess it's none of my business!" I ranted.

True, I hadn't even bothered to ask about my parents or even discuss visiting them with Gregor. There wasn't much love lost between us before they basically sold me to him, but still, he should have told me.

Giving her another quick hug, I headed to the door, tossing over my shoulder, "I have to go! I'll come by again tomorrow!"

Nadia cried out, "Wait, Samara! This isn't a good idea!"

Ignoring her, I pulled open the glass shop door and headed straight for the black SUV, hopping in before the driver opened the door for me. The moment he was behind the wheel I gave him my parent's address. Then sat back and went over in my head what I was going to say to Gregor—and my father—when I arrived.

If this marriage had any chance of surviving, I would need to show Gregor that his high-handed handling of every aspect of my life had to change.

It was time Gregor knew what it felt like to be chased and ran to ground.

CHAPTER 35

Gregor

"GREGOR ROMANOVICH, it is good to see you, my friend," Boris said. He gave me a quick embrace and gestured to a couple of chairs in his study.

I remained standing.

Despite Boris' warm greeting, he was anxious. There was a tightness around his mouth, and his eyes were open too wide.

Shrugging, Boris reached for a cigar, then turned and offered me one.

I declined, unbuttoning my suit jacket and leaning against his desk. Watching.

Boris sat before the dying embers of a fire and flicked open a silver lighter. Although he pretended to be absorbed in the task, his beady gaze traveled to me repeatedly. By the time the cigar was lit, he had burnt the end, adding an acrid sting to the sweet smoke that briefly enveloped his head.

Taking a long puff, he brushed some ash off his pant leg before saying, "I was happy to learn you found my daughter. We can now conclude our business. We both have got what we wanted, no?"

"And Novikoff?"

Boris lowered his cigar. "Novikoff? What does my old friend have to do with this?"

"Boris, are you going to try to tell me you didn't make a second deal for your daughter's hand in marriage to Egor Novikoff?"

He dropped the cigar onto the rather expensive Persian rug. Without caring, Boris rose and crushed it out with his shoe, grinding the hot ash into the fibers as he raised placating hands.

"Please, Gregor. Please, you must believe me. I would never betray you or your father's memory that way."

My brow furrowed. I was very good at reading people. I needed to be in this line of business. Complete trust was impossible but knowing when I could trust someone just enough not to kill me was important. I could almost believe he was telling the truth. Boris was not that good of a liar. Plus, it might explain why none of my surveillance picked up the two old bastards plotting to kidnap Samara or even talking about her.

I kept my voice low and controlled. "Someone has given Egor Novikoff the dangerously misguided impression that Samara belongs to him. As I am sure you can understand, this greatly angers me. *Bad things happen when I'm angry.*"

Boris wiped his brow with the sleeve of his suit. "Gregor, I swear on my dear mother's grave, I know nothing about... Wait. No, no, no..."

I straightened. "What?"

"It's not possible. It would be too great a betrayal."

"Start talking, Boris."

All my attention was on him. I needed to resolve this issue, and quickly. I wouldn't stand for my wife to be in danger for another moment.

Just as he opened his mouth, he looked over my shoulder. "What are you doing?"

I turned my head… then everything went black.

CHAPTER 36

Gregor

BLOOD-CURDLING SCREAMS.

Each one piercing my brain like an ax.

All I wanted to do was sink back into the deep, quiet darkness, but a primal, survival instinct had me forcing myself onto my knees. Lifting my hand to brace myself against the corner of the desk and rise further, I realized I was clutching a .38 Special revolver.

What the hell is going on?

"He killed your father! Oh God, the monster killed your father!"

Samara's answering cry propelled me to my feet.

Tossing the gun on the desk, I rubbed my eyes to clear my blurry vision. When I finally looked up, I followed Samara's horrified gaze. My shirt was soaked in blood.

On the floor at my feet lay her father. His eyes were open

and his mouth hung open at a grotesque angle. There were at least three bullet wounds to the chest and one to the head.

Fuck.

"Samara, I...."

Alena Federova raised her arm and pointed an accusatory finger at me. "You killed my husband. I saw you."

"Malyshka, you know I didn't do this."

"Of course he did! He's a criminal. He's probably murdered hundreds of men in cold-blood," sneered her mother.

Samara stood rigid in the doorway, her hand over her mouth and her arm wrapped around her stomach. She stared at her dead father with horrified eyes.

Needing to protect her, I took several steps toward her but froze when her head snapped up to train terrified eyes on me.

Fuck. This couldn't be happening. Not now. Not when I finally convinced her to truly be mine. I couldn't lose her this way. I tried to keep my voice calm and steady. "Samara, listen to me."

"Don't listen to him! He's the monster who chased you away from your home and your family for *years*. He took advantage of your poor father. Forced him into that despicable arrangement. It broke your father's heart to do it. We both loved you so much," cried Alena as she brushed away non-existent tears.

This finally broke through Samara's shock. Her head slowly turned toward her mother. Her brow furrowed. Her words came out barely above a whisper. "That's not true."

Her mother's voice faltered as she smoothed back her hair. "Of course it is! Your father and I didn't want you to marry this... this thug! He threatened to kill us if we didn't agree to the arrangement."

I held my breath as I waited for Samara's reply. It was

more than I deserved if she agreed with her mother. I *was* the monster who had been chasing her for years. I did force her into all of this against her will. And no amount of tailored suits or art acquisitions would erase the fact that at my core, I was nothing more than a criminal, gun-running thug.

She could do way better.

She deserved way better.

Unfortunately, none of this changed the fact that I would fight to the death to keep her by my side. She was mine and not just because of some deal with her father or because of the money. She was mine because I loved her. Against the odds and the sins of our family's pasts, I loved her.

And I had to hold on to the belief she loved me, too. I wasn't fooling myself. I knew she loved me beyond her better judgement. I knew she still had doubts about the truth of her feelings and whether I was the right future for her.

We could work through all of that… if given the chance.

Samara shook her head. "I don't believe you. I remember that night. The night of Nadia's party. You and father were insisting I marry him. Telling me I had no choice. You're lying."

Alena dove for the gun on the desk and swung her arm between Samara and me.

I lunged across the room, blocking Samara's body with my own.

Samara's hands fisted into the fabric of my shirt. "Mother, what are you doing? Put the gun down!"

My gaze narrowed. "It was you, wasn't it?"

Her mouth twisted, but she didn't say a word.

I continued. "That's why Boris had no idea about Egor. You're the one who arranged the second marriage deal."

Samara looked around my upper arm. "Mother, how could you!"

Alena rolled her eyes. "I'll give you five million reasons.

Your useless father pissed away the money Gregor gave us. I did what I had to do to survive."

"Well, it's over. Samara's mine, and I'm going to make sure you never lay eyes on her again."

"You men are all the same. You think you're so smart. Well, I got news for you—it's not over."

"There's a ring on Samara's hand and a dead body on the floor that says otherwise," I fired back.

Alena threw her head back and cackled. "You think Egor still wants to marry Samara? She's damaged goods now. He's moved on."

"What do you mean?"

Alena shrugged. "My deal with Egor wasn't about marrying Samara. It was about selling her to the highest bidder in the Middle East. You ruined that when it became obvious you were fucking her. Now he'll have to settle for selling her to some brothel I suppose. She can work off her fee."

My stomach twisted. I had seen and done some messed up things in my life, but nothing came close to hearing Samara's mother casually talk about selling her daughter into the sex trade.

At Samara's shocked gasp, I reached my left arm back and pulled her in closer.

I took a deep breath. Now I was on familiar ground. At its core, this was about business, and I now had leverage over Alena. She had screwed over a powerful and dangerous family. She would now need my help.

This wouldn't be the first time I had to negotiate a deal staring down the barrel of a gun, but this was the most dangerous because of Samara. I needed her safe. Nothing else mattered to me.

"So, it looks like you and I need to make a deal. You need to repay Egor for his investment. I'm guessing you don't have the funds… but I do. Let Samara leave, and you I will come to our own arrangement."

Her gold bangles rattled as she raised the gun higher. "I've already made my deal. Fortunately for me, Egor blames you. I wouldn't be surprised if he took your little bride from you before the honeymoon is over."

"You know that happens over my dead body."

"Suit yourself."

Alena pulled the trigger.

CHAPTER 37

*S*amara

I SCREAMED as I clung to Gregor but there was no powerful discharge, just a hollow metallic click.

Misfire.

The gun must not have been fully loaded.

I doubt even a second had passed. My mind caught up quickly.

Four bullets at my father.

One misfire.

Six chamber revolver.

The laws of probability theory

First rule of Russian roulette: The sixth shot *always* fires.

My mother raised her arm again.

Shaking off his grasp on my hip, I threw myself in front of Gregor.

"No!" I screamed.

"Samara!" Gregor grabbed me by the shoulders and

swung me violently around, shielding me just as the gun discharged. His body pitched forward but absorbed the blast. He had taken a bullet for me.

"Oh, my God!"

I clung to him as he stumbled against the desk. My mother ran out of the room, but I didn't care. My thoughts were only of Gregor.

Fresh crimson blood blossomed just below his right shoulder. I pressed my hand against the wound trying to stop the blood but it kept coming so fast. Oozing over my fingers in thick, sticky streams. My gaze distorted as my eyes filled with tears.

"Gregor, please you can't die. Please, don't die!"

His left arm wrapped around my shoulders as he grasped my hair and leaned in to kiss the top of my head. "I guess I have my answer," he rasped. "Those pretty green eyes of yours would cry for me if I died."

I sobbed as I tried to press his wound harder. "I... I... have to get to a phone. You need an ambulance."

"No ambulance. No cops," came an assertive voice from the doorway.

Startled, I whirled around as Mikhail stormed into the room, followed by several of Gregor's men.

They swarmed about us. One tried to pull me free, but I would not be moved.

"Are you crazy? He's been shot! We have to get him to a hospital now!"

Mikhail wrapped his hands around my upper arms and physically pulled me away from Gregor. He then nodded to the men. One man pulled off his shirt and held it against the wound as another supported Gregor under his good arm. "Let's get him to the car. We have to move fast."

"I'm going with you."

Mikhail shook his head, "I don't think—"

"I'm not leaving him," I asserted.

My doubts were gone. This was Gregor's life... and now it was my life, too. It was messy and bloody and violent but between us there was still beauty and light and love. I was done running. I had found where I belong and with who, and now it was time to fight for us.

Mikhail looked at Gregor who managed a slight smile despite his pain. "You heard my wife."

We bustled outside and into one yet another of Gregor's intimidating black SUVs. Once they had settled Gregor slightly prone on the backseat, I joined him, cradling his upper body as I pressed the makeshift bandage to his wound.

Transparent Earth Red. The color of blood.
Cadmium Red Deep. The color of blood.
Perylene. The color of blood.
Italian Pompeii Red. The color of blood.

I rocked back and forth. One of my tears fell on his cheek. I went to wipe it away and left a trail of blood on his face, not realizing my hands and clothes were soaked. Soaked with his blood.

"Please, don't die, Gregor. I love you. Please!"

His voice was low but still strong. "It will take more than a bullet to take me away from you, malyshka."

Mikhail looked over his shoulder from the front passenger seat. He had been on the phone giving terse instructions to someone. "We're almost there."

"What hospital?"

"I told you, Samara. No hospitals. That's not how we do things."

"Who's going to take care of Gregor?"

"I am."

"You?"

Gregor reached his left arm across his chest to place his hand over mine. "Mikhail is a man of many hidden talents.

Don't worry, baby. It's going to be… it's going to be…" His eyes closed, and his head lolled to the side.

"Gregor? Gregor?"

Mikhail glanced back. "He's lost too much blood. We don't have much more time."

The security gate to Gregor's home was already open and ready as the SUV careened past. Before the vehicle had stopped, Matilda was rushing down the front stairs. "I have everything ready. Bring him through the hallway into the kitchen."

They forced me to release Gregor and let his men carry his body into the home. Matilda wrapped her arm around my shoulders and led me inside. "You should go upstairs and change while the men work."

I shook my head. "I'm not leaving his side."

When we got to the kitchen, they lay Gregor out on a blue tarp covering the kitchen table. The shades from the hanging lamps had been removed so the bare bulbs could cast more light. Off to the side was a sinister-looking tray of medical instruments.

Mikhail stripped off his jacket and ran to the sink to wash his hands.

I rushed to the end of the table to stroke Gregor's hair and cheek. "I'm here. I'm here."

He didn't respond. His usually tan and robust skin had a pale, purplish pallor.

One of his men rolled up his sleeves and inserted a needle attached to a long tube, which another put in Gregor's arm.

Mikhail gave me a reassuring wink. "Battlefield blood transfusion. As good as any hospital."

Another man tore away Gregor's shirt. I cried out at the jagged exit wound.

Mikhail pulled one of the standing lamps positioned

around the table closer and inspected the wound. "Fucking bitch used a RIP."

"RIP?"

He shook his head. "Radically Invasive Projectile. It's a hollow bullet designed to break into eight fragments to cause the maximum amount of damage."

"Oh God." My stomach twisted. I had to swallow down the bile in my throat.

Mikhail probed the wound. Gregor groaned, and his body shifted.

"The good news is the bullet went clear through his shoulder. I can see only two fragments but they must be dug out."

Gregor regained consciousness the moment Mikhail began. Waking with a curse, he complained, "Jesus Christ, what are you using a spoon?"

"Shut up and let me work," groused Mikhail in return.

It took five men to hold Gregor down, but eventually Mikhail got both jagged pieces. He placed several stitches over the exit wound, and then Gregor was carefully turned so he could stitch up the entrance wound.

One of his men walked into the kitchen carrying a bag with the logo of a local veterinarian. "Got the antibiotics and bandages."

I cast an annoyed look at Mikhail, who only shrugged, "It's how we do things around here."

"What about… what about my parents? Don't we need to call the police?"

Gregor and Mikhail exchanged a look.

"That is being taken care of."

Gregor reached up to run the back of his knuckles down my cheek. "The less you know, the better, *malyshka*. You're just going to have to trust me on this."

Clasping his hand, I held his open palm against my cheek. "I trust you."

And I meant it. We may not have started our relationship the normal way, but normal was overrated. Gregor had more than proven to me that he did truly love me. He had more than earned my trust.

As Gregor liked to say, our choices had consequences. My parents chose greed over love, and now my father had paid the ultimate price. I guessed my mother would, too. I tried to feel sorrow but only felt the pang of regret of what could have been if they only returned half the love I tried to give them.

"So, Doc, will I live?" Gregor joked.

"You'll live. You're too stubborn to die."

With help, Gregor slowly rose off the table. Brushing aside any further help, he made his way up the three flights of stairs to our bedroom with me by his side.

"We need to get you out of those pants."

Gregor smiled. "Thought you'd never ask."

The hard outline of his cock pressed against his upper thigh. "Seriously? You literally have a bullet wound in your shoulder!"

"Nothing wrong with my cock," he said with a wink as he pulled me in for a kiss.

"You really are impossibly stubborn, you know that?"

Using his good arm, he wrapped his arm around my waist. "It's a good thing for you I am so stubborn. Only a stubborn man would pursue the same female for three years."

Slowly lowering to my knees, I flicked open the first button of his jeans.

Gregor inhaled. His dark eyes on me.

I flicked another button than another till his erect shaft sprang free. Wrapping my hand around the hot length, I flicked the head with the tip of my tongue.

"I think we both need to get out of these bloody clothes and into a hot shower," he said gruffly.

Taking in his powerful chest, the tattoos showing more brightly against the white of the gauze, I warned, "You'll ruin your bandages."

Driving his fingers into my hair, he pulled me to my feet. "Fuck my bandages!"

My mouth opened in feigned shock. "Language, *husband*!"

"Guess, you'll just have to give me a tongue lashing, *wife*."

CHAPTER 38

Samara

ONE WEEK LATER.

I TOOK A DEEP BREATH. This would not be easy. I'd thought about it long and hard over the past week, and I really saw no way around it.

I had to divorce Gregor.

The manner of my father's death had been skillfully covered up. It was listed as a home robbery gone wrong. The news reported that my mother had left the United States to grieve with family. From what I understood, she was shipped back to Russia and had not left willingly.

Unfortunately, the whole thing reeked of a cover-up scandal. There were salacious rumors running rampant.

The Federov name and prestigious reputation were now irreparably tainted.

The very reason why Gregor had married me in the first place was gone.

I gave Matilda a stiff smile as she dropped off a lunch tray set for two on the small table by the window inside my painter's studio. Of course, his injury had not slowed him up one bit over the last week. In addition to his own affairs, and helping cover up my family's scandal, he had overseen turning a side room in his house into another studio for me. When he was home, he joined me each day for lunch. Outside of our time in the bedroom, it really was my favorite time with him.

"I like your use of orange."

I turned my head as Gregor walked into the room. He came up behind and wrapped his left arm around my waist as we both studied my current work. "It's very Toulouse-Lautrec of you."

I loved when he talked Impressionist art with me. It was so sexy.

Screwing up my nerve, I set my paintbrush aside. "Gregor, we need to talk."

He stroked my cheek. "What is it, malyshka?"

"I think we should get a divorce," I blurted out.

His eyes narrowed. "Excuse me? What did you just say to me?"

In a rush, I told him all the reasons we should divorce. I tried to reassure him that I would stay his girlfriend as long as he would allow, but that he shouldn't be forced to link his name with mine.

With what could only be described as a growl, Gregor grabbed my arm and pulled me forward just as he bent down. Tossing me over his good shoulder, he proceeded to carry me out of the studio.

"Gregor! What are you doing? Stop! Put me down! You'll hurt your shoulder!"

His only answer was to swat me on the ass. "Apparently, *my wife* needs to be reminded that she's mine to have and to hold until death do us part."

Sometime later, as I was curled up in his arms, he said, "In case you were wondering, the answer is no. There will be no divorce. Not now. Not ever."

I sighed dramatically. Tracing one of his tattoos with my finger, I couldn't resist teasing him. "I should have gone with my first plan and run off and just mailed you the papers."

He shook his head. "That wouldn't have worked."

"Why not?"

"Because you beautiful creature, I would have chased you to the ends of this earth. You're mine, malyshka. Now say it," he demanded savagely.

I reached down and grasped his already hardening cock. "I'm yours, Gregor. All yours."

EPILOGUE

Yelena

Picking up my phone, I listened to Samara's voicemails.

They all had essentially the same message.

Run!

I knew what that meant. We would scramble for our safe house in Montreal. Until then, we would have no choice but to go off the radar. Radio silence. No phones unless absolutely necessary. Taking a deep breath, I reminded myself to focus.

I needed to get the hell out of town. We would figure out our next move when we were safely in Montreal. It was a shame. Like Samara, I was starting to like Chicago and the idea that maybe we could stop running.

Heading to my desk, I withdrew every scrap of paper. All important documents I kept in a lockbox in a bank in Los Angeles, but you never knew what the authorities or anyone else for that matter could glean from a few receipts or scraps of paper.

Carrying the bundle to the sink, I opened my junk drawer and searched for matches. Lighting one, I held it to the corner of several papers till it started to brown and curl. Eventually, it caught flame. I lit another match and repeated the gesture. As it started to smoke, the fire alarm went off. Grabbing a broom, I smashed it with the handle till it went silent.

I snatched a bucket from under the sink and went into the bathroom, where I wrenched the top drawer out and dumped its contents into the bucket. I did the same for the second and third, watching all my expensive Mac and Chanel makeup pile up. It broke my heart, but it was bulky, and I needed to travel light. I then took my make-up, hairbrushes, toothbrush, and curlers into the kitchen.

I opened the dishwasher door and pulled out the dish racks, then dumped all my beloved beauty products into the bottom. Opening a bottle of bleach, I poured it over the pile. Closing the door, I started the dishwasher. I stripped the bed of its sheets and put them in the washer. *That should take care of any DNA. You can never be too careful.*

It would be better to just burn the whole condo, but that wasn't really an option.

Wrenching open the door to my closet, I headed to the secret panel behind a shoe shelf. I pulled free the black backpack—my go bag.

Checking its contents, I opened up a few shoe boxes which contained some hidden cash and jewels and shoved them into the bag. I also made sure the gun Samara and I picked up in Mexico, and my pink pearl-handled stiletto knife, were there as well. On second thought, I snatched up the knife and put it in the back pocket of my jeans so I could access it quickly.

Next, I went into the living room and ran my arm along the mantel, tossing my favorite lucky charm Happy Meal toys into my bag. Although, admittedly, the little plastic toys had yet to bring me much luck. Taking one last look around, I picked up my car keys and pulled open the door.

And screamed in terror.

TRADITIONAL RUSSIAN RECIPES

Here are the recipes for some of the delicious foods mentioned in Savage Vow.

Сочиво (Sochivo) Christmas Porridge

2 Cups Whole Wheat Grains
(Sub. barley, rice or oats)
3oz Honey
6oz Poppy Seeds
6oz Walnuts
(Can substitute different nut option)
6oz Dried Fruit
(Raisins, Dried Apricots or Cherries)
Salt to taste

Prepare Whole Grain Wheat (or other substitute whole grain per instructions). Stir in honey, poppy seeds, walnuts and dried fruit. Salt to taste and serve.

Сбитень (Sbiten) Wintertime Hot Beverage

10c water (Sub. red wine)
16oz Blackberry Jam

(Sub. another flavor of your choosing)
1/2 cup Honey
1/4 Tsp Ground Nutmeg
1 Tsp Ground Ginger
4 Whole Cloves
3 Cinnamon Sticks

Combine water (or wine), jam, honey, cloves, cinnamon sticks, ginger, nutmeg into a saucepan. Bring the mixture to a boil over medium heat, stirring frequently until honey and jam completely dissolve. Remove from heat, strain and serve!

Zefir Marshmallow Cookies

Just kidding. These are a pain to make. Just buy them. ;)

ABOUT ZOE BLAKE

USA TODAY Bestselling Author in Dark Romance
She delights in writing Dark Romance books filled with overly-possessive Billionaires, Taboo scenes and Unexpected twists. She usually spends her ill-gotten gains on martinis, travel and red lipstick. Since she can barely boil water, she's lucky enough to be married to a sexy Chef.
www.zblakebooks.com

ALSO BY ZOE BLAKE

RUSSIAN MAFIA SERIES

SWEET CRUELTY

Dimitri & Emma's story

It was an innocent mistake.

She knocked on the wrong door.

Mine.

If I were a better man, I would've just let her go.

But I'm not.

I'm a cruel bastard.

I ruthlessly claimed her virtue for my own.

It should have been enough.

But it wasn't.

I needed more.

Craved it.

She became my obsession.

Her sweetness and purity taunted my dark soul.

The need to possess her nearly drove me mad.

A Russian arms dealer had no business pursuing a naive librarian student.

She didn't belong in my world.

I would bring her only pain.

But it was too late…

She was mine and I was keeping her.

SAVAGE VOW

Gregor & Samara's story

Ivanov Crime Family Trilogy, Book One

I took her innocence as payment.

She was far too young and naïve to be betrothed to a monster like me.

I would bring only pain and darkness into her sheltered world.

That's why she ran.

I should've just let her go…

She never asked to marry into a powerful Russian mafia family.

None of this was her choice.

Unfortunately for her, I don't care.

I own her… and after three years of searching… I've found her.

My runaway bride was about to learn disobedience has consequences… punishing ones.

Having her in my arms and under my control had become an obsession.

Nothing was going to keep me from claiming her before the eyes of God and man.

She's finally mine… and I'm never letting her go.

VICIOUS OATH

Yelena & Damien's story

Ivanov Crime Family Trilogy, Book Two

When I give an order, I expect it to be obeyed.

She's too smart for her own good, and it's going to get her killed.

Against my better judgement, I put her under the protection of my powerful Russian mafia family.

So imagine my anger when the little minx ran.

For three long years I've been on her trail, always one step behind.

Finding and claiming her had become an obsession.

It was getting harder to rein in my driving need to possess her… to own her.

But now the chase is over.

I've found her.

Soon she will be mine.

And I plan to make it official, even if I have to drag her kicking and screaming to the altar.

This time… there will be no escape from me.

BETRAYED HONOR

Mikhail & Nadia's story

Ivanov Crime Family Trilogy, Book Three

Her innocence was going to get her killed.

That was if I didn't get to her first.

She's the protected little sister of the powerful Ivanov Russian mafia family - the very definition of forbidden.

It's always been my job, as their Head of Security, to watch over her but never to touch.

That ends today.

She disobeyed me and put herself in danger.

It was time to take her in hand.

I'm the only one who can save her and I will fight anyone who tries to stop me, including her brothers.

Honor and loyalty be damned.

She's mine now.

DARK OBSESSION SERIES

Free to Read in Kindle Unlimited

WARD
Dark Obsession, Book One

It should have been a fairytale...

A Billionaire Duke sweeps a poor American actress off her feet to a romantic,

isolated English estate.

A grand love affair... except this wasn't love.

It was obsession.

He had it all planned from the beginning, before I even knew he existed. He chose me.

I'm his unwilling captive, forced to play his sadistic game.

He is playing with my mind as well as my body.

Trying to convince me it is 1895, and I'm his obedient ward, subject to his rules and discipline.

Everywhere I look it is the Victorian era.

He says that my memories of a modern life are delusions

which need to be driven from my mind through punishment.

If I don't submit, he will send me back to the asylum.

I know it's not true... any of it... at least I think it's not.

The lines between reality and this nightmare are starting to blur.

If I don't escape now, I will be lost in his world forever.

It should have been a fairytale...

GILDED CAGE
Dark Obsession, Book Two

He's controlling, manipulative, dangerous... and I'm in love with him.

Rich and powerful, Richard is used to getting whatever he wants... and he wants me.

This isn't a romance. It's a dark and twisted obsession.

A game of ever-increasingly depraved acts.

Every time I fight it, he just pulls me deeper into his deception.

The slightest disobedience to his rules brings swift punishment.

My life as I knew it is gone. He now controls everything.

I'm caught in his web, the harder I struggle, the more entangled I become.

I no longer know my own mind.

He owns my body, making me crave his painful touch.

But the worst deception of all? He's made me love him.

If I don't break free soon, there will be no escape for me.

TOXIC

Dark Obsession , Book Three

In every story there is a hero and a villain… I'm both.

I will corrupt her beautiful innocence till her soul is as dark and twisted as my own.

With every caress, every taboo touch, I will captivate and ensnare her.

She's mine and no one is going to take her from me.

No matter how many times my little bird tries to escape, I will always give chase and bring her back to where she belongs, in my arms.

Each time she defies me, the consequences become more deadly.

I may not be the hero she wanted, but I'm the man she needs.